Love in Time

A Tale of Love,
Death and Redemption

Cathie Dunn

Ocelot Press

Shadow Kitten

(16th July, 2017 – 12th February, 2019)

You brightened up our lives but left us too soon.

About the Author

Cathie Dunn writes historical mystery and romance.

She loves historical research, often getting lost in the depths of the many history books on her shelves. She also enjoys exploring historic sites and beautiful countryside. Over the last three decades, she has travelled widely across Scotland, England, Wales, France and Germany.

After having spent many years in Scotland, Cathie now lives in the south-west of France with her husband, a rescue dog and two cats. She is a member of the Alliance of Independent Authors, the Romantic Novelists' Association, and the Historical Novel Society.

Find her at **www.cathiedunn.com**, and on **Facebook**, **Twitter** and **Instagram**.

Books by Cathie Dunn:

The Highland Chronicles series:
Highland Arms
A Highland Captive

The Anarchy Trilogy:
Dark Deceit
(A sequel is in progress)

Standalone:
Love Lost in Time
Silent Deception (a novella)

Coming soon:
The Loup de Foix Medieval Mystery series

Love Lost in Time

A Tale of Love,
Death and Redemption

Prologue

The hills near Carcassonne, Septimania

She woke to complete darkness.

As she tried to blink, earth covered her eyes. The dull thud of pain pounded in her head. She lifted it, only to find that she could not move. Her hands were tied behind her back, and her full weight bore onto her wrists and fingers. She could not feel her legs, as if they had dislodged.

Breathing was impossible. She opened her mouth to cry out, but all that emerged was a bare whimper, a sound suppressed by earth and stones. She spat but there was nowhere for it to go. The earth turned to sticky mud as it mingled with her saliva.

In desperation, she swallowed, gagging. But with every short breath she took, more earth blocked her nose.

Then her memory returned. And with it the terror.

He had buried her alive.

'I curse you and your offspring in perpetuity…'

Chapter One

Late February, 2018
Languedoc, south-west France

Madeleine Winters blinked back the tears as long-hidden emotions shook her. Anger. Envy. Yes, even love. A love that she'd considered lost a long time ago.

Elizabeth Beauchamp was dead. After nine years of no contact, Maddie had missed her last chance to make her peace with her mother – and to discover once and for all who her father was.

She stared at the heavy yet simple oak coffin, willing it to release its inhabitant for a final talk, an acknowledgment, the revelation of a secret which Elizabeth had now taken to her grave. Nothing moved, except some stray brown leaves swirling around Maddie's feet. Apart from her mother's elderly French neighbour, Bernadette Albert, a handful of villagers had attended the funeral, and after the ceremony, they all had left Maddie to her own memories.

Ever the pragmatic realist, Maddie knew that nothing would ever bring her mother back, but she mourned her unexpected death.

The breeze whipped at her coat, and she wrapped her scarf closer around her neck.

Madame Albert had called her ten days earlier, to let her know that Elizabeth was in hospital with a lung infection. Maddie had booked herself on a flight to Toulouse. Expecting her mother to be alive and improving thanks to the excellent health service, it distressed her to discover her close to death on her arrival at the hospital in Carcassonne in the

5

south of France, though through no fault of the medical team. It had been too late.

Maddie swallowed hard, fighting back the tears, as she remembered the doctor's words.

"Madame Beauchamp has bowel cancer. She has refused chemotherapy or any other treatment." He paused, giving her time to let the bad news sink in. "We have this in writing whilst she was still fully cognitive, should you wish to see it."

Stunned, Maddie shook her head, unable to utter a word. Why had her stubborn mother not called her before it got too serious?

"Her condition is serious. The lung infection she caught recently has weakened her beyond recovery."

The words echoed in Maddie's ears. "Cancer?" she whispered. "Since when?"

The doctor cleared his throat and raised an eyebrow. "Did your mother not tell you?"

The surprise in his voice made her shake her head in place of a response. Although he acted professionally, careful not to give any indication of his opinion of patients' personal relationships, a sense of guilt washed over her. People would judge her. How could she not have known her mother was dying?

A nurse had taken Maddie to her mother's room where she could stay with her undisturbed. She stared at Elizabeth's beautiful face, criss-crossed with fine lines. Leaning forward, she held a frail hand between hers, her mind in turmoil. Why had her mother not told her she was ill? She knew Elizabeth was stubborn, obstinate, but to refuse to contact your only living relative, your daughter, during a time of need shook Maddie. Their estrangement had gone beyond reason. Her eyes dry, Maddie could only watch her mother's breathing grow more ragged. In the end, Elizabeth died calmly in her sleep just over six hours after Maddie's arrival.

And now Maddie was here, by her mother's grave, saying her final goodbye.

The biting *tramontagne* wind chilled Maddie's bones, and she huddled deeper into her coat. Elizabeth had loved the winds that sweep the plain between the Montagne Noire and the Pyrenees during all seasons. They brought winter and rain to a land parched by the sun, and cooled you down during the long, hot summer days.

"*Au revoir, Maman.*" Maddie dropped the bundle of red roses she'd been clutching onto the coffin, then turned away.

One thing was certain. She would never know her full parentage now, but she had no time to ponder about the past. Her mother's house in the Cabardès village of Minervens twenty minutes' drive north of Carcassonne was her priority. She wouldn't want to keep it. What would she do with it other than pay bills that would add up? No, the old pile of stones had to go.

Maddie knew that any potential British buyers would snap up a property like...well, hers, now, she supposed. People seemed to love rustic French renovation projects. She would speak to her mother's *notaire* the next day when she had an appointment for the reading of the will. Being an only child should make it straight-forward, and Maddie did not expect any nasty surprises – under French law, children could not be disinherited.

On leaving, Maddie stopped to close the wrought-iron gate behind her, casting a final glance over the small graveyard with its beautiful gravestones and old mausoleums. Framed images of loved ones, often accompanied by poems of love and loss, adorned almost all the graves, except for those where no relatives or friends were left. It was a lovely touch, and she admired the French for their way of caring for their relatives after death.

Her mother's grave was now out of sight, tucked into the south-western corner, and it would yet be weeks before a simple stone slate bearing Elizabeth Beauchamp's name and her favourite poem, as already organised between the funeral company and the *notaire*, could be put in place. Her mother had arranged everything. Maddie wasn't sure whether to be relieved, or saddened.

Pulling a key from her coat pocket, Maddie turned towards her small hire car, a bright red Fiat 500, parked a few yards away from the entrance. The central-locking clicked open – too loudly in her ears after the tranquility of the graveyard.

She was about to get into the car when a dull thud reached her ears. Then another. She halted. It came from the graveyard. A slow rumble of earth followed. Of course. They were filling the grave. Maddie shuddered. Her mother was lost to her forever. She snuggled into the seat and firmly shut the door to the chilling sound.

Deep breath! The past is gone.

Her resolution firm, she started the motor and took the village road up to the windy slope towards the Cabardès hills, passing by a row of old houses. Some of them looked like they had sat vacant for decades, their shutters closed, front doors dusty. A sense of abandonment hung over them. But she knew this was normal in rural France. To her right, the small office of *La Poste* had closed for the afternoon, and even the local *épicerie* looked deserted.

Eventually, she came to a halt in front of a stone house near the northern exit of the village. An overgrown front garden greeted her. Dating back to the early 1900s, like many houses along this long village road it was two storeys high, with sweeping views over the village and the hills all around. To the north, the slope rose steeply into the forests of the Cabardès in a blend of evergreen and brown.

Sighing, she peeled herself out of the Fiat and locked it. Then she stopped to look more closely at the house. It would sell quickly, no doubt, even though it needed complete renovation inside.

Maddie turned and let her gaze scan the majestic view. The low sun to the west cast a lingering auburn light over the landscape, as if the trees were burning. She knew that from the top of the hill, where the winery was, you could see across to the Pyrenees in the south.

'Suffocating.'

What? She shuddered and shook herself out of her reverie. Her fantasy was running away with her. It was a beautiful winter sunset; nothing more.

"Suffocating, ha!" With a nervous laugh, she unlocked the front door and switched on the dim corridor light. A musty smell lingered, even though she had aired it earlier in the day. How could her mother have lived like this?

Maddie locked the door behind her with a large, slightly bent key – the lock being likely as ancient as the house itself! She let out a deep breath as she slowly wandered past the staircase and looked around.

The old, peeling floral wallpaper that had never bothered her mother; the dark corners on the ceiling where God knows what had settled; the basic kitchen with its heavy, ornate sideboard and 1990s gas cooker; and the bathroom upstairs with its ancient bathtub.

Maddie laughed. In England, people paid premium prices for such antique baths, with their curved sides and ornate feet. Impractical for a modern family, but likely beloved by expats. With a little updating, the house would do well on the market.

She went into the kitchen and dropped her bag on a chair. Lighting a gas ring on the hob, she waited for the flames to settle. Then she filled a heavy copper kettle with water and set it to boil. Elizabeth had always favoured the simple things in life. No new-fangled electric kettle for her! Maddie decided to buy one the next day, however brief her stay would be.

Opening the creaky door of the sideboard, its glass front clouded with age, she was met with shelves full of China. Delicate cups, saucers and plates vied for space with large mugs and pots. She ignored the delicate 1950s teapot with the chipped spout, and instead grabbed a mug and rinsed it thoroughly in the chilly water from the tap. Princess Leia, pouting angrily at her from the front of the mug, would not appreciate the cold shower, Maddie was sure. She remembered the day she had given it to Elizabeth for her birthday. She'd been ten and very proud of having spent her pocket money on something so special. Quickly, Maddie wiped away the stray tear that dared threaten her composure.

Outside, dusk was settling, so while the kettle took to boiling, she closed the shutters. "Don't want any creeps sneaking around the house!" she half-joked to the Star Wars heroine patiently awaiting her tea on the sideboard.

Maddie went into the adjoining living room and firmly secured the shutters there too. The idea of someone skulking in the shadows of the overgrown garden made her shudder.

This house was so different from her own small one-bedroom flat in the centre of York, in the north-east of England. Overlooking the river Ouse from the comfortable and flood-safe height of her new-build, she considered herself fortunate. The short two-minute walk to shops and bars suited her well when she felt too cocooned into her world and needed to mingle with people. Writing history books about Vikings had its advantages – never-ending tales of courageous men (and women) conquering the world – but the isolation needed to meet tight deadlines and conduct in-depth research regularly reminded her that she was indeed a woman, living alone in her early thirties.

The kettle whistled shrilly. Startled, she rushed back into the kitchen, turned off the gas, grabbed a dishcloth to wrap around the hot handle, and poured water into the mug. The space princess seemed content now.

She let the green tea bag steam a few minutes before ditching it on the side of the sink and, balancing the mug with one hand, she flicked off the kitchen light and went back into the living room. Her laptop lay unopened on the table. She'd not dared plug it in yet, not trusting the old electricity, but she may not have much choice were she to stay longer. And there was no internet. Her mother had a simple old phone line. More for those future buyers to invest in.

Maddie settled on the mauve velvet sofa and leaned back, letting out a deep breath. Her hand holding the mug shook, and she quickly steadied it with the other. Staring at the painting on the wall opposite – an oil canvas of a young lady, dressed in an intricate gown in late Regency style, surrounded by an elaborate gilt frame – she unwittingly mimicked the unknown beauty's sad expression.

"I know how you feel," she said. "I'm alone, too, now."

No longer able to control her shaking hands, Maddie apologised to the fictional princess on her mug and set it down, tea untouched, onto the worn wooden floor. Then she collapsed on the sofa. Although she hadn't spoken to Elizabeth in over nine years, she'd always known her mother to be there. Now, she was gone, and with her the last of her own family. Maddie had no siblings, and neither had her mother, and as for her father…well, that would now remain a mystery.

She sighed. Even her own marriage hadn't lasted beyond five years. Brian and she separated when he was offered a lucrative post at the University of Valencia in Spain, and she didn't want to leave York. It wasn't the only reason, but the final straw, as they'd been drifting apart for almost a year before his move. Fact was, she was as focused on Viking research as Brian was on his. Unfortunately for her and their marriage, his specialty subject was Mediterranean archaeology.

'Alone…'

The word echoed around the room. Or was it in her head? Maddie let the tears run, uncaring if they sank into the musty velvet.

She would be fine. Eventually.

Chapter Two

The feast of Easter, AD 777
Carisiacum, Neustria, Kingdom of the Franks

"I beg your pardon, lady."

Hilda took a step to the side, hitting her shoulder against the wall as the maid rushed past her through the narrow corridor, carrying a large plate full of steaming lamb cuts. She watched as the girl, barely older than her own six-and-ten years, almost dropped the heavy load onto the table in front of King Charles. With the king's sharp eyes berating her silently, the poor maid curtseyed and rushed past Hilda, and out the open door behind her, towards the kitchen annex.

Transfixed, but too self-conscious to venture into the noisy room, Hilda stared in awe at the court gathered before her. Never in her life had she seen such magnificence.

The great hall of the royal stronghold was decorated beautifully for the celebration of the Easter feast, marking the end of weeks of fasting. The most intricate tapestries covered the bare stone walls, keeping out the still frosty evening air. Rushes held in sconces on the walls cast the large room into a myriad of shadow and light.

The only child of a Frankish count, Hilda was used to some comforts, but nothing compared to the splendour of this palace. The king had invited important lords from Septimania, a region adjoining the western Mediterranean Sea, in which he wanted to reinforce his control. As some men gathered were already his vassals and others yet to become such over the course of the holy days, he displayed his power and influence in full measure.

The mood in the hall was convivial. The wine, freely on offer and regularly replenished, helped mellow minor disagreements. From where she hid, she had spotted her father, Milo, the count of Vaulun, in deep discussions with a group of men.

Earlier in the day, at a solemn ceremony, King Charles had received homage from his new vassals. In honour of the event, he wore a silk tunic interwoven with gold thread, a wide leather belt decorated with large jewels sparkling in an array of colour in the light of the fires, and his gold crown, adding to his already grand persona an air of high status. His back straight, he sat on an intricately crafted throne in the centre of this great hall, where men of all ages kneeled in front of him, took an oath and swore their allegiance. Men of Visigoth, Merovingian and even ancient Roman heritage who had travelled north on his invitation. They sought the power and the safety that the Franks brought with them as part of their expansion. And she had heard those southerners were desperate for peace.

One by one, the ancient cities of Septimania had accepted or fallen to the Franks: Béziers, Narbonne, and more recently, Tolosa. Now, the good people of the region could look towards a more peaceful era – under Frankish protection.

King Charles already ruled a vast realm and brought prosperity to hitherto war-torn regions. Men and women dressed well, their grain stores were bulging, and they treated their non-free vassals fairly. With Charles' royal stance, shrewd intelligence and strong features partly obscured by an imposing moustache and beard, she knew him to be a formidable character – but one she could never share her secret with.

Her people were great warriors, civilised, and clever administrators, but they were also brutal, short of temper, and often without mercy. They were Christian. And therein lay Hilda's biggest fear.

Some women, like her and her late mother before her, were known as wise-women, whom the Church had recently begun to pursue. Her calling was no longer widely accepted, although at home, people still asked for her help. But the usually affable priest at her manor at Vaulun had suddenly berated her, calling her practices dangerous. So it began…

Shaking off her thoughts, her gaze drifted to her father, a close adviser to the king. Although older than Charles by a score years, Milo, count of Vaulun could hold his own, looking resplendent in a fine silk tunic, a simple, yet beautifully carved leather belt, and his aristocratic face with a slightly long nose and dark-blue eyes.

Bursting with pride, Hilda regarded her father, now talking at ease with a young man of a darker hue, clearly of Visigoth heritage with his black hair falling over strong shoulders, bright eyes, and a moustache reaching to his chin. There was something uncivilised about him. Shivers ran down her spine when he laughed at something her father said and patted him on the back. They raised their cups and took deep draughts of wine. Her father's complexion reddened as the spirit took effect. She smiled.

"Lady…"

Rolling her eyes in mock annoyance, Hilda jumped out of the maid's way again. This time, the girl carried a tray bearing two large bowls and several loaves of freshly baked bread which she deposited in front of Charles and other strategic places on the grand table, before she rushed back past Hilda with an apologetic smile.

"Nanthild! Daughter!" Father's voice reached her. He waved her over. Disappointment hit her briefly, as she had enjoyed watching the preparations from the side. Hilda did not crave the attention other girls here present cherished.

As she crossed the room to join him, the eyes of the young man by her father's side never left her. It unnerved her a little – she was unused to male attention – and her heart beat a solid drum in her ears.

"My dear daughter, come," her father said affectionately, his eyes full of joy, as he bid her sit on a stool beside him. Turning to the young man who was on Hilda's other side, he added, "I will be lost without her. She has been looking after me well since my wife, her mother, passed away."

A frown shrouded his features briefly at the memory, and she wanted to reach out to him, but refrained. Three years earlier, her mother had died giving birth to her only brother – who himself had only survived for a sennight. Both Hilda and her father had felt their loss strongly, and the count had thrown himself even more into diplomacy and warfare for the king.

"I'm sorry to hear," the young man responded solemnly, his voice a low hum. "We have seen so much death and sadness, too, including the loss of of my parents last summer."

Nodding, Hilda kept staring at the table, uncertain how to react.

"Here, let me…" The stranger filled a goblet with wine and handed it to her.

She looked at him from under her lashes. "I thank you, lord." She raised it and took a small sip. The pungent scent of berries and grapes blurred her senses, and the full taste of even the one sip made her head spin.

"'Tis strong, this wine they brought up from Septimania." Her father laughed. "But you will get used to it, daughter."

She carefully placed the goblet onto the table, trying not to reveal her trembling hand, and pulled her brows together, before risking a glance at him. What did he mean? Father was overly cheerful, his demeanour jovial. She saw contentment in his features as he gazed at her. And relief.

Her heart froze. Had he not said earlier he '*would* be lost' without her?

Father smiled and patted her hand. "We will talk later, my child. But first, I must introduce you to Bellon. He is a young lord from a noble family from Septimania who has been taking part in our recent campaigns. Charles has promised to create a fiefdom for him. Soon, he will appoint this brave warrior as Count of Carcassonne!"

She turned to the Visigoth. "My felicitations, lord. King Charles must think you a worthy ally to heap upon you so much responsibility."

"Nanthild!" She need not see her father's face to sense his fury at her sharp tone.

But Bellon only laughed. "Indeed, he might, Lady Nanthild. In fact, I sincerely hope he does." He still grinned and looked straight at her. His eyes were of a deep, mossy green, and the light danced in them with humour. How insolent! This was an absurd situation.

Thankfully, Charles' *senescal* announced the beginning of the meal, and, once the king had begun to eat, everyone at the tables helped themselves to ladlefuls of cuts of game and bird.

Bellon broke the gaze and offered to fill her trencher. What was the world coming to? Hilda cast a glance at her father who nodded. She inclined her head, having suddenly lost her voice. And her appetite.

***

Bellon placed a roast lamb cut and a small ladle of vegetable stew onto the lady Nanthild's trencher and smiled. "Would you like another spoonful?"

"Thank you. This is quite enough." Her cheeks turned a becoming red as she protested mildly, keeping her gaze firmly downcast.

He tilted his head and watched her as she took a piece with her knife and blew on it. The steam rose from the morsel, infused with the aroma of rosemary and thyme. Her delicate nose breathed in the scent, and her face lit up. The girl knew how to savour a moment. Then her eyes met his, and the look of bliss vanished.

"Are you not eating, lord?" She put the meat in her mouth, chewed, and stabbed another. Watching, Bellon felt sorry for the attacked piece – and relieved it was not him on the receiving end.

"I shall momentarily." Reluctantly, he broke the eye contact and helped himself before he passed the bowl along the table to his neighbour, Clovis, a Frankish nobleman from

Charles' entourage. The knight took it swiftly, laughing as he filled his trencher to the point of overflowing.

"A pretty wench, but with a sharp tongue." Clovis smirked. "She'll learn…"

Bellon felt his anger rise. He narrowed his eyebrows and glared at Clovis who, oblivious to his fury, tucked into his meat, still chuckling. It was one thing discussing strategy with Charles' men, but another to have them insult the ladies present. He ignored the oaf and pulled a chunk of soft meat off the bone.

When Charles had first discussed the new earldom with him, he was extremely pleased. Over recent years, he had worked hard for the king, trying to bring peace to war-torn Septimania. His home town of Carcassonne had been under attack from the Saracens and the Basques time and again, and he knew the loyal Visigoths were fighting a losing battle without the help of the powerful Franks.

Bellon admired their administration, their culture and the trained skills of their warriors. Whilst he had learnt much from dealing with the Saracens at Béziers and Narbonne, he had sought an ally to ensure his region was finally safe. And he was making good progress.

With Bellon appointed as *comes* of Carcassonne, Charles gained a reliable vassal and a staunch supporter. He would protect the people who fell into his responsibility, so they could live their lives safely. In truth, Bellon felt a little daunted by the task, but as he had gained great experience in warfare and strategy, he was ready for it.

All that was missing, as Charles had drily pointed out, was a wife of good stock. So, to consolidate their relationship, Charles introduced Milo to him, a nobleman from the far north-east, whose daughter, Nanthild, was of Frankish blood and, apparently, a beauty. Bellon had shrugged it off as a father's talk. He fully knew of what was expected from him as part of his new position, and he was prepared to do his duty for peace in Septimania.

Then he had set eyes on her.

He shook his head, grinning, and took another bite of lamb.

"What amuses you?" Lady Nanthild asked, gazing at him through lowered lashes.

Had she been watching him, like he had watched her earlier? He swallowed and reached for his wine. "Fate, lady."

Her eyes opened wide, and she put her knife down and wiped her fingers on a piece of cloth. "Why, true. You have reason to celebrate being appointed to rule over your own lands."

Bellon nodded. "I have."

Milo leaned forward, a smile playing on his lips. They had yet to complete their discussion, so Bellon knew the girl had no notion of what awaited her.

But having watched her over the preceding days, he was certain of his choice, and grateful to God for his good fortune. He would never want another. Her dark-blue eyes resembled a stormy lake and showed a fierce intelligence hidden behind her demure demeanour – a trait soldiers like Clovis clearly did not appreciate. But Bellon did. He found the company of babbling women tiresome, and much preferred a good conversation about the estate, the countryside, and what needed to be done. The lady beside him appeared promising.

Only three years younger to his twenty, Nanthild was tall for a girl, almost his height. He had noticed that men of smaller stature felt uncomfortable in her company, which made him laugh. Tonight, her long blonde hair was loosely tamed in a plait and covered by a delicate veil. He found her figure a little too thin for his taste, but it did not matter. Bellon considered himself fortunate.

But what if she did not return his growing feelings? He shook his head. He would handle it when the time came. First, they had to finalise the agreement and announce the betrothal.

"Lady," he began, "would you tell me of your home?"

Bellon knew little of the northern territories other than the usual impressions from his brief excursions. Unsurprisingly, he had found it dull and cold compared to the brilliant sunshine of his own region.

He saw her swallow, then she offered him a smile. "Of course. My home village of Vaulun is surrounded by forests and meadows." She cast a glance at her father who nodded in encouragement. "The land is more hilly, and you find plenty of wild boar and deer roaming. I always chase them away as they eat my herbs…" She blushed.

Bellon smiled. "You have a herb garden?" Vaulun sounded more idyllic than he had given it credit for.

Her gaze became closed. "Yes. I grow all kinds of herbs, even though the winter's chill often destroys any the deer leave behind."

"I apologise. I did not mean to insult you. In fact, my mother grew herbs and also vines. She loved adding new aromas to our food and drink." He leaned back a little, allowing her to regain her composure.

Lady Nanthild nodded enthusiastically. "How wonderful! The famous Septimanian sun must help them grow. So you know how much work it takes to—"

"Work?" Clovis snorted from Bellon's other side. "Womenfolk have no sense of work."

Bellon saw both Nanthild's and her father's backs straighten. Milo's expression turned thunderous. Bellon slowly put his knife down and shifted to glare at the man. "Please explain yourself, Clovis. If you must insult a lady, you may at least give her your reasons."

Clovis laughed, a harsh sound that did not reach his eyes. "Women are only good for two things: child-bearing and, well, I won't go into the other as the lady might still be innocent."

"Do you have a wife?" Bellon's voice was curt, his temper rising, but steadying his breathing, he decided not to allow the brute to rile up his humour.

"Yes. And she has no fancy pastimes like the lady Nanthild. She works the house, keeps it in good stead, and raises my offspring. That's all she's good for. The rest I seek elsewhere."

The lady stood, toppling the stool over with a clatter. "If you will excuse me, my lords, I have lost my appetite." She stepped over the obstacle and marched from the room, her back straight, without another glance at them.

"If I were you, I would learn to keep my mouth shut when near ladies," Milo suggested, his tone low and threatening. "'Tis my daughter you were insulting."

Clovis downed his wine. "They're all the same under their fancy silken gowns."

Bellon rose quickly, prepared to drag the odious man outside, before Milo would do anything stupid.

"My lords, I beg you." Charles' voice came loud and clear from the royal table to their left. "We are celebrating Easter, the feast of the resurrection. A feast of peace. I will have no disagreements at tonight's gathering in here nor, as it were, out-of-doors." The king, his eyebrows raised and his mouth set in a firm line, brokered no contradiction.

Seething inside, Bellon acknowledged the command with a nod, clenched and unclenched his fist, then sat down slowly as Clovis called for a nearby servant boy to refill his goblet. When the lad spilled a little wine, Clovis slapped the back of his head. "Useless cur!"

Watching the boy retreat, Bellon took another deep breath. A stern glance from the king pre-empted any retort.

His appetite lost, he picked up his own goblet and turned his back on Clovis, edging closer to Milo instead. The man was trembling with fury. But both knew that unleashing Charles' wrath over a personal disagreement would be disadvantageous. Disastrous, even.

"We must talk," Milo whispered.

Bellon nodded. It was time.

Chapter Three

Maddie woke with a start. Pain shot into her neck. She blinked, trying to get her bearings.

Oh, yes. She was in her mother's house, lying on the old sofa. A coil spring poked her rib. She pushed herself upright. Crack. Crack.

"Ouch!" No surprise her back was hurting. She slowly stood and stretched, then jumped when she knocked the mug over with her foot, spilling tea over the worn oak floorboards.

"Damn!" She picked up the mug and dashed into the kitchen, ditching it in the sink. "Where's the kitchen roll when you need it?" She glanced around the bare surfaces. Her mother had lived with very few possessions.

Grabbing a worn dish cloth hanging on a hook beside the sink, she went back to the living room and mopped the liquid off the floor. There was nothing she could do about the water trickling through the gaps between the floorboards.

"Great!" She sat back and sighed. "Deep breath."

Her words echoed around the walls. Apart from a few paintings and select pieces of her grandmother's large furniture, Elizabeth's large house was bare. Maddie wondered again how her mother could live like this. She must've had the money for a relatively comfortable retirement, so why hadn't she sold up and moved into a nice, modern place?

The silence of the house unnerved Maddie. Only in remote places had she experienced such quiet. Out in the open countryside she'd welcomed it. The past was talking to her there, in ancient ruins or painted caves.

Here, within the confines of the thick stone walls, it was different. Goosebumps rose on her skin, and she quickly brushed her hand over them. "You can hear yourself think," she joked, her laugh hollow. In York, there was always noise, even when she closed her double-glazed windows. Trucks, drunk students, barking dogs. Day and night, York was alive. This place was dead.

'Dead.'

Maddie stared at the lady in the painting, the only picture in the room. Yes, she was dead, too, so she was in no position to whisper. Shrugging off the uneasy sensation as a trick of the mind, Maddie looked away and snorted. Most likely, the poor woman had died of boredom.

Her stomach rumbled, and she checked her watch. 7.25 pm. "Time for food," she said loudly to break the silence. She went into the kitchen and opened the fridge – another relic from the 1980s. Its humming was a welcome sound.

Last night, she had found that the pre-made pizza she'd bought at *Carrefour* supermarket was a waste. The oven, connected to a portable gas canister, could not heat it into an edible form. At first, it was still frozen. Then, half an hour later, it had become burnt on the surface, and the base was rock hard. Eating it would have seriously threatened even the healthiest set of teeth! So tonight, she would cook.

Maddie hated cooking. But in the absence of a decent oven, or even a microwave, she had no choice. She lit two rings on the gas hob, put some butter into a much-used frying pan, set it on a ring and placed a saucepan filled with water on the other. She found a worn chopping board and discarded it immediately. The germs on that must be having a ball!

She took two plates from the dresser and scrubbed them under the slowly-heating water of the tap before using one to cut up mushrooms, tomatoes, and one half of a huge green pepper. "Nice to see tomatoes are less watery here," she quipped. Then she chucked them into the pan, followed by ready-made tomato sauce from a jar. Finally, she stirred the bubbling mass.

"Oh! Forgot the herbs."

She poked her nose into the small larder behind the kitchen, not looking too closely into the dark cobweb-covered corners. Elizabeth's spice rack revealed salt, pepper, paprika and a closed ceramic jar of dried *herbes*. This would do. She grabbed the jar and the spices and returned to the kitchen.

Thud.

Maddie nearly dropped her load on the kitchen table. Behind her, the larder door had slammed shut. Having stood open throughout her scrutiny of the small room's contents, it startled her. There was no draught. She opened the door again, glanced around, then turned off the light at the old black switch inside the larder.

She shook off her discomfort, shut the door firmly and returned to the cooker. By now, the water was bubbling in the saucepan, and she quickly stirred it, then grabbed a handful of tagliatelle from a pack before returning the rest of it to the fridge. She'd have the second half tomorrow, with more fresh vegetables, perhaps. She was eating better here than back home!

Whilst her food was cooking, she laid the table and poured herself a glass of wine from the bottle she'd bought – and opened – the night before. Taking a sip, she looked around the room. It was still too quiet. Then she spotted it, half hidden behind a tray on the sideboard.

A radio!

"Woo-hoo!" Connecting the plug to the power socket by the door, Maddie let out a loud whistle and searched the channels. Soon, the sound of classical music filled the room. She didn't recognise the piece, but it didn't matter. "That'll do," she confirmed to the radio, and turned it up a notch. Better! Silence banished.

Once ready, she mixed the sauce into the pasta and poured the mass onto a plate just as the 8.00 pm news came on. The political announcements passed her by. She wasn't interested in modern-day Machiavellian shenanigans. Absent-mindedly, she sprinkled small chunks of Camembert over her dish and tucked in. Mmh.

Eventually, the announcer warned of frosty weather with a risk of snow and frost in lower areas. Snow, this low?

23

Despite being fluent in French – like her mother, Maddie held both French and British citizenship – she considered herself to be English after spending all of her adult life in Britain, at first in London, and later in York. She was thinking in English, and listening to and speaking in French messed with her head now. .

Memories of her childhood in Normandy came flooding back. Rouen hadn't been a bad place to grow up in. A typical French town with plenty of history. From a young age on, her mother had dragged her to the historic sites in the area and beyond, which meant every weekend spent exploring a different place. She'd learnt much over the years. Her fascination with the Vikings and their conquests had begun in Normandy – after all, the Norsemen had invaded the land and left their mark for centuries to come, not only in name but also in culture. For that, she'd be forever grateful to her mother. History had been Elizabeth's interest as much as hers.

"Mmmhhh…" She slowly savoured the gooey feel of a warm cheesy bite and tomato. Bliss. She'd forgotten how good fresh French produce tasted. Guilt raised its ugly head when she remembered what she ate at home: frozen pizza, pre-made lasagne or a fairly taste-free chicken bake were her normal diet. "I must get into proper cooking." But how often had she said that to herself when convenience – and research – took over?

The first notes of *Ave Maria* sent a shiver down her spine. It always did. Elizabeth had loved classical music, another trait Maddie inherited from her mother.

She lowered her fork, closed her eyes, and let the music wash over her. It added a peaceful atmosphere to the house, made it turn more…homely? It seemed that she shared more with her mother than she'd realised. A disturbing thought!

Slowly, the air grew thick with the scent of rosemary and lavender, and a warm feeling washed over her. Maddie blinked and stared into the room, her vision zooming in and out. Black dots appeared in front of her eyes. Strangely, she didn't feel alone. Goosebumps rose on her skin, and she put her fork on the plate. The music drifted into the background, and a loud buzzing noise took its place.

Always the level-headed academic, she didn't believe in ghosts, but she thought she would recognise her mother if she decided to visit. This wasn't Elizabeth. It was…different.

Maddie pushed away her half-empty plate with the cold pasta and leaned back, taking a deep breath. Her work involved dealing with real, historical data, not mumbo-jumbo. She shook her head, and with that, the room smelled stale again, of locked, unattended house. Of a deserted home.

'Home.'

Icy shivers crawled on her skin.

"No! Stop!" She banged her fists on the table, the cutlery on the plate clattering in response. This wasn't her house – it was her mother's. It contained no items of her own life, as far as Maddie knew. And it certainly wasn't her home.

She rose, chucked the leftovers in the bin, and dropped the plate and cutlery in the sink. Her glance fell on the radio, and she switched it off mid-sequence. The sooner the house went on the market the better.

A draught made her shiver, and she checked the window. It was old, with six panelled sections each side, but it was closed fully.

"Bloody hell, Mum!"

Maddie left the kitchen, turning the light off along the way. Then, she checked the main door was locked.

In the absence of a TV, she grabbed a book from the overflowing shelf under the stairs before switching off the living room lights. *A History of the Languedoc*. Oh well, she would learn something new before going to sleep tonight.

Sighing, she climbed the stairs to the first floor. It had been one long, exhausting day.

Downstairs, the scent of rosemary and lavender returned and settled in the kitchen.

***

"Hello," Maddie said, staring at the stranger who had knocked on her door. Seeing him raise an eyebrow, she quickly corrected herself, "Umm, *bonjour*."

"*Bonjour*," he replied and smiled. "Welcome to Minervens, Mademoiselle *Beauchamp*…?" He pronounced her maiden name the French way, not 'Beecham' like in English.

"Who wants to know?" She placed one foot on the inside of the door. Maddie wasn't one to trust easily. Despite the man's friendly looks, she was naturally wary of strangers. Living in a city had taught her valuable lessons in looking after herself.

He shuffled his feet and grinned apologetically. "My name is Léon Cabrol. My family live a little further up the hill." He pointed to the outskirts of the village. Then he offered his hand in greeting and she shook it. A warm, firm grip enveloped her fingers. His smile vanished as he continued. "I wanted to convey my condolences. I knew Elisa, your mother, a little. We met at the odd fête in the village. We – I and my parents – were very sorry to hear of her passing."

"Thank you, Monsieur Cabrol. My name is Madeleine Winters. I'm Elizabeth's daughter…as you already know." She began to relax in his company. "You're from the *Château de Minervens*?" She'd seen the signposts for the large *domaine*.

He nodded. "Yes, it is our family business. We have a stand at many fêtes in the area."

Fêtes were the lifeblood of French towns and villages over the summer. Elizabeth would have visited some of them, she was certain. "Mum felt at home here," she mused. Then she remembered her appointment. "Oh, I'm sorry I can't offer you a coffee, but I'm just about to leave for a meeting at the *notaire*'s."

"Please don't worry, Miss Winters. I'm sure we'll meet again. Minervens isn't such a big place." He half-turned before he added, "I hope all goes well."

She smiled. "Thank you. I'm sure it will." She let the 'Miss' slide.

"*Au revoir.*" He waved and walked to an old Land Rover parked on the street just outside her gate, clicking the central locking open when he approached the driver's door.

"*Au revoir.*" Maddie raised her hand briefly, as she watched him get into his car.

She shut the door, ignoring the little flutter in her heart that she hadn't felt for years. Léon Cabrol was just a friendly neighbour, and she, a mere visitor, never to return after the sale of the house. Nothing more.

"*Bonjour,*" the *notaire*'s assistant greeted her on her arrival at their office in Carcassonne. "Please take a seat. Maître Martin will be with you shortly."

"*Merci.*" Maddie smiled her thanks and sat on a leather-covered chair in the small waiting room. She glanced at photos on the walls of the famous *Cité* – Carcassonne's rebuilt fortress – and the surrounding countryside. Vineyards where the eye could reach, behind them the distant, snow-capped peaks of the Pyrenees. The area was beautiful, she had to admit. Blue sky, green vines, and brimming with history. She understood why her mother had loved the area so.

"Madame Winters?" A suave man, probably in his mid-fifties with grey streaks running through black hair, appeared and looked at her expectantly. She nodded. "*Suivez-moi, s'il vous plaît.*"

Maddie took her bag and made her way to his office where they shook hands before he closed the door behind her. "*Bonjour.*"

"*Bonjour.* Please."

She took the seat he indicated on one side of his desk before he settled into a comfortable-looking leather office chair.

"Thank you, Maître. I appreciate you seeing me at such short notice."

"It is perfectly understandable, Madame Winters. I'm very sorry about your mother's death. Madame Beauchamp was not only a client but also a dear friend." He tapped a blue file on his desk. "She has entrusted me with her will and left very clear instructions about her property where, I believe, you are currently staying."

"Yes, I'm at her house whilst I'm here."

"Would you care to share with me what your plans are for it?" He tilted his head and looked at her expectantly.

"Well, I have to sell it. I live in England, where I work. I can't afford to keep two houses, and I have no links to Minervens."

"That's a pity," Maître Martin said, a hint of sadness in his eyes. He fished a pair of narrow, black-rimmed glasses from a case on his desk and placed them on the tip of his long nose.

"Why?" Maddie's defence went up. "There's not a problem with it, is there?" Visions of demolition and subsidence sprang to mind.

"As a matter of fact…" He opened the file and removed a few sheets tied together with ribbon, the front entitled, *Testament*.

Maddie's heart plummeted. What devious plan had her mother concocted to make her life miserable even after her death? All she wanted now was for it to be over.

The *notaire* looked at her over the rim of his glasses. "I will read out your mother's final testament in its entirety. I trust your French is good enough to understand all implications?"

"Yes, it is. I grew up in Normandy and lived in France until I went to university in England." She had been in her late teens, and keen to start her own, independent life. "My mother and I always spoke in French."

"So I gathered, but I needed to be certain. Now, please listen carefully, then ask any questions you may have. The will explains everything…"

As Maddie listened, her despair grew as the notaire relayed her mother's last wishes to her. Incomprehension warred with disappointment and anger.

"What the—" She shook her head and held up her hand when he halted mid-sentence. "*Je suis désolée*. Please continue."

Inside, she was seething. Elizabeth had done it again. She had always thwarted Maddie's progress. At first, her mother hadn't wanted her to move to York when the offer of a university place came in, then she developed a keen dislike of Brian, Maddie's ex-husband, for no clear reason other than having avoided men all her life after giving birth to her. Over the years, she had repeatedly asked her to join her in France, which Maddie always declined.

Maddie had no idea what had motivated her mother, but she had grown tired of her manipulations – and of Elizabeth's continued silence about who Maddie's father was. Not surprisingly, there was no mention of him at all. This small but most important fact disappointed her the most.

Maître Martin concluded the reading. "Your mother signed this testament on 26th August, 2017, in front of two witnesses in form of Madame Bernadette Albert, her neighbour, and my assistant. Later, when she was in hospital for her cancer treatment, she called me to confirm that this would indeed be her last will. Now, do you have any questions?"

"Absolutely." Maddie's blood pumped in her ears, and she took a deep breath to calm her ragged nerves. "Can I just confirm…that I have to stay in my mother's house for a year before I can sell it? I mean, actually *live* in it for a full twelve months? And that I have access to her bank account only to pay for any renovation works for the duration, with you authorising the payments?"

"Yes, that is correct, Madame Winters. That was your mother's wish." Maître Martin kept his voice neutral, but he showed a hint of a kind, understanding smile.

"And what happens if I'm unable to oblige her? Am I disinherited?"

"No. You can't be removed from a French will, as you are automatically entitled to the estate. However, if you are unable to proceed according to Madame Beauchamp's conditions contained herein," he tapped the paper, "then the house will remain empty."

"Forever?"

He nodded, then sighed. "Madame, your mother made it very clear that she wanted you to experience life here in the south of France. It was her greatest wish."

Anger soared through her, and it took all her efforts to stay civil. "But I can't afford to take a year out of work and not earn any money. It's ridiculous."

"Then you will have to keep the property empty until such time that you can do so."

"But…I can't. It's impossible. I'm involved in projects at the university in York. And I'm in the process of writing a book, for which I need to be there to conduct my research."

"The Languedoc is the perfect region for writing—"

"But not about Vikings!"

Maddie sighed, then quickly apologised. It wasn't the *notaire*'s fault that Elizabeth had let her down – again. She felt like telling him to stick it, but instead, she said, "*D'accord*. I'll have to think about how to do this."

"That is perfectly understandable, Madame. But I must know: you do not contest the will?"

"No, what would be the point?"

He nodded. "Then may I ask you to sign and date here as proof that you have understood – and you accept – the implications of the *testament*?" He pointed at duplicate documents, both requiring her signature.

Maddie obliged, then took one copy he handed her. "And if I need permission to buy stuff for renovations…"

"…please contact me anytime. Here is my card. I'll be happy to assist you."

She tucked the offered card into a pocket inside her bag. "Thank you for your time."

"Thank you, Madame Winters. And *courage*!" He smiled as he shook her hand. "You may come to like our beautiful area as your mother hoped for."

She let out a dry laugh. "True. Who knows!" she said half in jest. "Goodbye."

Passing through reception, she waved a polite '*Au revoir*' at the assistant, and left the office.

Outside, she paused and took a deep breath. She was still seething. What utter nonsense! Elizabeth had added that condition to spite her. So now, Maddie had to either sit on an empty house for the rest of her life, or do her work from here. Yes, the dig was almost finished, and she didn't have to visit the site any longer, but her next history project about the discovery, with all the new-found knowledge about that settlement, required suitable internet access. She would need to Skype and to research online, and she doubted the connection in her mother's house would be any good.

But more importantly, did she really want to swap city life for this backyard, however pretty it was?

She walked briskly to her parked car and pressed the key fob.

"Blast!"

Frustrated, she steered the little Fiat out of the parking space, and within a few minutes, she had joined the town's one-way system which was leading her around in circles. She laughed hysterically. "The wheels on the bus go round and round..." she howled, ignoring questioning looks from other drivers. Sod them!

Once she was home, she would call Brian. She had to let steam off somewhere.

Chapter Four

The Feast of Easter, AD 777
Carisiacum, Neustria

The knock on the door startled Hilda, and she nearly pricked her finger with the needle. She looked up from her embroidery and exchanged glances with Amalberga, her mother's cousin and her companion since her mother's death. Widowed at a young age, Amalberga had made it her task to look after her.

They had just settled into their morning routine. At times, attending the court could be exciting, but it also meant long spells of boredom – such as when the men withdrew to talk of warfare and such. Used to her father discussing all manners of issues with her at Vaulun, and seemingly valuing her opinion, she craved to hear any tidings, but she had barely seen him since their arrival.

"Who could it be?" Hilda wondered, as she watched Amalberga open the latch.

"Lord." Her companion stepped aside to allow Milo to enter.

Though his visit pleased Hilda, it also surprised her. Had Father not to attend the king?

"Thank you, Amalberga. Would you let me speak with my daughter…alone?"

Had something gone awry?

Amalberga nodded. "Of course, Lord Milo." She cast a quick glance at Hilda before she left the room, closing the door behind her.

Hilda secured the needle, then placed her embroidery into a basket at her feet and stood to extend her hands to him in welcome. "I wish you a good morn, Father. Please sit. What brings you here so early?"

The benign smile on his face made her skin prickle. She knew him too well. Smiles and chatter always preceded something unexpected.

Milo sat on the stool vacated by Amalberga, close to her, rather than on the comfortable armchair. Something was amiss. She took her seat again.

"Dear daughter."

Oh, sweet Lady! She swallowed, her gaze focusing on a dropped needle on the floor. "Father?" She did not dare move.

"I've come with news, child. Good news," he added, raising his hand as her eyes met his and she opened her mouth to speak. "Please let me finish."

Hilda knotted her hands in her lap. He couldn't have... She nodded, regarding him with wary eyes.

Milo sighed. "This brings me pain, but also happiness, as I won't have to worry so much anymore. I believe you may have an inkling, but I would like a chance to explain, first." He leaned his elbows on his thighs and folded his hands, his expression solemn. "You are now almost seven-and-ten years old. A young lady. A pretty lady who would no doubt soon gather a growing group of admirers. Men from all over the kingdom."

Hilda took a deep breath. She was aware of the effect she had on the courtiers here in Carisiacum. Not that she knew why – she did not find herself beautiful – but she guessed her age and Father's status and wealth added to the lure. "So..."

"So, in order to see you looked after by a husband I can trust, the man in question and I have come to an agreement." He paused, his eyes lit up, full of hope. "By the autumn, you will become the wife of young Bellon, who will be Count of Carcassonne. He is a fine man, a brave warrior, and you shall never want for anything."

A throaty laugh escaped her. "Shall I not? How about a husband I would know? A man who loves me – and whom I love in return?" Tears pricked at the back of her eyes, and she glared at her father. "How about a new home near...our home, not a fortnight's journey away!"

Milo shook his head. "You are blind sometimes, Sweeting. The lad is besotted with you. I thought it was evident at the meal last night. He could not take his eyes off you."

"Then he is very fortunate in that *he* gets what *he* wants!" Hilda quipped. "But what about me? What am I to be in all this?"

"Don't you find him attractive, Nanthild? I thought at one point you were quite taken, too."

She blushed. 'Twas true. Bellon was a handsome man: fairly tall, broad in shoulder and back, his flirty smile, and the sparkle in his green eyes. And he was only a few years older than her, not like other lords at court, with wives who could have been their granddaughters. "He has a moustache."

Milo burst out laughing. "Well, I have one. In fact, most men wear moustaches. You would not find a suitable husband without one." He chuckled.

"Thank you for taking my concerns so seriously, Father." She crossed her arms in front of her chest.

Milo sobered. "I am taking you seriously, Hilda. That is why I agreed to this match. It is not only strategic – and no," he pre-empted her response, "there is no point discussing that reason as it is what marriage is about – but he is also a man I can trust. He is young enough to make a good husband; he adores you; and he is warrior enough to protect you in the volatile area of Septimania."

"It is more peaceful at Vaulun," she pleaded, her hand seeking his. He took it in a firm grasp.

"I cannot keep you at home forever, daughter. I'm afeared for your safety, even there. Hordes of lawless men roam the country, trying to undermine Charles' attempts at bringing peace. Alas, nowhere is safe at all for an unwed lady."

"I am sorry, Father." She swallowed hard. "I will... I'll miss you."

"I will miss you too, Sweeting. With your mother gone, and you married, our home will be but an empty shell. Thus is the life of a father." He wiped away a stray tear with the back of his hand. "In the coming months and years, I will be with Charles, forging new alliances and protecting our borders. Aquitania is as always a hotbed of trouble, and the Basques to the south-west are a major threat to our peace, as are the Lombards. In the meantime, Charles has appointed Bellon as his *missus dominicus*, his main representative in Septimania. He will act on the king's behalf and be given full control of Carcassonne, the Razès, and the whole surrounding area. It shall restore calm after the upheaval of recent decades."

"Charles is a conqueror. So, with Bellon's help, he will subdue Septimania."

Milo jumped up and paced the room. "Child, do not say such things. Not to me, nor to anyone else. 'Tis but dangerous chatter. Charles is a good king; a man of peace – you said so yourself the other night, or have you forgotten? Ruthless, yes, that he is. You have to be as king to keep your head. But he is also fair."

"He subdues tribes—"

"Because, at times, it's necessary," Milo interjected. "To bring about a truce. Tribes are always fighting each other. But in Septimania, there are no rivalling tribes. The inhabitants yearn for peace. And that's what Bellon will bring."

"But at what price?" Hilda stood too, hands on her hips. "My life?" The fury inside her was raging.

"Daughter, watch your tongue!" Milo chided her.

She blinked at him, too upset to speak.

"There are reasons why women should keep their noses out of warfare. Your way of thinking makes little sense. You must stop this nonsense before your wedding." He sighed, his shoulders dropping. "I have let you have your own way for too long. 'Tis time another man takes up the task. Bellon is the man I chose, and he has accepted. I'm sorry that you appear to despise him, despite him defending you last night against that brute, Clovis, whose attitude shows nothing of the noble blood he carries. And I don't know what Bellon has done to deserve your disregard. I trust him, and with that, the matter is closed. You shall be wed in the autumn."

Tears ran down Hilda's cheek and she let them fall unchecked. Hanging her head, she turned away from her father. Leaning against the sill of the narrow window looking out over the roofs of Carisiacum, she sobbed.

"Nanthild, don't be afeared. You will be safe. And loved." Milo stood behind her, enveloping her in his arms, a sigh escaping into her neck. She leaned back against his warm chest and closed her eyes. 'Twas like in the old days. Oh, how she yearned to be a little girl again, carefree, roaming the fields and forests of her homeland. Instead, she was a bargaining tool. Charles and Father had secured Bellon's support with her womb. She realised then that her life as she knew it would end.

Her childhood was over.

***

The great hall of the king's *palatium* was welcoming, Bellon thought as he entered, glad to escape the cool breeze of the northern winds. Easter was a time of blossoms, of new flowers, of vines beginning to grow. But also of heavy rain – as it was tonight. He shook out his cloak and patted the moisture from his tunic. Pushing his wet hair behind his ears, he wiped away the small rivulets of water trickling down his neck. He had taken great care to wipe his leather boots on a narrow if drenched mat inside the door, but at least he was not the only one caught out in the downpour. Muddy footprints from dozens of other guests caked the tiled floor.

He waved at three lords huddled by the large fire pit in the centre of the room. They looked as bedraggled as he was. It made him feel better. He was about to step forward to join them when Milo called his name. The older man was already sitting at a trestle table laid out for the evening's meal, nursing a clay cup.

Bellon cast a final, longing glance at the fire, to raucous laughter from the men, and lowered himself on a stool beside Milo, pulling at his damp leggings to stretch them over his thighs. Reaching out, he checked the contents of a pitcher on the table. Dark ale.

"Please," the older man said, gesturing to it, "help yourself."

"Thank you." Bellon picked up an unused cup and filled it. He took a deep draught of warm ale. "Ah, these northern lands do nothing for my mood. The weather is awful." He grinned.

Milo chuckled. "Aye, I was caught in a rain shower earlier when I visited the camp. I take it that's where you've just come from?"

Bellon nodded. "It is. I spoke to the king and his advisers about the geographical advantages of Carcassonne as a strategic point against the Saracens and the Basques. Our combined presence should ensure no further attacks."

"Unless they came from south of the mountains?"

"We'll be preparing for all eventualities."

"I wish you much success. There are still dangers, but with the new agreements in place, we should make easy progress westward."

"I have no doubt." Bellon's face fell. "'Tis a shame I won't be taking part until later. I'll be heading to Béziers first."

Milo smiled and placed a hand on Bellon's shoulder. "You may still have many chances to prove your worth when you join the campaign in the summer. As it is, you already have. You are guarding a vital outpost of the Frankish kingdom against the Basques and the Goths." He winced, then withdrew his arm as Bellon's back straightened.

"I'm not defending Carcassonne against the Visigoths. I am one of them. 'Tis our home. That is why the leaders from south of the Pyrenaei will not attack me. Their blood runs through my veins. We won't stand in Charles' way. We have been fighting for too long."

Milo took a sip and leaned against the back of his chair. "I hope what you say is true. With Charles taking control over the region, there may be trouble brewing amongst some people." He looked Bellon in the eye. "But I have faith that you will handle them the way you have to, young man. 'Tis God's will."

"And the king's." Bellon winked, letting the argument pass. They were after the same goal. He raised his cup. "To peace."

"To peace," Milo repeated. "And to a successful marriage."

Bellon choked on his ale and started to cough. Milo laughed and patted his back until he calmed down. Once his breath had returned, he dared look at his future father-in-law. His cheeks were burning, and he was certain Milo knew it was not down to the liquid.

"So be it," he finally whispered. Then he took another draught, soothing his throat.

"I meant to tell you…I have spoken with Nanthild."

Bellon raised his eyebrows. His stomach was in knots. He had considered himself fortunate when Charles and Milo approached him about becoming wedded to the girl. It was a tactical match. But once he had cast eyes on the lady, he knew she had captured his heart. Still, her reaction to him had not been as expected.

"Bellon?" Milo was watching him through narrowed eyes. "Is all well?"

Bellon nodded, embarrassed with himself for feeling like a boy in his first rush of passion. "Yes, lord, I'm fine. But tell me – how did the lady Nanthild take to the…umm… tidings?"

Milo glanced at his empty cup. "It would seem you have some work to do. But whilst she isn't happy with the plan, she has a fondness of you. I have seen it in her eyes. 'Tis only that she knows how to hide it well."

Bellon let out a sigh of relief. Not all was lost. "You won't need to fret. I shall always treat her well. She'll want for nothing."

"I know, Bellon. I know. But like her dear mother – God rest her soul – she is of strong mind and opinion. Unbecoming at times, but," Milo chuckled, more to himself, Bellon thought, "I have always found that trait endearing."

38

"So do I, lord, so do I." Bellon picked up the pitcher. "Would you care for another?"

The soft sound of a lute drifted to his ears as Bellon watched the gathering of warriors, lords and ladies. Franks and Visigoths sharing a table, sharing food and wine. It was a good sign; it brought hope.

Beside him, the lady Nanthild pushed a small roast piece of rabbit across her trencher with a finely carved knife, her face too pale for his liking. Truth was, he worried about her. The news had been a shock to her, so it was clear she needed time. He was content to grant it.

A scraping sound pulled him from his thoughts. Nanthild had dug her knife deep into the dry bread that held the meat, and it had sliced into the table.

"I apologise, lord." Her eyes were wide as she kept staring past him. She shuddered.

Concerned, he followed her gaze and frowned. Clovis glared at them from across the hearth. The soldier's eyes were dark with anger in the flickering light of the central hearth. The clod still bore a grudge.

Bellon shook his head and touched the girl's wrist. "Don't fear him, lady. I will not let him come near you."

She blinked, then smiled at him. "Thank you," she whispered. "His words from last night shook me."

His heart melted under her concern. "I know. Please put no importance to them. Clovis is a great warrior – but not a man to deal with ladies gently, as would be their right. Despite his noble birth, his tastes lie in other, less savoury, directions…"

"As do many men's tastes," she said drily, withdrawing her hand from under his.

The table felt cold to his touch, and he quickly picked up his cup. "Not all of us, Nanthild." His sideways gaze held hers. "Not all of us." He sipped his wine.

"No, you are correct. I was always hoping my future husband would not…" She fiddled with the tassels on her belt, avoiding his gaze.

Of course, she knew. How could he forget? The reason she was subdued tonight was because of Milo having told her of their betrothal. Trying to soothe her fears, he smiled. "You have no reason to worry."

Her body shook for a moment before it relaxed. She raised her cup and held it to him, her eyes glinting in the light of the central hearth. "I take vows seriously, lord."

He nodded. "As do I."

A strong hand gripped his shoulder. Reluctantly, he broke the eye contact, prepared to glare at the intruder. Then he quickly put down his cup and kneeled to the king. "Sire."

The lady Nanthild curtseyed beside him.

"'Tis wonderful to watch young love." Charles acknowledged them with a nod, a smile on his lips.

"Sire," she whispered, keeping her gaze lowered.

Charles smiled and signalled to them to stand. "I shall announce the fortunate event in a moment."

Beside Bellon, Nanthild's body shuddered. Uncertain of how to react, he took her hand in his, surprised at her skin so cold to his touch. He entwined his fingers with hers.

"You have nothing to fear, my child," Charles said, his voice low, his gaze flicking from her to Bellon. "This young man is a fine warrior, of sound and brave heart, and he knows how to treat a lady. You shall be safe with him."

Bellon caught her eye, and he nodded. "All will be well, lady."

She swallowed hard and tried to extricate her hand from his. He let her go. "If you say so, sire," she said to Charles as she folded her hands.

The king took a step back, and Bellon quickly lowered his head in reverence.

"I do. Well, if all goes as planned during this summer's campaign, we shall celebrate your wedding in the late autumn. Bellon. Lady Nanthild." Charles turned and strode to his seat on the dais where Queen Hildegarde greeted him with a wide smile. Even now, her belly well-rounded, the young queen shared the king's high table. After having given birth to a girl the year before, rumours said she was carrying a boy. Witnessing the strong bond between the king and his wife, Bellon wondered whether he and the lady Nanthild would ever be as happy together.

Turning his gaze to his betrothed, he caught her staring at him. Had she read his thoughts?

He waited until she sat down again, then lowered himself onto the bench they shared. "Tonight will be over soon. Then we can look forward to our own feast."

He took a tentative sip of wine. The girl's subdued manner worried him. Her smile was brittle, and she seemed scared. Did his mere presence do that to her? When all he wanted was to protect her! He was pulled out of his reverie when Charles pushed his large, ornately-carved chair covered with comfortable cushions, back and stood.

"My lords and ladies here gathered." Charles' voice boomed across the room. Standing tall in the centre of the dais, he held his gemstone-encrusted goblet aloft. "Today, we are delighted to announce a happy event, one that shall be upon us in the autumn. Bellon of Carcassonne, Lady Nanthild, please." He gestured to them to stand before his table.

Bellon took her hand in his and led her towards the dais, supporting her shakiness with his warmth. She showed a shy smile, yet her eyes were wide, and she glanced across the room. She felt uncomfortable being the centre of everyone's attention. The queen was watching them with a curious expression on her face. Did the noble lady perhaps recognise herself in the girl?

Charles coughed. "Between all this talk of strategy, of expansion and co-operation, we are delighted to share the good tidings that Bellon, who will soon be installed as count of Carcassonne," Charles pointed at him, and Bellon lowered his head in acknowledgment of the royal favour, "will wed the lovely lady Nanthild, only daughter of my dear friend and adviser, Milo, count of Aulun, before the feast of Christ's birth. Furthermore," the king pre-empted shouts of surprise, "Bellon will act from today as Commander of Carcassonne, the Razès, and all the surrounding area which will form part of the county which his father had already administered in all but title. I am particularly satisfied with this result, as it proves that Franks and Visigoths can work together in making our southern border a safer place, bringing peace and stability. Let us drink to the young couple – and a safe Septimania!"

The king took a long draught, to much acclaim by all, then held out his goblet to Bellon who took it with his free hand and sipped the rich wine.

Shouts of felicitations echoed around the decorated stone walls of the hall, and Bellon acknowledged them. "Thank you. To a safer Septimania, where people can live and work the land in peace," he added. Beside him, Nanthild smiled at people too. Good. Despite her fears, she knew her duty, and her role as future countess. He passed the goblet to her, and she took a small sip. Bellon then passed it back to the king who nodded approvingly.

When they returned to their table, his eyes met Clovis' on the far side. The warrior's face was contorted in anger. Ahh, now Bellon knew. The man's obnoxiousness was not down to his betrothed, but because of his enhanced position. Had Clovis held hopes for the role of commander in the south? He was not of the region of Septimania, so had very little to offer other than what he was good at – the brutal suppression of unwilling tribes. Bellon broke the contact and watched Nanthild instead. They sat as the shouts abated and folk returned to their wine and food, without doubt discussing the unusual union of north and south, of Frank and Visigoth.

Milo pressed his daughter's free hand, then raised his cup to them. Bellon returned the gesture. Then Milo's neighbour pulled at his sleeve, demanding his attention with words of congratulations, and he turned away.

"'Tis all out in the open now," he whispered in Nanthild's ear, the scent of lavender from her luscious hair playing havoc with his senses. "I promise to be a good, faithful husband. You have nothing to fear from me."

She looked at him through half-lowered lashes and nodded. "Thank you, lord."

He smiled. "Please say Bellon from now on. We're betrothed now…Nanthild."

The lady cocked her head, her gaze firmly locked with his. "Then please call me Hilda."

"I shall, Hilda." Relief flooded through him. Perhaps he was fortunate, after all.

Keeping a close eye on the lass for the rest of the evening, it saddened Bellon to see the nervousness in her demeanour. When they were first introduced, before Milo had told her, she had seemed lighter, more self-assured, bolder. He had liked that in her. But this Easter had not gone well for her. To be married to a stranger before the year is out had come as a shock. Bellon prayed that she would, in time, develop the same feelings for him as he already held for her.

Chapter Five

On her way back from the *notaire*, Maddie stopped off at a large *Leclerc* supermarket on the outskirts of Carcassonne. She needed milk and bread – and wine! Especially after the shock…

She parked her car outside the big store and entered the lobby, dazzled by its size. Searching for a carrier, she found a small basket-on-wheels-like contraption. Uncertain where to start, she wandered up and down the aisles before she came to a halt by the large area for fruit and vegetables. Cold steam rose from between displays of boxes of loose courgettes and peppers, mushrooms and tomatoes and a great variety of other vegetables. On the other side, a choice of packed strawberries from Spain and other fruit from farther overseas was waiting for shoppers to pick them up. Her basket filled quickly with a selection of healthy foods. Good for her five-a-day!

The meat counters displayed choices she hardly ever saw in York: rabbit, wild boar, horse. Horse? Maddie stared, then passed by quickly. Other countries, other…umm…choices! She picked up a pack of organic *bio* beef mince and moved on. Now her basket was filling up fast. Fruit juice, biscuits, coffee, milk. *Mmmh, madeleines.* As always when she saw the delicious French cake bites that shared her name, she grinned, and grabbed a pack. Sorted!

Once she had all the items she needed, she moved to the large wine section.

"Wow!" she whispered, unsure where to start. A French lady passing her raised her eyebrows before moving on, slightly shaking her head. No doubt she was thinking, *tourist*! Displayed before Maddie were rows of wines from various

French regions, with a few small overseas sections thrown in. Up until now, she had not been a wine drinker. All she knew was that she liked Italian wines, easily accessible in York. But French?

Now, where to start?

"*Puis-je vous aider, madame?*" a strong, deep voice asked behind her.

Maddie turned and found herself staring into Léon Cabrol's dark grey eyes. She took a step back. Dressed in a biker's leather jacket and jeans, he exuded confidence. Quickly, she pulled herself together. She was a divorcee in her thirties, and French men were renowned to be great flirts. Still…

"*Oui, s'il vous plaît, monsieur.*" She smiled. "Thank you. I'm sorry, but I'm clueless. I was too young to appreciate wine when I left France, and northern England isn't exactly a hotbed for fine Languedoc grape juice."

"Yes, I can imagine. I lived in London for a few years, and although they serve French wines in bars and restaurants, they preferred overseas brands. Those imports were often the cheap stuff, with little taste – in my humble view," he added with a grin.

Maggie giggled. "I probably have to agree. So, what would you – as a local wine producer and drinker, I presume – recommend?"

"That depends. Do you prefer red, rosé, or white?"

"Well, I usually like my white, but I can't see too many here."

"That's right. It's because of the grape varieties the *vignerons* use here. Red grapes grow better in our hot summer climate, as do several kinds of rosé."

"Then I'll be happy to try a red or two. It looks like there are plenty of choices."

"Ahh, now, if I may lead you over there?" He pointed further along the long shelf where bottles of red wine stood lined up.

Maddie followed his lead. "Thank you. So here we have wine from the area, right?"

Léon Cabrol nodded. "*Oui*. Most of these here are from our regions." He pointed at the whole shelf half the width of the store. "The Cabardès is where we are from, as you know; the Corbières lie to the south and east of the Cité; the Minervois reaches towards the Mediterranean; and some others beyond. Many *domaines* sell directly to local restaurants and stores, and smaller ventures tend to who pull together under so-called co-operatives. It makes the whole business more affordable, especially the smaller your own vineyard is."

"Yes, I've heard of that. Very interesting. Now, which would you recommend? I'm looking for a couple of reasonably-priced wines, where you don't end up with a sore head after a glass..." She glanced at him with half-closed lids.

He laughed out loud. "A good point. Now, here we have a light *Pouzols*, easy to drink, from the Minervois..." He pointed at one bottle, at a surprisingly cheap price, and moved up the aisle. "There we have a delicious *Ventenac* that tastes of spices and berries. And this is a lovely wine, a *Château de Pennautier*. Excellent quality. Those last two lie closest to us."

Support your local produce. It made sense. "Thank you. They sound lovely." Maddie nodded, then glanced across the shelf. One label made her stop. She cocked her head. "Oh! And here's a *Château de Minervens*. I presume that's yours?"

Léon Cabrol shuffled his feet. "Ahh...*oui*. As it happens, yes. This is one of ours."

"You are not embarrassed about it, are you?" His reaction intrigued her. Usually, owners blurt out their credentials from a mile off. Sales tactics. This man suddenly seemed distinctly uncomfortable in his skin.

"*Non*! Not at all." He shrugged his shoulders in a typical French way, matching the stereotype. "I didn't want to push my luck." His mouth twitched.

Maddie raised an eyebrow and laughed. "So, you intentionally veered away from it."

"Well, I don't want to – how do you say – steamroll you into buying my wine."

"In that case, I'll have a *Ventenac* and two of yours, please. I'll try the others later. What does it taste like?" she asked as he handed her the bottles. She pushed aside the bag of apples at the bottom of her basket to squeeze in the bottles.

Léon Cabrol's face lit up. "Of ripe blackberries and cranberries, the wind and the sun."

"Is that your marketing slogan?"

"Umm, something like that, yes."

"Then it works very well, at least for me," she said. "Thank you for your help. I'll now know what to look out for next time."

"I'm delighted to hear. Please come and visit us for a tour if you'd like. I'd be happy to show you around."

Don't even go there. He's French, like your father – who left your mother when she was pregnant!

Reality brought her back. "Thank you. That's kind of you. I may take you up on your offer one day. I wasn't planning on staying long, but my mother had other ideas."

The smile died on his lips. "I'm sorry to hear. Is there anything I can help you with?"

Maddie tilted her head. "Perhaps. I have to mull it over before I decide."

"That's perfectly understandable." He fished out a business card from an inside pocket of his jacket. "Please call me or pop in. We're just a couple of kilometres up the road from you."

"I shall." She took it and tucked it into her bag. "And thank you for your help. I hope I haven't held you up."

"Not at all. It's been a pleasure." He winked. "*À bientôt.*"

"*Au revoir.*"

"Elizabeth did *what*?" Brian asked.

"She stipulated that I have to stay in the house for a year before I can sell it," Maddie repeated, clutching the receiver to her ear. Her ex could be slow at times. The typical nutty professor!

47

"But…whatever for?"

"I don't have a clue, Brian. I think she wanted to make a point. Mess with my life. Her last chance to."

"Don't say that, Maddie. She was your mother."

"Who never really got on with you."

"I know. Guess we'll never know why, now. So, what are you planning to do?"

"I've no idea. I can do my writing from here if I can arrange decent WiFi. But I'd miss the bustle of York."

"I've missed York too, for a long time. But, as you know, I still think this move was the best decision in my life."

"Yes, I'm sure you do. It finished our marriage," she added drily.

Brian laughed. "Sadly, it did. Just wasn't meant to be. But we are both happier now."

"True," Maddie conceded. Their friendship worked better than their short-lived marriage. "But I haven't lived abroad in years. Almost half my life."

"You'll get used to it, hun. The Languedoc is a beautiful place, full of ancient history."

"Ahh, the history professor at the university of Valencia is speaking." Maddie snickered.

Their one shared passion, history had been more important to them than marriage.

"I know, Brian. But no Vikings!" She shook her head. "How am I going to keep up to date with my research?"

"The worldwide web?" He made it sound so easy.

Maddie sighed. "I know it would, but…I'm happy in York. It's a pretty town. People are friendly. Historic sites all around. Lovely pubs…"

"But the wine isn't as nice as where you are," Brian quipped.

"Ha, cheers!" Maddie clinked her wine glass against the receiver and took a sip of the *Château de Minervens*. "Mmh…" That man shouldn't hold back about his business at all. The wine was delicious.

"Hahaha, you're on it already. I knew it! But seriously," Brian sobered, "it's a great chance to experience life elsewhere. You've not done that since you moved to York. Why not take it and see how it goes?"

"Seems like I have no choice."

"Look, why don't you speak to Jane and see if you can arrange Skype sessions with anyone at the uni you need to talk to? And ask her to take videos of any new discoveries for you. They often do that anyway, to record new findings. In fact, many consultants work like that."

"Again, provided I get WiFi here."

"It's a tourist area, the Languedoc. They'll have WiFi – at least, enough for what you need to work."

"True," she conceded. "OK, I'll give Orange a call to see what's what."

"That's the spirit. I'm sure you'll enjoy it there. It's hot and dry in the summer!"

"Trust you to mention the weather. Valencia has screwed with your head." She laughed.

Brian chuckled. "Yes, likely too much sun, I admit."

"Well, it would be a big change."

"You don't have to decide on the spot. Have some wine. Relax. Sleep it over. Maybe tomorrow it won't seem too absurd. Though I wonder about Elizabeth's motivation."

"So do I. I'm still going to sell the house when the year's up. But at least, I can do some cosmetic work to it to make it more attractive to buyers."

"Attractive to expats, you mean."

"Shh! To anyone willing to buy a 100-year-old French village stone house with wonky electricity and old pipes. Mum has a nice sum of money in her account, but I can't access it – unless for renovation reasons – until I've lived here for a year."

"Elizabeth had money? Who'd have thought." Brian joked.

"Tell me about it! Bet you wouldn't have divorced me so quickly had you known I was a rich heiress…" She chuckled and took another sip. The smooth liquid went down like velvet.

"Now, now!" She could hear the laughter in his voice. "I rather blame the Yorkshire weather."

"Muppet! Off you go, then. And thanks for listening."

"Always, love. Give me a shout if you need help."

"Thanks, Brian. And give my love to Ana and huggles to Felipe."

"Will do. Take care. Bye."

"Bye."

She put the receiver down on her mother's 1990s telephone and sat back. Brian was right. It didn't matter where she wrote, and she could always contact Jane for updates of the dig. Should they unearth something dramatic, she could fly out at short notice.

Maddie sipped her wine and looked around. Decorating the rooms would be her priority. She smiled, her head already filling with ideas of how much better the old place could look. Maybe it wasn't such a bad idea at all.

It was only for a year, after all...

***

Arranging to stay took over much of Maddie's time. The next morning, she visited the post office to apply for an account at the *Banque Postale*. Then, she popped into the *épicerie* for some fresh baguette and cheese. Walking back, she was already munching a ripped-off corner off the tasty, still-warm bread. The sun beat down on her back, and, despite the chilly temperatures, the rays warmed her. Maddie welcomed the pleasant feeling of heat and fresh air.

Passing Bernadette Albert, she saw her neighbour was busy tending flowers in her garden. The grey-haired lady crouched on the ground, her knees on a gardening pad, adjusting a rosebush in a patch of loose earth.

"*Bonjour, madame.*" Maddie waved as she closed her own gate behind her, shopping bag in hand, and looked over the fence. "*Ça va?*"

"Ah, *bonjour.* I'm fine, thank you." Madame Albert returned her smile and rose slowly, pushing herself upright, and brushed off the earth from her hands. "And please call me Bernadette." She waved a hand at the patch around her. "Some plants toppled over in the storm we had two weeks ago, so I had to tuck them in again." She proudly pointed at a neat row of cut-back roses planted along her wall, now firmly held in place again, tied to a trellis.

Come May, her neighbour's garden would give Monet's at Giverny a run for its money, Maddie thought. It was already vibrant with colour, and bursting with scent, even this early in the year. She had planted perennials next to big round tubs of lavender, a small grove of olive trees stood on the side of her house, and Maddie knew that she had fruit trees at the back. She'd seen them from her bedroom window.

"Ah. Oh, thank you. I'm Maddie," she offered. "Your garden looks beautiful. I can't wait to see what it'll look like later in the spring. My mother didn't seem too bothered about her own." She shrugged apologetically and pointed at the overgrown shrubs around her. Weeds grew from the gaps in the stone-walled border from months of neglect.

Bernadette came forward and leant on the fence. "Your mother preferred to occupy herself with other things, like reading. She was forever sitting in a chair on the little terrace over there – before it became too overgrown – with a book in her hands. Gardening wasn't her priority. André cut the grass and the bushes every few weeks for her over the summer. I can ask him to help you if you'd like." She put her hand to her mouth, her gaze full of worry. "I'm so sorry. I hope I wasn't too personal."

Maddie laughed. "Not at all. I would be grateful if you could ask him. I'm a useless gardener. I can just about pot a plant, but trying to get it to survive is tricky."

"Ahh, I can help you with that. *Pas de souci*."

"I would appreciate it. Thank you. It looks like I'll be staying here for a while, doing some work on the house, so to have someone keep the garden nice and pretty would be great."

Her neighbour nodded, a big smile lighting up her face. "Yes, that makes sense. So you've decided to stay? It's what

Elisa wanted the most. And it'll be lovely to have a neighbour again. The owners of that one," she pointed to the large house bordering her garden on the other side, "live in Lille, and they show their faces maybe twice a year for a few weeks." She tutted to show her disapproval. "*C'est une dommage.*"

"Yes, I guess so." Maddie kept her reply intentionally vague, not wishing to give the woman false hopes. "I must return to York first to sort out some work stuff, but then I'll be here whilst I'm decorating. The house needs an upgrade."

Something in Bernadette's expression concerned her. She'd barely met the lady, yet she already knew her to be friendly, helpful – and very direct. Maddie promptly received confirmation of her thoughts.

"Oh, you are planning on selling it?" An eyebrow went up, the smile slowly vanishing.

Why did the woman have to make her feel bad? This place meant nothing to her. It had Elizabeth's name written all over it! The memory of her mother brought back unwanted, distant memories. Maddie brushed them aside.

"To be honest, it's very likely."

Bernadette's face fell.

"I'm sorry," Maddie added. "This was Elizabeth's house. I haven't…hadn't spoken with my mother for years. The reasons go way back." Maddie felt she had to justify her position.

Why? I can do what I want with the place.

A crash made them both turn towards the house. Something had moved. Maddie peered over the shrubs. Several roof tiles lay on the overgrown terrace, shattered into a myriad of little pieces. A shiver ran down her spine as she looked up. How did they get unstuck? The weather was completely calm.

Baffled, she glanced at Bernadette who was watching her. "Did you see that?"

"Yes, dear. I was just about to point out that it looked like they were sliding when they fell off the roof. All by themselves." Bernadette frowned. "Elisa only had it re-done two years ago. It should be in perfect condition."

"Well, it's no longer." Maddie's gaze went back to the splinters. "I'll have to get it checked. Do you know by chance who did the work?"

It slowly dawned on her that she'd have to ask her neighbour and other villagers about a lot of things concerning her mother's house – and life here. She knew nothing at all about the place, or how life in France worked these days. Twenty years were a long time to be away. And France was a country where the rules change with the *Cévenol* winds. Often.

"It was an English guy," Bernadette said. "I'll find out his number for you. He must fix it, for free!"

Maddie grew even more baffled. "English? That's unlike my mother."

Her neighbour laughed. "Very true. The roofer in the next village had just retired, so she called Jake."

Maddie smiled at the soft pronunciation of 'j'. The lady obviously had little to do with Brits.

"But your mother made him work twice as hard for his money." Bernadette winked. "Oh, *bonjour*, Léon!"

Maddie turned around to find Léon Cabrol running up the hill towards them, dressed in a loose-fitting t-shirt and baggy jogging pants.

"*Bonjour*, Bernadette. Hello again." He stopped near them and, leaning forward, propped his hands on the fence, trying to catch his breath. Despite the chill hanging in the air, a thin layer of sweat covered his exposed skin.

"Oh, hello," Maddie returned his greeting. "You're not running up that hill, are you?"

He nodded. "Yes. Every morning, if I can."

"Impressive." She grinned. She'd tried hill-walking now and then, but running was firmly outside her capability.

From the corner of her eye, she saw her neighbour watching her carefully.

"I see you're making friends," he said, straightening up, hands on hips. His lips were twitching.

"Yes, I hope so." Maddie exchanged smiles with Bernadette.

"Someone has to show the young lady how things work here. She'll be renovating the house, you know."

"Oh, really? As I said before, please let me know if you need any help."

"That's very kind of you, Monsieur Cabrol, but I think I'll be fine once I know where to get what."

His eyes lit up with humour. "Well, the offer stands, madame. And please call me Léon."

"Léon is your man if you need a hand in the house," her neighbour said, a shrewd gleam in her eyes. "He renovated his parents' rooms in the old manor, and they look beautiful now."

The woman was positively selling him to her. As expected, the man himself shrugged it off in typical Gallic fashion. "It took years, mind. And I didn't do it all on my own…"

"Oh, but it is lovely." She grabbed Maddie's wrist over the fence. "He knows *everyone* who can be of help."

"Says the woman who has been the heart of the village for longer than I've been alive."

Bernadette blushed, beaming with pride.

There was a high level of affection and respect between them. Maddie felt a warm glow descending on her. She felt accepted, welcomed – something she hadn't felt in many years.

"Well, thank you very much, Monsieur Cab—"

"Léon."

"Bien sûr. Léon. And I'm Maddie." She held out her hand over the gate, before the awkwardness of her gesture hit her. Just as she was about to withdraw it, he took it in a warm grip and held her gaze, his grey eyes full of warmth.

"Enchanté!"

The man was a real charmer. She had to be careful.

A Mini screeched to a halt beside them and they turned as a window was lowered.

"*Salut*, Léon. Can I give you a lift up the hill?"

Maddie withdrew her hand, breaking the contact.

The woman spoke with a slight foreign accent. Spanish, perhaps? Or Italian? Her face covered in a layer of makeup, with strong black eye liner and ruby red lipstick, she exuded feminine city chic. Just what did such a dolled-up figure do in a sleepy village like Minervens? She woman ignored Maddie and Bernadette, but kept beaming at Léon.

Was she his girlfriend?

"Hello Gina." Léon's tone was neutral as his gaze went slowly from her to the glamour puss. It seemed almost like he regretted the disruption. He consulted his watch. "Actually, I'm running a little late, so, yes, that would be great." Turning to Maddie and her neighbour, he added, "I'm sorry, mesdames. Duty calls. *À bientôt.*"

"*Au révoir,*" Maddie said, smiling politely.

Bernadette waved. "Too right. Time to earn your living," she joked.

Laughing, Léon opened the door on the passenger side, then paused. "Remember my offer, Maddie, will you?" Not waiting for her answer, he got in and shut the door.

Gina revved up the engine and sent Maddie a dark look. Without a word, she put her foot on the gas and shot off up the hill.

"She's trouble, that girl."

Maddie turned to see her neighbour glare after the car.

"Umm, is she? In what way?"

"She's the marketing assistant at the *domaine*, but would love to become Madame Cabrol."

"Oh, and what would be so bad about that?" Maddie shuffled her feet. Léon's private life was none of her business.

Bernadette's eyes widened. "Everything! She never speaks to anyone here in the village, only to the Cabrols. She is bossing the other staff around, and whilst she is polite to his parents – to their face – she slags them off to other people. I've heard her, you know!" The old lady tutted. "They're too working-class for her. You see – they don't mind getting their hands dirty in the vines, nor does Léon, but *mademoiselle* wouldn't lift a finger in the dirt." She shook her head. "No, she's not a good person, that one. Though, sadly, she excels at marketing…"

"So he values her work?"

"Yes, but she wants him to value her…as a wife. Never! Besides," she added with a sly smile, "he seems to like you."

Maddie gave her a sweet smile, then turned to her house. "Now, back to those fallen roof tiles…"

Chapter Six

Late autumn, AD 777
The mountains of southern Francia

A thick flurry of snowflakes swirled around them as Hilda's
retinue trundled its way through the thick forest covering yet
another hill. The pine trees barely kept the snow at bay, and
the horses' hooves were sliding on the slushy ground. They
had been travelling for a fortnight, through rain, sleet and,
most recently, snow, and within a few more days, they would
cross into the usually dry plain that led to Carcassonne. On
their way, they had found accommodation with noble
families of her father's acquaintance, where possible. At
other times, they had stayed a night in a tent. The chill had
crept through her bedding and furs, and she hated it.

Though Father's planning of the journey had been
meticulous, Hilda was weary of the long days spent
travelling, of the cold and the rain, and she had lost her
appetite days earlier. With every step that took her farther
south, she longed for the comfort of her home, with its
inviting hearth, hot food, and warm bedcovers. She already
missed the familiarity of her family manor. When would be
the next time she saw it again? Would she ever return? Her
thoughts grew more and more morose.

Father had finally sent for her after she had waited for
months, and the conditions for travelling could not have been
any worse. Hilda huddled deeper into her mantle. 'Twas not
Father's fault her journey had begun so late in the season. He
and Bellon had spent most of the year repelling the Saracens.
And whilst some of their leaders kept to their concluding
agreement with Charles, others were still leading raids across

the high peaks of the southern mountains, and even into the plain. In the end, they had all been pushed back.

In honour of Bellon's hard work, Charles had at last installed her betrothed as Count of Carcassonne during a what Father had called 'memorable if brief ceremony' in his letter. Finally, they had established a tentative peace in Septimania, and confirmed the date for the wedding. She would marry Bellon of Carcassonne on the day of St Adela, on the eve of the feast of Christ's birth. The celebration would be brief, lasting only one day, but Father had promised her an unforgettable event. Apparently, the town and castle were already busy preparing for the big day, with plans for a sumptuous meal, and Bellon had summoned storytellers from across Septimania and Aquitania for their entertainment.

Unforgettable? Christ wept! Hilda rolled her eyes. She'd had many months to think about that one day. In fact, she had thought of little else. And whilst Amalberga had not stopped singing praises of Bellon and his heroic pursuits on the king's behalf, Hilda's own thoughts had been less complementary. 'Twas true – he was a fine warrior, and a handsome one, too. She had to admit it. Heat seeped into her cheeks, a suddenly pleasant feeling against the suffusing cold. Instead, she gritted her teeth, banishing any positive thoughts of her husband-to-be. 'Twas the end of her life as she knew it. With Father away so often, the responsibility of running the manor household had fallen to her, and she had thrived in it, and the independence it had given her. She could come and go as she pleased, although an escort was always on call ensuring her safety. And therein lay her problem.

She would lose her freedom, and likely someone would uncover her calling. Even though Bellon would without doubt be away often from her new home, she would not be alone. There would be servants watching her every move as countess of a bustling, strategic town. At her childhood manor, she was used to moving unhindered, unobserved. As she needed to be.

Like her mother before her, she had a deep love for herbs and their effects. So, known only to Amalberga, she had learnt the ancient skills from a wise-woman living near her home, who was delighted to see her young charge succeed her. Once Hilda had gained sufficient knowledge, she had taken over the old woman's work. People met her, arranged through Amalberga, in secret locations not too far from the manor, and Hilda would offer to help. They travelled far for her guidance and some called her a saint for her skills as a healer. Villeins and nobles alike swore by her potions. Even wounded warriors came to gain her advice and help.

Yet, here she was now, moving to a place she did not know, far from her home and those she trusted. Hilda had never visited the south, so finding out where to collect herbs would be her first task. It was a different climate, hotter and drier, so it might be difficult to gather some. Amalberga would help her.

But who else could she trust? Bellon, the Christian warrior affiliated to Charles, lord over all equally Christian Franks, would not permit her to follow her path. She was certain of it. The mood in the Church had changed in recent decades, and rumours had reached her of attacks on wise-women, and some were even banished or killed. Unlike the early saints, with their visions and skills, the role of ordinary women had become more defined in recent years. Defined – and restricted – by men!

So Hilda had to keep her calling secret from her future husband.

Her thoughts bleak, she pushed the worries from her mind and focused on the route ahead. The ground was treacherous, with leaves beneath a layer of wet snow a dangerous footfall for the horses. The group had slowed to a walk as they followed a narrow path through the thick forest. A hill beside them rose steeply, its forest covered in an even thicker layer of snow. Ahead of her, she saw men struggling to keep their horses from sliding. Oh, why could they not have waited till springtime? She gritted her teeth and kept her head low against the biting flurries of ice. Inside, her anger against Father, and against Bellon, rose unhindered.

"Halt!"

She raised her gaze, shielding her eyes against the falling snow. The men at the front had stopped. She exchanged a glance with Amalberga, riding in silence beside her, then nudged her mare forward. "What appears to be the problem, Dagobert?"

The captain of her escort turned to face her. "There is a small clearing not far ahead, lady, sheltered to all sides by thick forest. With dusk settling, we will make camp here for the night. The remaining light will fade fast in these hills in autumn."

Yet another cold night in a tent. Hilda nodded, sighing. "Thank you. Please see it done."

She signalled to a lad younger than her to help her from her mare. Then he assisted Amalberga before leading the horses away.

They stepped aside as mayhem ensued around them as the men set to putting up tents and building campfires, whilst two sturdy women who accompanied their group pulled several dead rabbits, caught and killed earlier in the day for the night's meal, from their bags and set out to prepare them. With deft hands, they skinned and prepared the small animals for roasting, putting aside the pelts for later. They would likely be made into gloves or trims for a hood or cloak. Setting a large pot on stilts across a brightly-burning fire pit, one woman added cut-up carrots, parsnips, dried herbs and water to simmer over the spreading heat whilst the other pushed the skinned rabbits on a spike, to roast across another fire.

Amalberga stood next to Hilda and wrapped her snow-covered arm around her shoulders. "Not long now, Sweeting. We shall soon arrive in our new home."

Hilda laughed, the sound too harsh in her ears. "You have already settled in, have you not?" She shook her head. "How can you be so calm?"

Amalberga nodded, smiling. "Because I know it will be a good place for us."

At a gesture from Dagobert, they walked towards a lit fire outside their tent, where two benches awaited them. Hilda sat, wrapping her cloak tighter around her, and stared into the licking flames, a sense of foreboding gripping her innards. Amalberga pulled the other bench closer and held her hands out towards the heat.

Hilda lost sight of the world around her as the front of her body veered from cold to heat. Visions appeared before her eyes. Darkness overcame her, menacing, clawing at her breath, choking her. She swallowed several times to rid herself of the taste of cold earth. Shaking violently, she blinked and gripped Amalberga's arm, her fingers sinking deep into the fabrics of her trusted companion's cloak. Still she did not take her eyes off the flames. It was all so clear in front of her. The sun. The forest. A faceless man. Earth. Darkness.

She stood, toppling the bench over, and blinked again. Amalberga's eyes were large with concern as she held on to Hilda. "What is it, Sweeting?" she whispered, not wishing to raise anyone else's attention. "What have you seen?"

Hilda swallowed hard, eyes staring ahead, unseeing. "Death. I have seen my death."

***

Late autumn, AD 777
The fortress at Carcassonne

"My lord, my lord." Frantic knocks on Bellon's chamber door accompanied the cry.

Having just changed into clean leggings following a day spent in the practice yard, Bellon secured them swiftly. Then he took a linen tunic from the bed onto which he had thrown it earlier. "Enter!"

The lad bolting through the door was out of breath. "Lord!"

"What is it, Lot?" Bellon slipped his arms into the sleeves of his tunic and gestured to him to calm, uncertain if it was danger or excitement that had made the boy so out of breath. "Has aught happened?"

"No. 'Tis just…they've arrived." A broad grin spread over his face as he was holding his side. "I… I wanted to let you know as soon as I spotted them."

"They? Them? Ahh!" Bellon smiled, as recognition hit him, and he quickly pulled the tunic over his head. "You mean the lady Nanthild's party has been sighted?"

The lad nodded, still bent double but delighted that he was the first to tell him.

"Thank you, Lot. That's wonderful news. Ask the lord Milo to meet me in the hall and have the kitchen prepare a hearty broth and hot spiced wine for the travellers. Oh, and have stones heated and placed into the lady's bed."

"Yes, my lord." Lot turned, his breath still ragged. "I shall." And he rushed off, leaving the door wide open in his haste.

Bellon laughed. Lot – Lothaire by full name which nobody used – reminded him of a young dog, eager to please and keen to learn. In late summer, the boy had lost both parents in an attack by rogue Saracens on their remote village close to where Bellon and his men had stayed during a foray into the mountains. On finding him amongst the few survivors, he had taken him under his wing. The lad, barely over three-and-ten years old, took his duties seriously. Hopefully, with suitable training, Lot would grow into a man he could trust.

Leaving his chamber, Bellon closed the door and clicked the latch into place. The cold breeze hit him as he took the wooden steps down to the ground. How he missed the hot summer! He entered the hall through its heavy oak door. With men training outside all afternoon, it was deserted, so he refilled the hearth with wood and lit it. It spat and crackled, and soon the heat spread across the hall. Hilda and her retinue would be chilled from their weeks of travelling and needed the comforts of a warm keep.

The door to the yard opened. "Greetings, Bellon." Milo approached him and took his arm in a firm grip. "'Tis a welcoming fire. Together with the new tapestries, and fresh rushes on the floor, this hall is most inviting. Nanthild shall be pleased."

Despite his words of praise, a frown crossed his brow.

"What troubles you, Milo?" Bellon filled two cups with red wine and gestured to a bench beside the hearth. Whilst he had servants he could call upon as lord of Carcassonne, he still preferred to undertake tasks himself, unless it was in an official role. He handed a cup to his future father-in-law. "Is it the wedding?"

Milo shook his head. "Oh no. Naught to do with that." He raised the cup to Bellon and took a draught. "To your health."

Bellon sat on the bench opposite and looked at Milo across the fire. "What is it, then?"

"I wondered if it was the right thing to do to send for Nanthild in the middle of this wretched season. They crossed through snow and rain for weeks. The journey must have exhausted her. Yet we expect her to be cheerful on her wedding day which is but a fortnight away. Perhaps it was wrong not to wait till the spring."

"I agree in parts, but that she should have travelled months ago and waited for us here in Carcassonne, in safety and comfort, rather than crossing the hills this late in the year. But what's done is done. They are due to arrive at any moment."

Milo nodded. "True. And I am right glad I will see her soon. Yet the fact remains that I should have travelled with her." He stared into his cup.

Bellon sighed. "But the raids have kept you occupied since the spring. Hilda is in good hands – you said so yourself when you chose her retainers – travelling on roads secured by Franks. And…she will not want to see her father morose on her arrival after her arduous journey." He raised an eyebrow, then took a sip, relishing the strong liquid tasting of berries and sun.

Milo looked up sharply, tensing for an instant. Then his shoulders slumped, and he smiled. "You are right. And I should rejoice in her safe arrival." He drained his cup.

"Indeed. The kitchen is preparing a hot meaty broth, and I have instructed to have Hilda's bed filled with hot stones. If she needs rest – and I do not doubt it – she will find it warm and, I pray, comfortable."

Bellon wanted to impress the young lady who was his bride, and who had not seemed as keen on the betrothal as he had been. He simply wanted her to feel at home, by his side, here in Carcassonne. Expecting her each day over the past sennight, he had ordered the maids to ensure her chamber was a lovely, cosy place, to make her feel welcome.

To make her appreciate your efforts.

Bellon took another draught of wine. He could not wait to see Hilda again. The memory of her face, with its strong cheekbones, blue eyes the hue of a winter's frozen mountain lake, and a deliciously curved mouth – her fragile beauty had stayed in his mind throughout recent campaigns. It had nurtured him through grim days of pitched battles in relentless autumn rains and through endless, tiring negotiations. During their last encounter, he had fallen in love with the shy but self-assured girl, and he still could not believe his good fortune.

He looked up to find Milo staring at him over the rim of his cup. A smile appeared on his lips.

"I am glad," Milo said.

"Why? What for?" Had the count read his thoughts?

Milo refilled their cups, then raised his. "My daughter will have a good life, of that I have no doubt. It seems she has found a husband who genuinely cares for her."

Heat rose into Bellon's cheeks, and he stared into the flames to rid himself of the embarrassment. "Hmm. I would hope for her happiness here."

"It will come." Milo nodded. "She doesn't know it yet, but it will. Give her time."

Bellon swallowed. "I shall gladly do so."

A commotion by the door made them turn.

"My lords, come quickly, if you will," Lot called, holding the solid oak door open, a broad grin on his face. "They're here."

Laughing, Bellon and Milo put their cups on a trestle table and followed Lot into the courtyard where a flurry of activity almost threw them backwards. Men were dismounting, and their horses were led away under the chief retainer's command; others were unloading the carts under sharp, vocal instructions from Hilda's maid who stood beside the first cart with her hands on her hips. "These chests bear the Lady Hilda's garments." Her voice carried loudly across the yard. "Make sure to take them to her chamber – intact!"

"Lot, show them where the lady Nanthild's room is."

"Yes, lord." The boy scurried to Amalberga.

Bellon glanced across the chaos and, eventually, he spotted Hilda near the end of the train, still on horseback, a look of wonder on her drawn, tired face.

"There she is." He gestured to Milo, and together they bypassed horses, men and carts to appear by her side.

"Hilda!"

Bellon took her mare's reigns, his heart thumping at twice the speed. Though weary from her long journey, she looked as beautiful as he remembered. But there was a new sense around her, one of vulnerability, that he had not seen at Easter. It made him want to embrace her firmly, to protect her for the rest of her life, to chase away all the things she thought would harm her. He guessed that would include him, though.

"Greetings, dear daughter," Milo said, holding out his arms to help her from the saddle. She sank into his embrace, clinging on for a moment.

"Father." Her voice sounded hoarse, yet Bellon sensed relief in it.

She stepped back and her eyes flicked from one man to another. Warmth showed in them when she looked at her father, but Bellon felt a chill when her gaze settled on him.

"Lord Bellon." She let go of Milo's hands and curtseyed to him.

"Welcome to Carcassonne, Hilda. We prepared for your arrival," Bellon said, disappointed to see her frowning.

Give her time. Milo's words echoed in his head.

"I am so relieved you made it safely, Nanthild," Milo said. "The length of your journey has worried me."

Hilda smiled sweetly. "No, Father. You never worry about me, or you would not have insisted we travel in this atrocious weather." Her sharp tone belied her smile.

Bellon cocked his head, still regarding her. Yes, despite the breeze, the sun was shining over the towers of Carcassonne, as it did so often. But a chill crept into his heart. Hilda was unhappy.

Months of waiting had not reassured her. She seemed more distanced than in the spring. And although he could not help how his body reacted to her mere glance, he was at a loss how to soothe her wounded pride. He was a warrior first, with a strong sword-hand and a bold mind, but his relations with women had so far not been worth remembering. Although sometimes, after the heady action of a skirmish, he had sought to release the pressure with one of the women who accompany those camps, he had been careful not to catch a disease or leave a trace where one could claim a child as his. It had always been a meeting of bodies, not of emotions.

His future bride was different, and he struggled to gain control over the unknown feelings that assaulted him in her presence.

Milo laughed and took his daughter's hand into the crook of his arm, holding it firmly in place. "Ahh, the vagaries of the weather are nothing compared to the preparations for your big day. Always remember, Nanthild, I have your best intentions at heart." He cast Bellon a knowing glance. "And I have no doubt that this fine young man will see you are safe and have all you need." Then he began to pull her towards the hall – a proud father and a bemused daughter.

Bellon's heart sank at the sadness in Hilda's stance, her shoulders slumped forward and her head bowed. He swore he would prove her fears unfounded.

Give her time.

He handed the reins of her mare to a stable lad and followed his soon-to-be wife and father-in-law inside.

He was a warrior. 'Twas time for battle to begin.

Chapter Seven

Mid-March, 2018

"Phew! Let's see." Maddie put the paint roller into the tray and stepped back, wiping her hands covered in drops of colour on an old cloth. Careful not to bump into any of the covered furniture huddled in the centre of her mother's living room, she looked up and around.

"Nice." She grinned.

The dark atmosphere of the living room had changed to a light, airy tone – a pale vanilla for the walls and a white ceiling – inviting in and reflecting the sunlight that filtered through the streaky windows. Those would be next on her list! The old cupboard would still loom dark against the wall, and she might have to consider selling it. It was a real pain to shift, scraping the floor. Surely, the antique piece and several other pieces of Elizabeth's furnishings would interest a *brocante* dealer. But the change might help make the house more modern – and sellable.

Maddie took a sip from the bottle of beer on the windowsill. Yes, she was pleased with the result. One room done, and the difference was already staggering. The place just needed a modern feel to find a happy buyer. It was all good news, wasn't it?

As she stood there, a tinge of sadness wove through her and tears welled up. Where had that come from? She shrugged it off and took another draught. Why would she feel sad?

The smell of paint became overpowering, so she opened the window. Leaning against the ledge, she breathed in deeply, her lungs relishing the fresh air. It would take a few days for the two layers of pain to dry properly. The warming sun rays did not reach into the depth of this room.

During her trip back to the UK, which involved a drive back with her own car loaded with two new cases full of clothes and five large boxes of books amongst other necessary things, Maddie had made preparations for her 'year out'. She'd met with colleagues and visited the site one last time, and she found a research student to rent her flat. As she'd already taken two years out from her teaching at the university to focus on her writing project, she merely informed them of her temporary new address. She kept her British mobile number, so they could contact her if needed.

When she arrived in Minervens late one afternoon, after a night-time ferry ride from Newhaven to Le Havre, and a twelve-hour drive south (after four hours of sleep on the ferry in blustery seas!), the house welcomed her like a long-lost relative. Various flowers had budded in the garden – it had sprung to life. But on closing the doors, the darkness inside became almost stifling, and it took a long time for her to get to sleep.

The next morning, Maddie set a reasonable schedule for the works the house, the roof and the garden required, and she'd started right away, keen to banish the dark, brooding sense the place gave her.

Jake had come to fix the roof, embarrassed. He couldn't explain the loose tiles, but replaced them without charge and double-checked that the complete roof was safe.

At a local *Brico* store, Maddie had bought several pots of light-coloured paint and various decorating utensil. Her mother had loved the dark corners, calling them cosy, but Maddie was keen to chase away her ghost from the house. Elizabeth had her say in her will, and now Maddie would do her part, as instructed, though not without giving the rooms a complete makeover.

She turned around and inspected anew her work. She'd been careful not to drip any paint on the power sockets or light switches, though these definitely needed to be replaced.

Cleaning wipes had not removed all the grime of the last twenty years.

Maddie discovered that she didn't know her mother at all. Yes, they'd been estranged, but Elizabeth had raised her to become an independent woman that she was today. Yet, she'd lived in a house full of dust and cobwebs, only with her books. More like a hermit. As if the real world hadn't mattered.

Maddie felt like a stranger catching a glimpse into the life of another person; not like a close family member. She swallowed hard. Perhaps, she should have made more of an effort.

"At least your home will look proud and happy again," she whispered into the empty, quiet room.

It was useless pondering about the past. Taking a deep breath, she picked up the beer bottle and went into the kitchen, letting the fresh air seep into the living room to dispel the smell of paint. Stopping in the doorway to the kitchen, she looked around. The Welsh dresser was desperately in need of a new varnish, as was the sideboard, but the heavy cupboard would have to go. A fresh worktop was needed. The walls needed brightening, just like the living room, and the old, unevenly-tiled floor required a new base, with fresh, modern tiles.

That meant either levelling and covering it or lifting the floor altogether. Yuck! She dreaded to think about the ensuing mess. She needed help with that.

Maddie crouched down on her heels and ran her hands over the old, red square floor tiles that left every piece of furniture in the kitchen wonky. Bits of cardboard shoved under the feet of the cupboard, dresser and dining table kept them stable, but the chairs all wobbled. Nobody had bothered to straighten the floor in the last century. The tiles beneath her hand felt poorly fitted. Not one tile was level with another. It was a shame, but these tiles would have to go.

A tremor ran across the floor, and it made her withdraw her hand quickly. She nearly lost her balance, catching herself on the doorframe.

"What the—?"

Curious, she put her hand down again, clutching the beer bottle with the other. The ground was solid. Had she imagined it?

She sat, waiting for more. Nothing happened.

Sighing, she rose and put the bottle on the table. Was the area prone to earthquakes? She'd never heard of any here. Tomorrow, she would ask Bernadette if she could recommend a builder. Dreading the cost of it, she walked the length of the room, then the width, measuring the room in her mind. "About twenty square metres. OK."

Not too big a job, but still messy. She expected dust would spread all over the house if she did not keep doors shut. In the meantime, she could paint upstairs before doing the corridor once the kitchen was finished. The wooden beams had to wait for their woodworm treatment until she could keep the windows open.

Elizabeth's savings would fade fast, but the sale would bring in enough to cover them.

She sat and took another sip, as she imagined what the house would be like post-renovation. With new furnishings and a cream-coloured tiled floor, the kitchen would look nice and fresh. The old sideboard would get a new coat of varnish and the Welsh dresser could be the *pièce de résistance* in her new modern, yet charming country kitchen.

Not that it would have to be to her taste! She shook her head in emphasis. Once the year was up, the house would go.

Another light tremor beneath her feet made her jump. She darted to the radio and dialled through the channels to see if there were any reports of earthquakes. But they either broadcast music or discussions, with the latest rugby results announced on *Sud Radio*. Surely, programmes would be interrupted for news about any unexpected earthquakes in the area?

"Bizarre," she murmured. Then she remembered her neighbour. She should check if Bernadette was OK.

Maddie emptied the bottle in a last big gulp, then rinsed her mouth with water from the tap. She didn't want to smell like a drunk.

Collecting the house key from the sideboard, she went to the door. As she threw it open, she stared at a man whose outstretched hand was inches from her face.

"Oh, hello. I was just about to knock." Léon Cabrol withdrew his hand and put it into his jeans pocket. "*Salut*."

Maddie blinked and stared at him. Besides tight jeans, he wore his black leather jacket. Why did such a man have to live in her village? She'd been single for too long!

"Oh, umm, *bonjour*." Maddie's hand went to her hair. She'd tied it in a high bun before she started to paint, and it was all mussed up now. "Did you feel that?"

He raised his eyebrow. "*Quoi*?"

My god, what a question to ask! "Sorry, I meant whether you felt the earthquake." His eyes told her he had no idea what she was talking about. "Just a minute ago, and couple of minutes before that. The ground was shaking."

"It certainly is now," he said. Amusement sparkled in his eyes.

Insolent sod! Maddie's temper flared. "A *real* earthquake. I...I sat on the kitchen floor to inspect the tiles, and the ground was moving beneath my hands."

Léon shook his head. "No, can't say I noticed anything. And I think I would have, given I was riding a bike. Why do you think it was an earthquake?" His tone had turned serious, and he looked past her into the gloom of the corridor, then studied her. "Are you alright?"

No earthquake? What had it been, then? Maddie swayed to the side. Léon's hand stretched out, and he gripped her arm to stabilise her.

"Are you OK?"

"I'm not sure." Her mind whirled. The earth *had* moved. Twice.

"The paint," she blurted out. It must have been the paint! She laughed, the sound a few notes too shrill for her own liking. "Oh, I'm sorry. I think the smell of the paint got to my brain."

He cocked his head and grinned. "You've been painting?" His gaze went from her hair,   and down her worn-out University of York t-shirt to her old, ripped jeans, then met hers. "I wouldn't have guessed."

Maddie looked down her front, laughter bubbling from inside her. Both her t-shirt and jeans were splattered with colour, as were the cheap trainers she wore.

"Oh dear," was all she could manage.

Léon smiled. "You're keeping busy, I give you that. Were you planning to go out like that?"

"Umm, I didn't think of it. I was going to see if Bernadette had noticed the earthquake."

Léon shook his head. "There really was no earthquake." He shifted his weight to his other leg. "May I come in and have a look?"

"Sure." She took a step back, and he brushed past her, close, but not touching. "Head to the kitchen; first door on the left."

He waited inside until she passed him.

"Grab a seat. Would you like a beer?"

"No, thanks. Not when I'm out on the bike." He pulled back a chair and sat. "But if you have any tea, I'd love a cup."

Maddie laughed and went to the kettle, filled it with water, and switched it on. "Very sensible." Then she turned to face him, leaning against the worktop. "But tea? Should it not be coffee? You're French."

Léon grinned. "I may be French, but when I lived in London, I developed a liking of a nice cup of English tea. Is that so unusual?"

"To me, it is. You see, where I lived in Normandy, when I was young, the fathers of my friends didn't drink tea at all. Everyone had coffee."

"So, you grew up in France? I thought I detected an accent, and it wasn't an English one."

"*Merci*," she said coquettish. At the click of the kettle, she poured two cups and swirled the Pyramid tea bags in each cup with a spoon before she removed them and dumped them in the sink. "Milk? Sugar?"

"Just sugar, please. That's the one thing I can't get used to – milk in tea."

So much for a proper cup of English tea! "Ever tried it?" she challenged him.

"*Oui*, and it was vile." He smirked when she threw back her head in laughter.

"Let's say…it's an acquired taste to those who haven't experienced it before."

"Well, then I must admit it's not a taste I've acquired yet…" He took a sip, looking at her over the rim of the large floral mug. "Though this is nice."

"Glad you like it." She glanced around the room, thinking of how to approach him with her request. "I wonder…"

"*Oui*."

"I've meant to ask Bernadette for recommendations for a builder, but perhaps you have a suggestion."

"That's the reason I stopped by, to see if you needed any help."

"Thank you. I need a builder or a tiler…for the kitchen," she added.

"Obviously." He smiled.

"Obviously," she repeated. "I can paint walls and ceilings, but I'd like a professional to re-tile the floor."

He put his mug down and leant to the side, sliding a hand over uneven tiles. "Yes, I see what you mean. These old red tiles are lovely. How do you say…rustic?"

"Yes, you could say that."

"But they're not very practical for a modern resident."

Relief flooded through her. Someone agreed with her vision! "I'm so glad you see it like I do. I was afraid of upsetting Bernadette. I know she has similar tiles in her house."

"Bernadette is a lady of a certain age, as was Elisa. No disrespect to either, just stating the obvious. Younger people like ourselves look for a more…modern look in our home, don't we?"

When she nodded, a strand of her tied-back hair came loose, falling into her face. She brushed it aside and blew into her mug. Léon swiftly averted his gaze and looked around the room.

"You could do something worthwhile with that rack over there."

"The Welsh dresser?"

"Is that what it's called? Yes, it's beautiful. I love the carving. With a new coat of paint, it could look incredible."

"So you like a bit of rustic after all?" She was teasing him now.

He laughed. "Yes, I appreciate beautiful furniture. I even love those old cherrywood cupboards. Just that I'm not keen on big pieces in my home. They suffocate a room."

"True. The living room would also be much more spacious without the heavy cupboard and big sofas."

"Yes, I see it in my parents' part of our home: all solid mahogany or oak cupboards and wardrobes, and then they put dainty tables and Louis XV chairs around the rooms. It's too much. I prefer things to be simple."

"So do I," she agreed. "I can see that I might call on you a few times for advice, like, where to get nice but bright furniture."

"I take it you won't want to go to Ikea?"

She giggled. "I like some of their stuff, but not everything. Their bedroom furniture would probably do, and their kitchens are OK. Is there a store nearby?"

"Not close by, but it's not too far to either Toulouse or Montpellier. It's handy for small items. Mother goes mad for candles, small side tables and kitchen utensils." He grinned. "But I know an *artisan* in Carcassonne who could do a simple fitted kitchen if that's what you like. He works with wood and has a small store. I'm sure he could sort it all at a good price."

"Are you sure? You always need to pay extra for these guys to instal everything. I like the idea, though. More individual than a chain store."

He nodded. "Then I'll get in touch with him. And what do you have in mind for the floor?"

"Simple dark cream tiles. Large ones. They look rustic without being olde-worlde."

"Without what?" He raised an eyebrow and grinned.

Maddie smiled. "Olde-worlde. Old world. Means like in the old days."

"Ah." He looked enlightened. "You have good ideas. I should take you to a warehouse just across the Spanish border. Tiles are cheaper there, and they have a fantastic choice."

"Oh, you won't need to…"

"But I insist. You'd hardly get a bunch of big tiles into your car. We can take the Rover."

"Hmm, true. My old VW Golf isn't solid enough for a large pile of tiles."

"That's agreed, then." He grinned.

"One thing at a time. I guess all these lovely tiles will go?" A tinge of sadness touched her face.

"Yes, unfortunately. They are brittle, and the ground needs to be opened enough to ensure that you could put an even layer of concrete underneath your new tiles, to make the floor level. It will mean digging."

The ground beneath their feet vibrated.

"What was that?" Léon stared at his half-drunk mug of tea on the table, the liquid moving from side to side.

Maddie jumped up. "See? It happened again." A shiver ran down her spine. The ground had definitely shaken.

"How bizarre!"

"So, you believe me now?" She stood in front of him, her arms folded in front of her.

He nodded slowly. "*Bah ouais*."

Twenty minutes later, Maddie stared at herself in the mirror. Her cheeks were flushed, and her eyes shone unusually bright.

Had she been flirting? It had been too long, but perhaps a little attention from a handsome Frenchman had done her good.

Then the earth had moved again. At least this time, there was a witness.

After his initial shock, Léon left to speak to the *maire* to find out if there had been any reports of earthquakes in the area today. Maddie was sure there hadn't. Bernadette would have come over to see her, no doubt. But in expectation of the *maire* – the most influential man in the village – coming to her house to see for himself, she had quickly tried to scrub the paint from her exposed skin. To not much avail. It would take turpentine to get it off. Now, what was that in French?

She changed into clean jeans, a red camisole and a checked shirt. As her shoes were covered in paint too, she opted for her flip-flops. They had to do. She would not need to go outside in them.

Brushing her hair, Maddie heard a knock on the front door. She threw the brush into the basket on a shelf beside the sink and rushed downstairs, the sound of her flip-flops echoing around the corridor.

She threw the door open and beamed at Léon and the *maire*.

"Hello again, Maddie. Let me, um, *presenter à vous Monsieur le Maire*, Bertrand Carnot. Bertrand, this is Madeleine Winters, Elisa's daughter."

"*Enchanté,* Madame Winters!" The short, rotund mayor took her hand and kissed it, a big smile on his face. Ahh, another flirt!

Maddie smiled. "Lovely to meet you, Monsieur Carnot. Please come in." She stood aside as Léon led the way to her kitchen.

He quickly explained the situation they'd found themselves in, whilst Maddie watched them from the kitchen door as both men studied the floor and then the wall.

Having assured himself that all was solid, the *maire* turned to her, a frown between his bushy brows. He must think her mad. "Madame, I am baffled. There was no seismic action here in the village, and the structure of your house is firm. It was built of solid stone." He looked around. "Does this happen in other rooms as well or just in the kitchen?"

Maddie blinked. "Just in here." Perhaps he'd sussed it. It was true – it hadn't happened in any other rooms. "It's usually when I touch the floor or talk about…my plans."

He raised an eyebrow and, propping himself up with his hand on the dining table, slowly lowered himself to his knees. Then he brushed his hand across the floor tiles. Dust clung to his fingers.

Damn! She should have quickly brushed the floor.

"So, you're planning to re-tile this floor?" he asked. "That means digging deep, to adjust the level of these unstable tiles."

The ground vibrated, and Maddie grabbed the doorframe to steady herself. Bertrand Carnot lost his balance and toppled onto his side. Léon, who was leaning against the sink, jumped forward and took the poor man's arm to help him up.

All was calm again.

"*Merci*, Léon," the *maire* whispered, eyes wide. "This is very interesting."

Maddie nodded and pointed to the chairs. "Please sit, monsieur. Would you like a drink of water?"

He lowered himself into a chair, and Léon sat next to him, keeping his thoughts to himself.

"*Ah non, merci*. I'm fine. It's just…"

She sat opposite him and exchanged glances with Léon. Intrigued, she turned back to the *maire*.

"It's what, monsieur?"

He cleared his throat. "Part of this village was built over an ancient cemetery dating back to Visigoth times. Err, do you know who the Visigoths were and when they lived?"

Maddie nodded. "Yes, I'm a historian." The *maire*'s eyes lit up, and she smiled. "I know they lived in this area around

77

the fourth to the seventh century. There are many remnants of their existence here, but I didn't know about this village."

"Yes," he said enthusiastically, clearly delighted to have found a fellow *connoisseur* of dark age history. "But the point is – the ancient cemetery here in Minervens is on the other side of the village, behind the *Cave Co-operative*. We found no other traces so far, and certainly not near where we are now. I wonder…" He stared at the tiles, as if to lift them with his mere gaze to reveal their secret.

Léon raised an eyebrow. "You wonder what, Bertrand? That beneath this floor lies something yet to be uncovered? Like more graves?"

"*Ouais*." Wild-eyed, the older man looked almost manic.

A shiver ran down Maddie's spine, and goosebumps rose on her skin. This was surreal. "So…you think there's something beneath my kitchen floor? Something… paranormal that shifts the ground?"

Monsieur Carnot nodded vigorously. "It is possible."

Doubts clouded her mind. She didn't believe in ghosts. "Well, we shall see, won't we? When the works begins…"

Chapter Eight

Eight days before the feast of Christ's birth, AD 777
Carcassonne

With a sennight to go to the wedding, Bellon was none the wiser as to how to woo his betrothed. Since her arrival, Hilda had remained in her chamber most of the time, except for a joint walk through the settlement where she greeted people as her station demanded, but showed no further interest in her new home.

It did not come as a surprise to him: she had crossed hundreds of miles in the coldest season, only to wed him, against her will. He would not begrudge her some comforts and much-needed time to recover. Often enough had he travelled with Charles' armies, and he knew well just how treacherous conditions could be during wintertime. But it was no excuse for her not to attend meals most evenings or to ignore his pleas to sit by the fire and talk about their future. Even Milo had become disgruntled with his daughter and had repeatedly voiced his displeasure. That, Bellon did not wish for – that her father would put pressure on her. So he had asked him to leave her in peace, to give her more time. Milo had not happily accepted his request, but acknowledged that it made sense. To a certain point.

Now, having allowed Hilda her own will for so long, both men had grown weary of her obstinance. But Bellon was not angry. It simply disappointed him that Hilda did not even try to get to know him. She was polite, yet shy and reserved in his company, and he could not break through the invisible wall she had built around herself.

Deep in thought, Bellon winced as the chilly winds stung his face, reminding him where he was: deep in the rolling hills, exposed to the elements. Yet he relished it. He needed this feeling of being alive. Whether his horse enjoyed it, he was not so certain. *Best to return to the keep to give the poor beast a rest.*

He guided his stallion away from the hillside he had been climbing and, with the wind in his back, turned towards Carcassonne. His home. A sense of pride rushed through him as the high walls, which he had reinforced over the past year, grew nearer. He could barely make out the sentries on the watchtower above the gate, but he knew they would have spotted him long before he had seen them. To the opposite side, the land around Carcassonne was flat, and the location of his fortress at the top of the hill granted him the perfect defence.

He had worked hard to get to where he was: count of Carcassonne, lord of the small, ancient, but strategic settlement he had grown up in. He loved his home with a fierce pride, that despite losing its independence to Charles as part of the king's seizure of Septimania, it gained protection and prestige. And the safety of Frankish swords. The alternative, to be at constant defence against the Saracens crawling across the Pyrenaei, and the uncertainties in Aquitania to the west, was not an option. Carcassonne had seen too much warfare over the decades. Together with the Franks, they had made treaties or beaten rogue parties back. Charles' hold over Tolosa granted Bellon a certain sense of security. The settlement would thrive under him. With Hilda by his side, they would found a dynasty that could hold sway in Septimania for generations to come.

The heavy winter rains would soon return, flooding field and path indiscriminately. Only this morning, he had spoken to his *majordomus* to ensure that preparations were under way, barriers created in places of danger, so the water would not flood the dwellings at the foot of the keep or the grain stores. Bellon had seen starvation many times before, and he knew the floods following the rains posed a danger. The river that flowed below the fortress had often caused damage to homes and crops. Under his guidance, Carcassonne would not suffer that fate again. He would see to it.

Nearing the gates just as dusk was settling, he slowed to a walk and waved at the sentries, who ordered the gate to be opened. Bellon crossed into the courtyard and behind him, the heavy gate was closing again.

"Sire." A lad appeared from the stables. He took hold of the reins and Bellon dismounted.

"Thank you. Brush him well." He grinned at the boy, whom he had known since birth. He knew he could trust him with his beloved stallion.

Pushing the door open to the hall, he found a fire lit in the hearth, much to his relief. Little had he realised how the cold had seeped through his cloak. But the sight that greeted him, made his heart pound in his ears. Sitting beside the hearth were Milo in one chair and Hilda in another, her arms outstretched towards the flames. Bellon threw his cloak over a bench beside her and sat.

"Greetings, Hilda. I would hope you will honour us with your presence tonight." He smiled at her as he rubbed his hands close to the fire. Turning to Milo, he added, "The wind is picking up. We are expecting a storm tonight."

The older man nodded. "I have seen them here before, and I am glad to know we are warm and safe inside." His gaze moved to his daughter, and Bellon's followed.

Hilda blushed under the scrutiny, keeping her eyes firmly cast downwards. Or was it the heat from the fire? Bellon knew not the answer. But he did not want her to withdraw again. He wondered if Milo had spoken to her.

"What say you, Hilda?" He kept his voice low, barely above a whisper. Her fragile beauty, her blonde hair, tied into a pleat, glinting in the fire's light. He was so fortunate.

She looked at him before her eyes darted towards Milo and nodded. "Yes, my lord. I shall join you and Father."

Ah, Milo had ordered her to attend. Bellon's heart sank. But at least he would be with her. Certainly, she must become used to him when they were sharing their trenchers.

"Then I am a happy man." Despite his words, he had to keep himself from making his voice sound critical. 'Twas a first step.

The torches were lit in the sconces, casting an eery light across the stone walls and tapestries. Several candelabra placed on the high table helped illuminate the room as darkness had long fallen. In addition, lamps containing olive oil had been placed on the lower tables, casting them in an eerie light, and sending a scent of olives across the room. Bellon, seated at his usual place at the centre of the high table, let his gaze roam across the hall. He loved this room, bustling with people and noise, its warmth thwarting the winter's chill outside. A lutist, sitting all by himself in a corner but supplied well with ale and bread, played a cheerful melody which added to the communal mood. His people were excited about the upcoming wedding. A feast like none other ever seen in this part of Septimania.

He wished he could be as joyful, but instead his mood was as foul as the weather outside.

He signalled to Lot to refill his cup again. "Thank you," he grunted, and the lad withdrew back into the shadows, no doubt replenishing the now empty clay jug.

Bellon glared into the deep red liquid before he took a large gulp. He had finished off a jugful already, and the food had not even been served. His head felt lighter, and he was certain the wine had taken away his doubts a little. Instead, his mood had darkened.

He had tried to be supportive, but how in the name of the virgin was he meant to get to know Hilda – and she him – if she did not wish to spend time with him. Yes, perhaps she was scared. So was he, with the prospect of being tied to a wife who so obviously despised him. He glared into the fire. Christ, it was easier to face an enemy across a field than woo this damn woman!

A firm hand closed over his wrist as he tried to lift the cup to his lips again. He banged it back on the table, sending a hush over the room.

"'Tis enough, son," Milo said in a calm voice barely above a whisper and sat down beside him. "Lot, bring his lordship a large cup of well water. As cold as it comes." The lad nodded and rushed from the room.

"What do you know?" growled Bellon. He glared at the gathered faces watching him, but his words were intended for Milo's ears only.

"More than you think, Bellon." Milo sighed. "I must confess I do not understand Hilda's erratic behaviour, but then I am not a good judge of women. Ah, thank you." He took the cup of water from Lot who had appeared behind them and put it under Bellon's nose. "Drink."

Bellon mumbled under his breath but complied. The chill of the water hit his senses like an axe. He coughed and blinked. "God's breath!"

Milo laughed. "You do not need to blaspheme. 'Tis your head that does it, not the Lord's."

"At least you did not throw it in my face." Bellon smirked. His senses were slowly returning.

"Perhaps I should have done so, but not in front of your court." Milo turned serious. "Nanthild's mother acted just like her – if that is any consolation to you. Before our wedding, Alda took great pains to stay out of my way. She was fiercely independent, which is sadly something the Church now frowns upon. To be honest, though," he added, "it was the trait I admired most in her after our wedding. Alda stood up for her beliefs. Even when it brought her into trouble with our priest, she stood proud."

Bellon's head shot up. "Your lady wife had issues with the clergy?" He sincerely hoped Hilda had not inherited all her mother's traits. It could be dangerous if you disagreed with the followers of Christ.

Milo nodded. "Yes, she did. You see, Alda was a wise-woman. And in recent Church synods, it has been made clear that such women are apparently in league with the devil. It was troubling for me to defend her. Her faith was absolute. She just wished to help people who were sick or injured…" His voice trailed off.

"Ahh." Bellon was at a loss. He did not believe wise-women – or any women involved in healing – were consorting with the devil, but it set a dangerous precedent. He would have to keep a close eye on Hilda, should she insist on following in her mother's footsteps.

"Ahh indeed. Alda died giving birth to our son – who was born dead – when Nanthild was still young. I sometimes wonder if it was God's punishment for her actions…but then, she had saved many people's lives before she died. Surely, even He would not disapprove." The last words were spoken in a hoarse whisper, and his brow furrowed with the pain of his memories.

Bellon patted Milo's shoulder. 'Twas as if their roles had become reversed. "I do not believe her death was His response to her actions," he said. "I believe that instead it was her time to join Him. She can help much more, in a different way, where she is now, in Heaven."

Milo gave him a wry smile. "Yes, 'tis possible. Though some priests would argue that she would not ascend. I…I do still miss her after all those years. And now I'm going to lose my daughter."

Bellon shook his head. "Nay, you will not lose her, Milo. She will always remain your daughter." He grinned. "And… you are about to gain a grown-up son!"

Milo looked at him quizzically. "Yes, it must be so. I have thought that if I had been granted a son, he would be like you. No, don't laugh, Bellon! In truth, I could not ask for a better man to wed my only child."

Gratitude washed over him. He was proud of Milo's association, of his approval. It meant so much to him. If only Hilda could see…

"My lords." A soft voice spoke behind them, and both men, absorbed in their musings, jumped.

Bellon vacated his cushioned chair and moved to the next one to allow Hilda to sit between him and her father. Then he gestured for Lot to bring her a cup of wine and smiled at her. "Hilda. It is a pleasure to see you here tonight. Your beauty brightens the darkest day."

On her other side, he could see Milo grinning into his cup, not saying a word. He was fortunate to have such a great man as his father-in-law.

Determined, Bellon sat down, finished his cup of water and pulled a face. He would win Hilda over. Tonight or never.

***

"Thank you." Hilda shuffled to sit comfortably on the cushion. She watched as Amalberga headed to one of the lower tables. Her heart beat a steady drum in her ears when she saw her confidante welcomed to a table of members of Bellon's household whom she seemed to know well already.

When Bellon handed her a cup of wine, their hands touched briefly. She was certain that it was intentional, but she had not expected her body to react in such a manner. Goosebumps rose on her skin, and she entwined her shaking hands on her lap. Casting a quick glance sideways at her betrothed, she found his gaze steady on her, a warm smile playing on his lips, and a glint in his deep green eyes. His scent of lavender and something else, more unusual – was it sandalwood perhaps? – hit her senses. She swallowed as she felt the heat rise in her cheeks.

It terrified her, and that terror had been her reason for hiding.

What was she expected to do? Was this how wives reacted to their husbands? She blinked and looked away, still aware of his scrutiny. What if he found her lacking?

Throughout her life, Hilda had been surrounded by women. Father was close to her, but often she wished he would spend more time with her. Since her mother died, Hilda had wondered if Father had had any regrets. Her little brother was dead, yet she had survived childhood with all its threats. But Father had never mentioned it. He had only forever been away from home since then, crossing borders and expanding the kingdom. Always with Charles. Always in danger.

She had dealt with warriors and hosted guests of honour alongside Father for several years and treated wounds that even many men would not dare touch. Yet none of them had such an impact on her mind – and her body – as Bellon did. This new heat in her blood betrayed her senses, and she did not know how to cope with it.

"I have a proposal to make, Hilda." His voice was barely above a whisper, and she was not even sure Father on her other side heard it.

"Yes?"

He took her hand between his. Scared this would reveal her shaking, the warmth flowing through his skin into hers as he massaged her palm surprised her. As if he wanted to calm her.

Little does he know…

"We are to be wed in a few days' time, and I would like you to get used to life here in the south."

She nodded. "Yes, Bellon." Encouraged by the kind glance he sent her, she could not help but smile. It lit up his eyes, sending shivers down her spine.

"I would like to show you my country, once tonight's storm has passed. These never last long. I'm certain you are by now recovered from your journey. And 'tis perhaps cold, but with the coming sunshine, we can ride out into the plain, so I can show you our vines and the orchards we have recently planted, and also the ancient ruins of my forebears. It would be an honour if you were to join me."

The ruins of his forebears? Of Visigoths like him? Ancient sites often held powerful energies. She shuddered with excitement. A shadow fell over his face, and she was quick to reassure him, a new hope rising in her heart. "Yes, I would like that very much."

It was time she learnt about the land if she wanted to continue on her path. She would recognise plants and remember where she found them. And she would discover plants unknown to her. But the prospect of being alone with him, in the castle or outside, still worried her. "Will there be an escort?"

He sighed. Had he read her mind? "Yes, we can take Amalberga or Lot with us. That way, nobody can accuse us of improper behaviour prior to our wedding. Does that reassure you?"

Hilda nodded, sending him a shy glance. "Yes, that would be kind."

"Then, provided the sun will appear, we shall head out in the morn after breaking our fast." He lifted his cup with a proud glimmer in his eyes.

"So be it."

They turned to see bowls of food arriving, and servants distributed trenchers. The scent of spiced stew filled the room. Hilda took a sip of her wine. Finally, she began to calm, and her wildly pounding heart slowed to a more steady beat.

The sunlight blinded her as they headed eastwards, in the direction of the sea, so Bellon had told her. She rode alongside her betrothed, with Lot following them at a discreet distance. Amalberga had declined to join them, citing the chilly wind and her advancing age. Hilda smiled. Amalberga was not as ancient as she at times pretended to be, although the long journey south had taken much of her strength. Still, with Lot as a companion, Bellon could not try anything improper.

As if he did, said a little voice inside her head. He was a warrior, but also a man of his word who appeared to respect women. She had noticed that he did not treat her, nor Amalberga, nor other women in the fortress, with the disdain some of his fellow knights did. The memory of Clovis insulting her at the Easter court sprang to her mind. No, Bellon was different. Or did she simply wish it to be so, as he was to be her husband? She had heard of many tales where men mistreated their wives after they had consummated the marriage. A shiver ran down her spine.

Looking at his profile, the head held high, proudly so, the broad shoulders and straight back as he rode next to her, his long hair not tied back but falling over his shoulders – he was a man to be reckoned with. A man women would die for to have as their husband. Handsome. Fierce. Proud.

And he would be hers.

Hilda shuddered at the thought. Of course, he would insist on his rights as a husband. He would touch her, share her bed, give her children. Heat shot into her cheeks, and she blamed the sun, strong despite the winter's cool breeze. Quickly, she averted her eyes towards the land laid out in front of her. In the clear air, she could see for many miles from her perch on a hill. Vines covered much of the landscape, replacing those burnt by marauders over the centuries, so Bellon told her. Between them lay orchards, waiting for spring to arrive. Yet in the distance, patches of charred black soil stood out, as raw as when the land was torched. 'Twas no wonder Bellon wished to rebuild the area from the ravages of skirmish upon skirmish. She admired his vision. He wanted the best for his people.

"Does this view please you, Hilda?" he asked, pointing towards rows upon rows of vines across the plain.

Her blush deepened. Had he read her thoughts? "I'm sorry?" She stared at him.

"This." Grinning at her, he slowed his stallion to a gentle walk and made a sweeping gesture with his left arm, encompassing the wide landscape. "The countryside. The vines, which, as far as we know, were first planted by the Romans. The views over to the hills in the north, through which you travelled, and the high mountains behind us to the south."

Hilda slowed alongside him, following his gaze across the plain. As she turned, she saw snow was crowning the tips of the high mountains. "And beyond those peaks, there is the Caliphate?"

"Yes, and along the coast. But we have our new treaties. To the west lies Vasconia, a small kingdom that has caused us much trouble. Most of it is now under our control."

The satisfied tone in his voice gave her a chill. The warrior in him was speaking.

"Ah," she said meekly. "And on the other side?"

Bellon turned away from her. "Beyond those hills lies the eastern part of the duchy of Aquitania. Also under Frankish rule," he added, "though not without its problems."

Hilda thought she was learning as much about his life as about the history of these southern, troubled lands. He was clearly proud of his heritage, as a Visigoth, now fighting for the Franks.

"What about your own folk?"

He stared at her. "My folk?"

She nodded.

He pulled the reins of his stallion to stop him, and she came to a halt beside him. "The Saracens, coming up from Iberia, clashed with my folk. Many people lost their lives during the frequent raids, and although we could maintain our faith, life was still harsh. That's why you see so few populated villages. The Franks freed us from decades of fighting. Many of us have fled, dispersed into faraway parts of Septimania, Iberia, and beyond. Those in cities like Narbonne fared better. They could adjust more easily and found life bearable."

"And now you're joining the king in his fight against them."

"Yes. Many of us Visigoths have lost our lands, and we are no longer strong enough to defend them against the Saracens. So, yes, it is safer to be on King Charles' side – despite the sacrifices we had to make." He cast her a glance that showed he respected her interest. Dared she hope that Bellon would be a husband who valued his wife's counsel?

All around her, the influence of women had diminished. Where they were once consulted for their wisdom, the Church now told them to stay by the hearth and tend to the children. And although wives were still in charge of households, it had eroded their independence.

Hilda silently prayed to the Goddess for Bellon to be an understanding husband. Although it was likely she would never dare to reveal her true calling to him...

Chapter Nine

Late March, 2018

The early spring sun was beating down on Maddie's car as she drove past rows of vines covering the landscape either side of the road. *Vignerons* were busy checking and pruning the thin branches to ready them for the summer months.

The drive from Minervens to Carcassonne was relaxing her, despite a boy racer overtaking her in a hairy manoeuvre near a sharp bend. Tutting, she kept her cool and paid attention to the oncoming traffic. Some things never changed, and racing along country roads was always a popular, if dangerous, pastime – not just in France.

After a couple of further visits from Monsieur Carnot to check on her kitchen floor and any potential paranormal activity, Maddie had decided to escape for a few hours. To her relief – and the *maire*'s clear disappointment – there had been no further earth-moving shenanigans in the house, allowing her to focus on painting the bedroom walls. Pleased with her progress, she deserved a treat.

A visit to the famous citadel in Carcassonne, followed by lunch, had been on her list ever since she arrived. But she'd declined Léon's kind offer made the previous evening to accompany her, insisting he would find her spending much time looking at historical exhibits and exploring the site at her leisure too slow. Fortunately, he had simply shrugged it off with a smile and wished her a nice day.

The speed with which she grew familiar with his presence frightened her. Yes, he was handy for answering all those questions she had about renovations and gardening, but in recent days she'd had the impression that he was far more interested in her company than she was ready for. Their trip to Spain had been successful, and she'd returned with a batch of beautiful tiles for the kitchen. Time spent chatting had flown by.

Small steps, she told herself, and tried to ignore the twinge in her heart when she saw his expression turn sad after her knock-back.

Now, skirting the town on the bypass, she turned into a road that eventually led her to the nearest car park, close to *Porte Narbonnaise* – the main remodelled entrance to the former fortress. Looking at the cost of parking, she gulped. It wouldn't be cheap, but today she didn't care.

This time of year, the car park was half empty. The Easter holidays were a week away, and she was under no illusion that by then, this place would be packed. Never mind during the summer months! Carcassonne was the second most visited tourist site in France, and she'd heard of huge crowds pushing their way through the narrow lanes in the height of the hot season. Not something she would relish, and she was grateful for the cool breeze.

From the car park, she crossed the road at a pedestrian crossing that led to the large square in front of *Porte Narbonnaise* and stopped short.

"Wow!" The words escaped her, and she quickly glanced around her to see if anyone thought it odd that she stood there talking to herself. But the sight that greeted her was too distracting.

The rebuilt walls and towers looked impressive from any distance, but up close she was lost for words. Dating from a range of centuries, their stones could tell tales. Maddie took a few photos with her phone, aware of resembling any other awestruck tourist seeing La Cité up close, then slowly walked up to the gate. She wandered over the bridge, its large wooden blocks creaking after decades of use, and crossed the grass-covered moat. Once through, she looked at the wide paths on either side of her between the outer walls and the inner ones that encircled the walls of the old town. From books she found on her mother's shelves, she had learnt that, merely over a century earlier, rows of shacks stood side by side, leaning against the inner walls. People had lived here. The poorest people of Carcassonne.

In her mind's eye, Maddie imagined these ramshackle buildings, complete with front doors, sometimes small, square windows, and chimneys. She saw children play in the mud as horses, stray dogs, donkeys and other animals roamed the lane. The images in the books had haunted her. So much poverty. Then, with the renovation of the towers and walls, people had to move down to the *bastide*, the lower town. They didn't fit in with the fairytale castle image of the 19th century. *Poor people never fit into rich people's ideas.* Maddie hoped that conditions had improved in their new homes…

A Spanish couple chatting loudly shook her out of her imagination, so she set off up the path into the old town. Never one to go for the tourist trail, she intentionally got lost in the narrow winding lanes over the next half an hour, savouring the atmosphere. Tacky stores selling cheap trinkets vied with craft shops, galleries and restaurants for the visitors' attention. She spotted some lovely gemstone jewellery and nudged herself to return for a better browse.

The Romans had established the citadel – including its inner walls – with unearthed signs of life dating back even further. A defensive settlement at first, over the centuries a town had grown around the *Château Comtal*, outside which she had now come to a halt. She quickly checked her watch. 11.30 am. Great.

"Just enough time for a little wander," she murmured before she headed through the barriers. After saying, "*Au revoir*" to the ticket seller, Maddie crossed another bridge and walked into the castle.

A tingling sensation ran down her spine, and she shrugged it off swiftly. "This is too exciting!"

She smiled at a tourist staring at her. Yes, she talked to herself. She always did when exploring ancient sites. And it usually attracted curious glances. Following the trail, she made her way through the inside of the château and along the wall walk of the original fortress and its towers. Their

92

foundations ancient, a sense of homecoming flooded through her. She often felt like this during her work, so it did not bother her too much.

Taking the tour from tower to tower, even the refurbishments of the 19th century could not spoil the atmosphere. she found the fact that they dated from across the last two millennia fascinating. Climbing in through narrow doors, she stared around, imagining the place teaming with Roman or medieval life.

As she approached a smaller tower, her hands began to shake. She stared at the sign. *La Tour Wisigothe*. Checking the leaflet, she realised that this was one of the oldest towers still intact together with several Roman towers, now fully restored, along the wall to the east of the inner fortress. Looking behind her, she found herself surprisingly alone.

"Phew! Let's see what you're hiding," she whispered, clasping her hands firmly to stop them from shaking. Swallowing hard, she took a few steps to the Romanesque doorway and glanced into the tower. As she moved, her throat constricted, and she began to feel queasy.

"Silly woman!" Maddie chided herself. This had never happened before, and she would not allow it to happen now, but where had the stale taste of whatever come from? It smelled like damp earth. She gagged and cast another furtive glance around. All was in order. No decomposing animals lying around.

"Sod it!" Balling her hands into fists, she entered the tower. As she walked through, staring at the wooden beams above, dizziness overcame her, and she sat down, leaning against the cool wall.

"Breathe…"

It was easier said than done. "I'm not in a thriller." Maddie tried to keep her voice steady, but failed. Instead, the words escaped like a hoarse whisper.

"I must get out!" she croaked, and tried to get up, but her wobbly legs didn't allow it. She slid down onto the cold stone floor and closed her tired eyes.

Visions of sparse furniture, pre-medieval, filled her mind. A few straw beds set against the walls. Shapes of men asleep, snoring, the sound roaring in her ears. Swords, belts and knives lay in a heap by the far door. Then a shape sat up and turned her way. Across the small space, his dark brown eyes bored into her. The chill in them froze her blood. With a smirk on his face, he rose and—

"Madame, Miss," someone gently shook her shoulder, "do you need help?" An English accent. Female.

Maddie drew in a sharp breath and blinked. "What? Where?" She stared at the woman kneeling beside her.

"You're English?" the woman asked.

"Yup." She nodded, trying to control her breathing.

"I'm so sorry to disturb you, but you were whimpering, as if you were in pain. Are you OK now?"

"Yes, thank you. I…I think so."

"Here, have some water." The woman unscrewed a small thermos flask, wiped a cup with a paper tissue she pulled from her bag, and filled it with fresh water.

Maddie raised her hand, but it was still shaking, so her helper held it to her mouth. Grateful for the cool liquid, she took a few sips. "Thank you so much. You're very kind." She spotted another woman and a man hovering behind the woman. "I'm so sorry to be an inconvenience. I've no idea what just happened."

Between them, they helped her up. Feeling a little steadier, she took the offered cup and emptied it.

"Not at all," her helper responded, as she shook out the last drops from the cup and bagged it with the thermos into her backpack. "Are you sure you'll be all right?"

"Yes, I'm fine. I just think I'll need to grab some lunch."

The woman laughed and pressed her upper arm. "Then I'd suggest you take a break from your walk… Take care."

Maddie smiled. "Yes, I'll do that. Thanks again. Bye."

But the walking direction meant she could only continue forward, to the next tower, and those beyond. Outside the Visigoth Tower, she leaned on the crenellations and looked out over the town below her, and the rolling hills of the

Montagne Noire to the north. Somewhere up there, out of sight, was Minervens. Taking deep breaths, she slowly regained her composure.

What had just happened in there? Who had the guy been? His memory of his glare still sent shivers down her spine. It seemed so real.

"Léon won't believe this…" She chuckled, before she realised that she'd thought of telling Léon first, rather than calling Brian. Something had changed in the last few weeks. Her ex was no longer the Number One to talk to. "Ooh…" she whispered, aware of a group of Spanish tourists passing her. Fortunately, they were talking too loudly to each other to hear her mumbling.

Not sure whether this was good news or bad, she shrugged off those dangerous thoughts as she waited for the group to move on.

When silence descended again around her, her gaze drifted into the distance. All this used to be part of the ancient county of Carcassonne. Perhaps tonight, she would first read up more about it before telling anyone. She needed proof of the historical era of the weapons and clothes in the…what? Vision?

"The county of Carcassonne," she murmured. Smiling, she appreciated the citadel's strategic location and undisrupted views for miles and miles. As she stood, her eyes lost focus, and the scenery began to melt into a hazy glimmer.

The unexpected scent of lavender filled her nostrils.

'My home…'

Chapter Ten

The feast day of St Adela of Pfalzel, AD 777
Carcassonne

Hilda tried to keep her hands from shaking as she picked up her comb, but she could not hold it steady. Her wedding day had arrived too soon, and it filled her head with thoughts of excitement and concerns, both at the same time.

Amalberga tutted and took it from her. "Sit still, or we will be late for the ceremony!"

Hilda caught a glint of humour in her companion's eye and shook her head in mock disobedience, before dutifully turning on her stool to allow Amalberga to brush her hair. She had washed it this morning, and the scent of lavender engulfed her as Amalberga ran the comb through her tresses. Today, she would wear her hair unbound, only covered by a thin veil. A delicate gold circlet, decorated with small precious stones, lay on its small cushion the table. It had been her mother's.

She smiled as she remembered her father giving it to her as a wedding gift before she retired to her chamber last night. He blinked back the tears, and his face had shone with pride. They had embraced firmly, before he abruptly left her. Only later had she realised the reason: he would be on his own now. No longer a woman awaiting his return at home – her old home. She briefly wondered if he considered to marry again. Strangely, the thought had never occurred to her before, and she was uncertain how she felt about it.

"Tilt your head back just a little, Sweeting."

Hilda did as asked and felt Amalberga tie two narrow strands of hair at the top of her head into small braids,

96

securing the ends with tiny threads and letting them loosely fall over her shoulder. She raised her hand.

"Don't touch!" Her companion's stern voice warned her. "I do not wish for the braids to fall apart."

She burst into a fit of laughter. At times, Amalberga sounded like a strict abbess. "Yes, Mother Superior," she teased.

A sigh behind her made her turn around. Amalberga took her hands in a firm grip, tears welling up in her eyes. Immediately, Hilda's humour turned to concern. "What troubles you?" She stood.

"Ahh, Sweeting." Another sigh. "Soon you will be wed, lead your life as Countess of Carcassonne, have children – and no need of old little me."

Hilda embraced her gently. "I will always have need of you, Amalberga. You are my rock."

Her companion laughed, the sound dry. Hilda moved back and held her at arm's length. "You are the only person I trust completely. Besides, if there are to be children, they will need a sage woman to guide them." The thought of what she had to do to have children briefly crossed her mind. Amalberga, as always, had prepared her for what to expect, and it had not sounded too pleasant.

Amalberga's face grew sombre. "I have thought about returning to Vaulun – if you preferred it. Your lord father would let me stay. He promised."

"In his household? Hundreds of miles away from me? No, no, no." Hilda vehemently shook her head. "I forbid it. No, you must stay." Tears were now threatening her too, and she quickly took a step back and wiped them with the back of her hand.

"Oh Hilda, please do not cry. A bride must look happy, not sad."

Hilda nodded. "Even if she feels sad?"

"Indeed, my child. If you wish for me to stay, I shall. Though your lord husband will have to agree, of course."

"Why should he not?" Hilda cast her companion a mystified look. "He has not indicated his displeasure at your presence, and if he wants me to remain in Carcassonne, he will have to allow you to stay." She crossed her arms under her breasts and tapped her foot.

Amalberga laughed and brushed away her tears. "Oh, Sweeting. You don't know yet what men are like."

Hilda felt a helpless anger stir inside her. Never would she allow a man to tell her what to do – and what not! "I do, Amalberga. I do." She glanced at her gown hanging over a rail on the far side of her room. She shrugged her shoulders and changed the subject before both dissolved in tears. "Will you help me dress?"

"With pleasure." Amalberga rushed to pick up the linen shift worn underneath, and Hilda slipped into it. Its tight fit and wide sleeves accentuated her curves. She grabbed the ends of the sleeves and held out her arms as Amalberga pulled a tunic of finest silk over her head. Careful not to dislodge the precious gemstones woven into the tunic whilst Amalberga adjusted it, she stood stock still. Then the maid placed a thin belt of carved leather inset with amber stones to lie loosely around her waist. Lastly, her companion placed the veil on her head, letting the fabric flow over her unbound hair.

"Hold this here." Amalberga guided her fingers to her crown to hold the veil. Taking the circlet from its cushion, she held it for a moment with a wistful glance. Then she looked up, blinking back the tears. "I have this now. Please let go."

As Hilda slowly removed her hand, Amalberga placed the circlet on her head. It fit tightly enough to keep the veil in place, yet not too much to cause her any discomfort.

Content with the result, Amalberga stood back. Tears still glistened in her eyes, but this time a broad smile accompanied them. "I wish you could see yourself, Sweeting! You are so beautiful. Count Bellon is a fortunate man." She clasped her own hands firmly. "Indeed."

Hilda blushed. She also wished she could see herself. "I feel…" she raised her hands then dropped them at her sides, "…strange. Not myself."

"'Tis no surprise you are anxious. But I truly believe you will be very content with your husband. He's a good man."

Hilda cocked her head. Was Amalberga only saying this to soothe her fears, or was she convinced of the truth? "We shall see."

She went to the stool and sat down, carefully adjusting her clothes. She adored the beautiful gown, but on this momentous day that would change her life, she could not be overly happy over it. Although she had to admit to herself that the seamstresses had worked wonders. The gems shone with an intensity she found reassuring. She knew of their power. It was no coincidence that the stones used included amethyst, quartz, amber, blood stone – and the rare blue stone flecked with gold from the orient. Father had spared no expense. She had not dared ask how many deniers this wondrous dress had cost him, and he had hidden the account from her with intent.

Alas, she was no longer in charge of her manor. A thought reoccurred to her, and she turned to her companion. "Do you think Father will marry again?"

Amalberga stopped tidying up their utensils and stared at her. "I suppose it would be possible. He needs someone to look after the county when he's going on campaign with the king. And he needs an heir for his title."

"I had not thought of that," Hilda admitted. "It would feel strange to me to hear of another woman looking after the home of my childhood."

"'Tis understandable, Sweeting." Amalberga put the brush on a small table near the window and glanced out. "They are gathering," she said. "We must hurry."

Hilda's stomach curled into knots, and she briefly closed her eyes.

"You will not faint, Hilda, will you?" Amalberga touched her shoulder. "All will be well."

"Hmm…" Hilda whispered, opening her eyes. "I will be fine." She swallowed hard, then dipped her feet into the fur-lined boots. Usually, a servant would tie the strings that bound them around her ankle, but before she could suggest such a course of action, Amalberga kneeled in front of her and took hold of them, winding them tightly around ankle and lower calf.

Satisfied with the result, she stood. "Good."

Amalberga straightened her own tunic and briefly touched her own head to find her veil securely in place, then went to open the door to the corridor. "I'm so proud of you. Now it is time."

Hilda stood, carefully dropping the tunic to fall loosely into place. The stones glinted in the beam of the sunlight streaming through the window. She allowed Amalberga to wrap her fur-lined mantle over her shoulders and secured it at the front with a brooch.

Taking a deep breath, Hilda tried to calm herself, and stepped into the outside world as Amalberga, now wrapped in her own woollen cloak, opened it, and an icy blast hit them. The chill made her skin tingle. Or was that the anticipation? She knew not the answer, but still she stepped forward, treading carefully on the hard ground. The morning's frost had lifted, and in the strong sun, the ground had become dry.

A gust of wind tagged at her veil, and she reached out to hold it in place. At the entrance to the chapel built of stones left by remnants of Roman *villae* her father looked resplendent in a tunic of dark silk she could glimpse through the gap at the front of his mantle. She found his smile encouraging. He would always want to see her content.

Amalberga stepped aside. "I shall be inside."

Hilda nodded, then joined her father.

His eyes shone with pride, and he grinned at her. "Dearest daughter, you are beautiful! The very image of your mother, God rest her soul." He engulfed her in a warm embrace.

His familiar scent soothed her raw nerves, and her breathing slowed. He held her at arm's length and with a thumb gently wiped away a tear lurking in her eye.

"You make me very proud today, Nanthild." He stepped to her right and cradled her arm in the crook of his. "Bellon awaits you inside, together with most of Carcassonne's residents. Are you prepared?" A shadow crossed his brow.

Hilda nodded. She must be brave for him. "Yes, Father, I am."

***

Bellon's heart beat a steady drum in his ears when Hilda entered the chapel. Her beauty took his breath away.

Her half-open cloak revealed a beautiful tunic, which suited her well. Through the narrow windows the sunlight reflected off the precious gems woven around the collar of her gown of blue silk and the fine amber pieces on her belt. She resembled an angel floating over the floor of this little church built two or three generations before. Her hair, framed by the veil, fell softly over her back, and her pale face seemed almost ethereal to him. He could not believe his good fortune. Fact was, he would have taken her as his wife her even without the generous dowry that Milo had bestowed on her, and which he would use to make their home a welcoming and comfortable place for her and their children.

He joined her on the threshold and took her hands in his. They felt cold to his touch, so he stroked the soft skin not only to warm her up but also to reassure her. Her gaze lowered, she smiled demurely, but with a soft squeeze of her thumb, she acknowledged his effort. They kept their heads bowed when the priest loosely bound their hands together as he followed the wedding litany. Barely listening to him, Bellon's thoughts tumbled through the brief history he had shared with Hilda. From Charlemagne's Easter court and the announcement of their engagement, her difficult journey south, their recent rides out which had finally seen her open up to him, and to their meal last night when they were exchanging childhood stories. She seemed at ease for the first time, much to Milo's – and his own – contentment.

Eventually, the priest pronounced them man and wife, before removing the physical ties. Following him into the chapel for mass, Bellon kept Hilda's hand firmly in his, unless for prayer. Her voice had been frail when she spoke, but her gaze held a reassurance he had not noticed before. It would all turn out well, his patience worth it.

The hall had been decorated beautifully for the occasion. He was glad that Amalberga had taken over the arrangements – a much-needed woman's touch in a fortress full of men-at-arms. Sunlight filtered through the plain windows, sending light dancing across the floor and torches had been lit, illuminating new ornate wall hangings Hilda had brought with her from her home in the north. Fresh rushes covered the floors, sending a heady scent of dried lavender and rosemary across the hall. A large fire burned in the central hearth, around which trestle tables and benches stood for the revellers. In a corner, the lutist played a cheerful melody the moment they entered.

Bellon gazed around the hall, nodding slowly in approval. It conveyed the warm, inviting atmosphere he wanted to achieve. Beside him, her hand still firmly in his, Hilda smiled.

"Amalberga knows how to make a hall comfortable," he complimented.

"I agree. I have always had a wonderful home thanks to her. Servants may think she's overbearing, but she knows how to turn a simple room into the most welcoming."

Sensing her contentment, he felt positive that they could make their marriage work. He gently pulled her along to the high table, the closest one to the fire.

"Please sit. We have a feast prepared for today. Lot?"

The lad appeared by his side, a jug of wine in each hand. "Lord?"

"Please make sure the lady Nanthild is comfortable. It is her day."

Beaming at his new mistress, he said, "With pleasure. May I pour you some wine?"

Hilda lowered herself into a cushioned chair and laughed, nodding. It broke the spell.

Sitting down beside her, Bellon held out his own cup for Lot to fill, then sent the lad on his way along the table.

Servants placed jugs of wine and baskets of freshly-baked bread on the tables as his retainers filed into the hall.

He took her hand and kissed it, ignoring the startled looks of some new arrivals. She cast him an unsure sideways glance, but quickly seemed to forget the world around them.

"This is the happiest day of my life," he said, surprised at himself for it was true.

He had won decisive battles, gained in status, but the most important thing he could think of was the girl sitting beside him. In recent days, her gaining in confidence had seen them enjoying heated discussions, exploring nearby parts of their territory and planing the continued fortification of Carcassonne.

Eventually, she had even agreed to leave Lot at home and ridden out with him alone. It had raised a few eyebrows, but Milo had simply nodded, certain in the knowledge that Bellon would behave with responsibility and in good faith. Although tempted beyond words, Bellon had kept his promise – and his reward had seen Hilda beginning to trust him. It had made this day possible and very special.

"Son!" With a clap on his shoulder, Milo shook him from his reverie. Had he really been staring into Hilda's eyes all this time? Heat shot into his neck and cheeks. He blamed it on the wine!

He stood and engulfed his father-in-law in a strong embrace. Milo had done so much for him, at the king's court and offering his daughter, and he was glad to see the knight content. "Milo. Be seated and have some wine. It will be a long day of celebrations!"

He winked, and Milo laughed. "Oh, I'm certain we can cope with a few days of festivities over the holy days. God knows how soon reality will return…"

Hilda shot him a sharp glance. "Father! No talk of warfare today."

Bellon sensed the tension returning into her frame and nudged her. "Do not fret, Hilda. There will be too much entertainment for him to have any morose thoughts. I promise!"

He smiled, and her breathing steadied, yet a sad look in her eyes remained when she took a draught.

Wine and ale were flowing freely all day, and although the food was rich – the usual rabbit stew replaced by a large roast boar and venison cuts in a strong red wine sauce laced with rosemary – nobody grew tired. After servants had removed the trenchers – to be given to the poor – and cleared the tables, jugglers entertained the gathering with their tricks.

Bellon was pleased with how the day went. Milo's earlier mood had evaporated, and he talked animatedly to Dagobert beside him. And after recent skirmishes, his men and their families enjoyed the feast.

As the sun set, more torches were lit and the mood mellowed. A storyteller took up the space in their centre, close to the fire. Lot handed him a tankard of ale, which he gratefully received before he began.

Silence descended when the strong voice cut through the chatter.

Bellon leaned back into his chair, stretching his legs. Watching Hilda brought a smile to his face. She had cocked her head, her gaze focused on the stranger.

"My mother used to tell me this tale when I was small," he whispered. "Do you know it?"

She shook her head. "No, but it's intriguing."

Content with her reaction, he reached across to take her hand. After a surprised glance, she sighed and gave his a light squeeze, then continued to listen as the *raconteur* shared more tales of heroic deeds from the proud warriors of Septimania. Yes, she fit in well already…

Eventually, he rose, pulling her gently up with him, and the crowd fell silent. He raised the hand that held hers in a strong grip. "My dear friends. The lady Nanthild and I wish to thank you for joining us today on this important occasion. Together, we will ensure that the county of Carcassonne and Razès will flourish under our rule and our guidance. I swear to defend the fortress with my sword, and the lady Nanthild will turn this rough shell into a warm and welcoming home for all of us. I thank God for his kindness in providing me with a beautiful and intelligent wife, and I'm certain that you will award her the same respect that I hold for her. To the future of Carcassonne!"

Bellon raised his cup with his free hand and glanced at his wife, still unable to believe his good fortune.

Showing her upbringing as the daughter of a count and a lady of the educated Frankish court, she smiled into the assembled crowd. "I promise that there will always be an open door for all inhabitants of the fortress and beyond. I am grateful for your support in building a home worth coming back to, wherever your paths may take you. I have much to learn about Carcassonne – and Septimania – but your interests are now close to my heart. Thank you."

The loud tapping of dozens of hands on the tables brought tears to her eyes, and Bellon squeezed her hand with growing pride. The smiles on the faces around them showed that people wanted to accept her, even with her Frankish origins. That small but obvious fact relieved him.

Having said their piece, it was time for them to withdraw to their rooms on the upper floor. Amalberga took Hilda into her arms, whispering words of…support? Encouragement?

"Milo?"

"Bellon." His father-in-law stood awkwardly and took his arm in a firm grip. He sensed the older man's nervousness.

"Can I trust you with this lot?" He gestured towards the rather merry crowd.

Milo grinned. "You can. I'll make sure they are on their best behaviour. And…" he hesitated, his gaze drifting to Hilda beside them and back to him, "you know I trust you too."

Bellon nodded.

"Daughter." Milo gave Hilda a kiss on both cheeks. "I'm proud of you. Always have been, and always will."

Tears glistened in her eyes and, lost for words, she merely gave her father a shy smile.

Straightening her shoulders, her gaze met his, and Bellon nodded. Her hand cool in his, he led her to the door to the yard where Amalberga waited with a cloak. He thanked her and wrapped it around Hilda's shoulders.

Leaving the old maid clasping her hands at her heart, they left the hall and took the creaky steps to the upper floor, hurrying to escape the chilly wind.

Without speaking, he led her into his chamber – their chamber now – and quietly closed the solid door behind him. On second thoughts, he drew the bolt into place.

At her alarmed glance, he held up his hands and smiled. "Don't fret, Sweeting! I just don't want any unexpected… interruptions!"

She gasped. "People do that?"

"Oh yes, when they've had a few cups too many. This way, nobody will disturb us. Now…" He turned to a small table where a jug and two goblets stood on a small tray. "Would you like more wine?"

Hilda took a deep breath. "Perhaps a little, yes."

"A good idea." He poured the ruby liquid into the intricate goblets and handed one to her. "It will help you…"

She took a few sips, then looked around the chamber. He could not tell whether she approved or not. "If there is anything you wish to change in here, let me know. I've only ever used the room for sleeping."

"I may have some ideas."

She smirked. "Great. I'm looking forward to hearing about them. Later…"

He put down his goblet and walked towards her. Pulling her slowly towards him, he put her drink aside and trailed the line of her face and throat with his fingers. The flickering candles cast shadows on her face. Her curvy body felt warm beneath his touch.

She shuddered, but kept her gaze steady. A surge of emotion washed through him. If she was afraid, she did not show it. He lowered his mouth to hers, probing gently. Sensing her response, hesitant at first, then growing in confidence, he drew her towards the bed.

Chapter Eleven

Early April, 2018

Maddie sat on the sofa with a cup of coffee, looking at the chaos at her feet. Papers everywhere! Sifting through old bills and other paperwork, she had created two piles: one for the bin, and another for the lever arch files. She knew French bureaucracy well and expected she needed to keep some documents for reference.

Her thoughts returned to her recent trip. After having researched the history of the fortress of Carcassonne, Maddie was convinced what she was dealing with were visions. As unlikely as it seemed, something – or someone – in the past called to her. She knew which time the weapons, helmets and clothing she'd 'seen' at the *Tour Wisigothe* stemmed from: they were early medieval, in the style worn by the Franks. But she couldn't explain the scent of lavender that had followed her there from the house.

Léon was baffled, too, when she told him over a café at their local *épicerie* one morning. But he took it seriously, even asking for details, and to her relief, he didn't laugh or make jokes. He'd felt the earth move in her kitchen, too, after all. Yet, like her, he had no solid, scientific response.

More and more, she found his opinion mattered to her. By now, they met almost every other day, and Maddie had to admit that it was more than a simple welcome of a 'new girl in town'. Still somewhat reluctantly, she enjoyed his company and open interest. Whatever lay ahead of her once her year in France was up, who knew…

For now, the renovations took priority, so today, the work on the kitchen would finally start. She had agreed the date with Jean Marti, the builder recommended by Léon. Given the strange goings-on, she was keen to get the floor done soon.

The *maire*, Bertrand Carnot – Bertrand to his friends to whom she now counted, too – had accompanied Monsieur Marti to explain the scope of the work required, but had beforehand urged her not to breathe a word about anything they might find. So Maddie kept quiet, as instructed.

Léon had brought boxes and helped her empty the large kitchen cupboard, sideboard and dresser, then moved the heavy pieces of furniture with her into the corridor which was fast becoming very narrow. She had advertised some items on *Leboncoin*, a French online sales site, and someone would pick up the cupboard the next day, together with a large wardrobe and ornate bed which clogged up the spare bedroom. As cruel as it sounded, she couldn't wait to get rid of them. They simply weren't her style, and they would suffocate any potential buyer at the time of viewing. Maddie didn't want much money for the heavy pieces, although she knew they would be valuable, but if people picked them up themselves, they saved her the job of taking them to the skip or wasting time with *brocante* dealers.

As it was, she hadn't progressed with decorating, as planned. Instead, decluttering became her priority. She had donated old crockery to a charity and taken curtains and carpets that looked like they could enjoy a second chance to the dry cleaners. The worn ones had gone to the skip, together with much of Elizabeth's faded 1980s utensils.

A knock on the door pulled her from her musings. Taking the mug, she checked her watch as she went to answer. Monsieur Marti arrived on time – most likely prompted by Bertrand who accompanied him again. Maddie had to smile. The *maire* seemed keen to discover if any secrets lay below the surface of her house even more so than she did!

He might end up sorely disappointed…

The builder outlined the first steps – lifting the tiles – and warned her that dust might filter through the house. She laughed and shrugged it off, but quickly closed the door to the living room with its bright new walls.

Once the schedule was agreed, she excused herself and left the men to their work: Monsieur Marti drilling the floor tiles, and Bertrand sitting on a chair in the corridor, not letting the kitchen out of sight. If the *maire*'s behaviour perturbed the builder, he didn't show it. She felt a pang of sadness at the loss of the beautiful red tiles, but they were impractical and out of kilter. Maddie went into the living room, closed the door behind her, and continued to sort papers.

By lunchtime, she emerged to find the men getting ready for their break. The sight before her made her stop in her tracks. The builder had made good progress, though it was Bertrand who had a trace of sweat on his brow, though not through exhaustion. One-third of the beautiful floor tiles was gone, and the exposed ground was now a few inches lower, to make it easier to lay a more solid concrete base for the new floor.

Both men returned after two in the afternoon with Léon in tow.

"*Salut*," he said, smiling. "Are you ready?"

She let them in, nodding, before she grabbed her handbag. There was nothing of value in this house, and she found that she trusted Bertrand not to pry amongst her mother's belongings. "Yes, let's go."

She turned at the door, calling out, "*À tout à l'heure, messieurs!*"

Bertrand, seated on his chair again, waved her off with a grin, then covered his ears with earmuffs just as Monsieur Marti began to drill again.

Following Léon into his Range Rover, she shook her head, giggling. "I hope Bertrand won't be disappointed. He's expecting something big, I think."

Léon laughed and, turning the key, started the motor. Gently, he eased the car into the lane towards Carcassonne before he sent her a sideways glance, the corners of his eyes creased with humour. "My very thought. He is very excited about finding something historically significant. He's the head of the local history association, and the members are – how do you say? – on tenterhooks."

It felt like a comedy, although Bertrand and his club of history fans were seriously intrigued. She knew she would be, in their place. In fact, she had felt excited about it, too, though mixed with trepidation. She was a historian, though the Visigoths pre-dated her era of expertise. Still, if there was something buried under her kitchen floor – which she had doubted to start with – then she would still be thrilled.

But if it were of importance, it might stall her redecorating project. Her mood turned sombre. "Well, whatever might or might not be there, I hope it won't delay the works too much. I need the kitchen in order."

Léon nodded, the smile on his face dying. "That's true. Let's wait and see, shall we? It might bring up nothing of note, and poor Bertrand would be bitterly disappointed."

Maddie felt a pang, a sense of loss. Why did she have to bring up the fact that she had to get the house ready – for sale? It always brought a sense of sadness to their conversations.

Especially as, in recent weeks, they'd become closer. She couldn't deny that she had found Léon attractive – very attractive, in fact – and she was enjoying his attention. He'd kept his distance, being the perfect gentleman, but she had to admit that the odd touch, whilst handing her a glass or a cup made her skin tingle. It was exciting, being at the receiving end of a handsome, intelligent man's charm. She'd not felt like that in over a decade. Not, she had to admit, since the very early days of dating.

She brushed aside her thoughts and focused on the now. No more talk of selling the house.

Léon cleared his throat. "Do you fancy going to *Chez Jean-Pierre* tonight?"

The restaurant in a village by the Canal du Midi was meant to be excellent. Maddie realised she'd not been out for dinner since her arrival. Her heart skipped a beat.

"Yes, that would be lovely. I've heard of it, but haven't had a chance to visit yet."

"Then that's settled. They do very nice seafood if you like that. I'll pick you up, say, around 7 pm?"

Nodding, she said, "That sounds yummy. Yes, 7 o'clock should give me enough time to get ready after our Indiana Joneses have left."

He laughed. "Good point. I wonder what treasures they'll dig up," he joked.

"If it's an arc, my career would take off." She grinned.

Glancing over at her, his eyes were full of mischief. "Yes, I can just see you welcomed at the Élysée…" He chuckled.

"Oh, God forbid!" Maddie was mortified. "I'd love to write about it, but I'd hate the publicity."

"I'd help you with that…" He winked.

Maddie smiled, content with their banter. She mustn't think about the future. A year would pass by quickly. For now, she was looking forward to a relaxed dinner tonight with Léon. Small steps.

But first, she had to decide on kitchen cupboards. And he knew just the place to go to.

An hour and a half later, they exited a showroom owned by a friend of Léon's. Maddie had chosen a small fitted kitchen with birch doors, in a mix of country style but modern enough. It would go on two walls, covering the sink, gas cooker and oven, but leaving enough space for the Welsh dresser and sideboard. The colour would go well with the pale floor tiles she had brought from Spain, and which were waiting in Léon's garage. Resisting the temptation to buy a matching dining table and chairs, she said she'd consider it later. Who was she kidding?

They had set the date for installation for fourteen days' time. Delighted with the deal, she grinned as Léon led her back to the car. When his mobile buzzed, he hovered by the driver's door and looked at her over the roof, his face serious.

"It's Bertrand." He connected the call. "*Oui, j'écoute.*" His gaze didn't leave hers while he listened to the *maire*, whose excited voice, though muffled, reached her ears.

"*Incroyable*… Yes, I will tell her… We're on our way back. See you at the house in twenty minutes."

A sinking feeling settled in the pit of her stomach. Her body began to shake, and she leaned into the car for stability. Léon ended the call and pushed his mobile into the inside pocket of his leather jacket.

"You might want to get in," he said, and lowered himself into the driver's seat.

Maddie sat slowly and pulled the door shut, clutching her hands in her lap.

His eyes glinting, he looked at her, his warm, firm hand covering her shaky ones. "They found something."

She swallowed hard. "Did he say what?"

He grinned. "No. He wants to tell us in person." Revving up the car, he asked, "Are you OK? You've gone a bit pale."

She nodded. "Yes, I think so. I…I didn't really believe that something was there."

"And now it feels strange that there is?"

"*Ouais*." Taking a deep breath, she let her thoughts wander. What would await them in Minervens?

Léon drove as if the hounds of hell chased them, and Maddie held on to the handrail.

"I've never known Bertrand to be so secretive," he mused. "It's bizarre he wouldn't say what they found."

Why did this leave her with a sense of dread? Usually, Bertrand was chatty, that much she'd gathered in the last few weeks. She kept her hands clasped firmly in her lap, and stared straight ahead, deep in thought.

"You OK?" Léon asked again.

She looked at him, then she nodded. "Yes, I think so. I…I just wonder why Bertrand hadn't told you what they'd found. Why wouldn't he?"

"It's very unlike him. I've not heard him this…serious since we had the big floods that submerged half the lower part of the village a few years back."

When he swerved wide around a bend in the road, she tensed and was relieved when he took his foot off the gas pedal just enough to slow to a reasonable speed. No need to kill themselves over something they'd find out eventually.

"Sorry."

She gave him a wry smile. "It's fine. I'm as curious as you are." She released her grip from the handrail.

"I'm thinking about the layout of the village, and I can't imagine the Visigoth graveyard reaching that far, to be honest. So I don't think it'll be linked to that."

"A good point," she agreed. "They usually place graveyards outside the living quarters, in a specific space, not spread out across a settlement. From what we saw on the map Bertrand showed us, it was roughly six hundred yards away from my house. So, it must be something else."

Léon nodded. "Indeed. But what? What could make him keep it secret?"

"Well, we shall see, won't we?" She grinned. "It might be a treasure!"

He laughed out loud. "True. How do you say in English… Finders keepers?"

"Yes, something like that. Though no doubt the authorities would take the lion's share. If there'd be enough left for me to renovate the house, I'd be happy."

They fell into a companionable silence again. Smiling, she was thinking of a treasure. Part of her wished it was true.

"It would be funny if they were cooking pots…" Léon quipped.

Maddie snorted. "How very fitting! A modern kitchen built on an ancient one. Well, history is full of quirks like that."

"True. Nearly there," he said as he swung the car around a bend. "We— "

His phone buzzed inside his jacket. He fished it out with one hand, keeping the other on the steering wheel. Casting a swift glance on it, he turned serious. "Sorry, I need to take this. It's work."

"No problem." She sent him a quick smile, despite her reservations about talking on a mobile whilst driving, and looked out of the window.

To her relief, he pulled into a drive off the main road and switched off the car. So he was a responsible driver, after all, which secretly pleased her.

Having missed the call, he pressed redial. "Yes, Gina? Everything OK?"

Gina's voice sounded through the phone, asking where he was. It was loud enough for Maddie to hear her.

"I'm just on my way back to Minervens. Why?"

"...straight back...mix-up...bookings...key...cellar..." She heard.

Sighing, he closed his eyes briefly. "Do we have a group today? I didn't see anyone booked in. The key should be in the cabinet in my office."

This time, Maddie didn't catch Gina's reply, but Léon started to look annoyed.

"It was there yesterday," he reiterated. Gina's response made him sigh again. "Yes, I have my spare key with me. You know I do."

Disappointment surged through Maddie, and she expected his next words.

"*Bon.* I'll be there in ten minutes." He ended the call, pocketed his phone and, gritting his teeth, looked at her.

"You need to go home?"

Léon nodded, starting up the car. "Yes. Apparently Gina can't find the key to the wine cellar, and a group has turned up that wasn't in the calendar. She knows I always have a spare one here." He pointed at his key ring.

"Of course, you must go back."

"I'm sorry," he said as he revved up the car and reversed into the main road.

She smiled sadly. "Don't worry, Léon. You can always join us later. I'm aware I've kept you from your work too much lately."

"Not at all," he said quickly. "I tend to catch up with business at night unless I'm needed. It's an interesting timing for a booking like that."

"Oh, why?"

"Can't say for sure until I know what happened here. I'm sorry."

"Me too. And you'll miss Bertrand's big revelation," she half-joked. "Just come round when you can."

He stopped the car outside her house and laid a hand on hers. "You'll be careful, yes?"

"I will be." She gave his hand a little squeeze, then slowly – reluctantly – extracted herself and got out. "I'll see you soon," she said through the open door.

"You will. I'll hurry. Text me if you need me."

Butterflies began to dance inside her, and she sent him a warm smile. "Of course. Thank you."

She pushed the door closed and went through the gate.

After a little wave, he set off. Feeling somewhat bereft, she turned towards the house. Now, what was awaiting her here?

Chapter Twelve

The feast day of Christ's Birth, AD 777
Carcassonne

Hilda woke to the rattling of the shutters outside the narrow window. She opened her eyes to almost darkness and propped herself onto her elbow. Only the glow of embers in the hearth to her left allowed her a glimpse at her surroundings. As her eyes adjusted to the dusky light, she scanned the strange room, bare except for the bed she lay in, a thick curtain – moving slightly in the breeze that filtered through – covering the window, several chests of different sizes lined up against two walls and clothes hooks near the door on which tunics and mantles hung like ghosts in the faint light.

The bed...

With a jolt, memories of the previous day returned. She glanced at the space to her right.

Bellon lay with his back to her, his body moving softly with each breath he took. He was fast asleep.

Her hand flew to cover her mouth. So it had happened. She was married. And not only that, she had...

Sweet Goddess!

As carefully as possible, she reclined, not wishing to disturb him. But now she was fully awake, and, with the sound of the high winds outside, her mind wandered to the night before.

Feeling the heat rising into her cheeks, she held her cool hands against the hot skin. Hilda suspected that she was fortunate. Bellon had been considerate, patient, and gentle with her before he had carried her away with him. Sensations she had never known before had soared through her, and she had allowed him to show her how what Amalberga had called 'the marriage thing' really felt like. Absorbed in his touches and kisses, she had soon pushed aside the discomfort and unfamiliarity that arrived briefly. That they had continued after a pause, during which he had rekindled the fire and handed her some wine to refresh herself, showed how much her view of him had changed in such a short time span.

Over the past week, he had taken her out-of-doors to discover this beautiful but rugged part of Septimania. She had acknowledged his pride in his heritage, and his plans for the future. His real interest in her opinion delighted her. Why, during the wedding feast he was talking about 'their' guidance, not 'his', and he had looked at her with contentment.

Turning her head, she glanced at him. She fervently hoped he would not change now they were wed, as she was slowly falling in love with this Visigoth warrior.

At that moment, Bellon shifted onto his back and let out a deep breath. Hilda held hers. In the gloom, she studied him: the deep-set eyes, the strong nose, his ubiquitous moustache... A giggle escaped her when she remembered how it had tickled her skin!

It took her a moment to realise that he had opened his eyes, giving her a quizzical sideways glance, and a broad smile spread slowly across his face.

"Were you laughing at me?" he asked in a serious, mocking tone.

A shiver of anticipation ran down her spine. "Me? Would I dare laugh at my husband?" She tried to mimic the expression of an obedient wife and squealed when he rolled over to cover her in a swift movement.

"You wouldn't..." He challenged her as he trailed soft kisses down her throat. "Mmh."

She wriggled beneath him and drew her arms around his back, relishing the heat emanating from his body. "Perhaps I would, just to see what he would do..."

"Ah, it's like that!" He propped himself onto his elbows, taking his weight. His gaze, full of mirth, slid over her face.

"Oh no! In that case, the lady will have to wait." He edged off her and rose. Her disappointment must have shown, as he added, "First, the fire. Then…"

Watching him, she snuggled deeper into the soft covers, drawing them over her chilled skin. "You'd better hurry. Your…reward…awaits!"

His frame shook with laughter as he placed a handful of twigs to the embers before stoking them vigorously into a small fire. Placing several large logs on top, the fire soon began to spread.

He stretched and turned back towards the bed. Her eyes feasted on his body, and she realised that any sense of shame or discomfort had gone. Instead, a fierce pride flowed through her. He was her man. Why had she had so many doubts? Had she known this would happen, she could have spared herself months of miserable thoughts and fears.

Brushing her earlier concerns aside, she lifted the covers.

Grinning, he slid into bed beside her. Propped up on his elbow, he cupped her face in the palm of his free hand, stroking her cheek with his thumb. "I'm very fortunate, Hilda."

She swallowed hard, then gently stroked his chest. "So am I." Letting her fingers trail along his ribs, she giggled when he gave a growl.

"Now, dearest wife, where is my reward?"

They had wanted to stay in bed late, but on this feast day they had to rise early.

Leaving the upper floor, she suddenly felt self-conscious. Outside, the yard was bustling with daily sounds – people and animals were mingling in the bright sunshine. A gust of wind almost lifted her skirts, something that was entirely inappropriate after a wedding night. Bellon took her hand and led her down the steps to greetings from guards and other retainers. He waved at them, returning the salutations, and she followed his example. Giving her hand a squeeze, he seemed to sense her apprehension, and she sent him a grateful smile.

"Let's see who awaits us in the hall."

"No doubt, Father will be waiting…anxiously."

Snorting, Bellon opened the door and ushered her out of the gales and into the warm room. All trestle tables but one had been moved to the side, and a small group of men, Milo amongst them, had gathered around the hearth, cup in hand.

Amalberga sat nearby, and, on seeing them, lowered her embroidery. She beamed when she realised that they were holding hands and continued her work, content.

"We may have to eat crumbs." Bellon grinned as he gestured to Lot who was refilling a pitcher on a trestle table. "Do you have something edible for us?"

But before the lad could respond, a loud cheer went up from the hearth.

Had Father partaken in too much of the local wine this early? On a holy day?

The group cleared a bench for them closest to the fire, and three men left after offering congratulations.

While Bellon spoke to Lot, her father approached her, his gaze assessing. "Nanthild." He took her hands. "I trust you are well?"

Her cheeks were burning when she realised what her father was referring to. She did not mind sharing her thoughts with Bellon now, but with Milo? Although she accepted that he had his paternal concerns.

She smiled at him. "Yes, Father. I'm well…and famished!"

Milo laughed and drew her into an embrace. "I'm glad, and I hope your previous worries will have been for naught," he whispered.

She stepped back and nodded. "It appears they were." A sense of awkwardness stayed with her. All these people would know what she had done last night, for the first time.

And the second and third…

Blushing, she pursed her lips, pushing aside such embarrassing thoughts.

Taking a cup of wine from Lot, she settled on a bench beside Bellon, elbow to elbow. Her heart expanded when they exchanged a long glance.

"So, the preparation for today's feast are continuing?"

Bellon nodded. "Yes, the feasting is not over yet. We'll have deer and wild boar tonight, before late mass. And on the morrow, we'll discuss our defensive strategies for Carcassonne and Razès. But most importantly, we'll celebrate our new countess." He raised his cup to her.

Hilda smiled. He wanted his people to accept her. To distract herself from being the centre of attention – something she was not used to, and which she did not really enjoy – she took a few careful sips of the hot, spiced wine. Its warmth spread through her, and she began to relax.

Lot returned with a tray of steaming oatcakes and a pot of honey. Bellon picked up a cake and broke it in half, handing her her share. Thanking him, she thought she could become used to the way he looked after her. She dipped a morsel into the honey. Feeling famished, she devoured the tasty treat quickly.

Only half-listening to the men making preparations for an excursion to the southern boundaries the next day, she startled when Bellon addressed her.

"Hilda, would you like to come with us?" His open gaze gave her a choice.

She heard several indrawn breaths and saw him looking sharply into the round.

"If you wish to know your home, and the dangers that lie lurking here, I thought it a good idea if you were to join us. But it won't be a leisurely ride as we'll be exploring a wide area."

"It might be better if Nanthild stayed here," Milo raised his concerns. "For her safety."

"Yes. I'll come along." She straightened her back, looking at each man in turn. "Bellon is right. This is my home now. I'm keen to learn of any threats, and I want to be certain all is in place to repel those."

Bellon nodded, then addressed his father-in-law. "Nothing will befall her, Milo. There are enough of us to defend our group if needed, and of late, the Saracens have stayed south of our borders." Turning to her, he added, "If you are sure?"

"Yes, I am."

***

The feast day of St Stephen

Bellon heaved himself off his horse and helped Hilda dismount her mare. He noticed tiredness in his new wife's features and felt a pang of guilt. Mass commemorating Christ's birth the evening before had lasted for hours, and, on return to their chamber, they both had been too awake to think of sleep. Lounging in bed under the covers, they had talked and drunk wine, and made love into the early hours, and now, he felt the lack of rest. As did she, without doubt. He was used to it, on his excursions across the country, but for a lady used to regular hours, getting used to a strange place whilst staying up late carried its mark.

But the look she sent him was one of wonder at the sight that lay before them, and he could well believe it when her gaze turned southward again, drinking in the beauty of the land.

They had left Carcassonne early after breaking their fast. The wind that had lasted throughout the previous days had lessened during the night, but a light cool breeze still hung in the air. Accompanied by an armed guard of eight men-at-arms and members of his own council, Bellon, Hilda and Milo had ridden hard across an old route leading south. They had only paused at intervals to scan the landscape for any dangers, but the weather kept many people indoors.

Passing tiny hamlets of huts nestled almost out of sight into the rolling hills – families of Visigoths displaced by decades of warfare – he had spoken to many and invited them to join him at Carcassonne. Wariness had clouded their

121

faces – they had become resigned to escape conflicts – but a palpable sense of relief spread across the small gatherings when he outlined his vision for the county. People should feel safe, able to pursue their work on fields and vines; the wars of recent decades were over.

Watching his wife with pride as she spoke to women and children, Bellon realised how fortunate he was. Hilda was perfectly suited to life as a countess: polite, a good listener, and a woman of sound judgment. When she played with a small girl, his heart felt like bursting, and he hoped that soon they would be gifted with children of their own soon.

Your own dynasty.

He swallowed hard as he followed her gaze towards the south. Snow-capped peaks rose high in the distance, but in a trick of bright sunlight they seemed close, looming to dizzying heights. Almost near enough to touch the icy cover. Many times had he travelled to the mountains, and even crossed them a few times, but usually in summer. Now, the blanket of snow covered the mountain-sides down to the valleys.

"It's beautiful," Hilda whispered in awe.

"It is. As often as I have seen these mountains, which we call the Pyrenaei – the burning hills – I can never get enough."

"They are impressive. But why 'burning'? What happened?"

"The name comes from the Greek word for fire. Ancient tales tell us the mountains were called 'the burning hills' after herdsmen ended up setting the whole range on fire. But we often have such fires here during our long, dry summers, so to me, it sounds plausible that they were simply named after an observation of such a regular occurrence rather than after a group of herdsmen."

"I see. And these fires, how do you fight them?"

He sent her a grim look. "You cannot fight them. If they are near rivers, we have vats and carts to quash them, but out here, in the wilderness, nature will take its course. A fire burns itself out, eventually."

"And the hamlets we have visited? People lose their homes!"

"You will see that people build their houses near streams, so, whilst there is water, they can fight the flames, but when we have droughts – which we have often – people must be careful and look after their hearth fires. Everyone here knows of the dangers."

"Ah, I see. I'll bear your words in mind." She gazed past him towards the towering peaks and made a sweeping movement with her hand. "And beyond these Pyrenaei lies Iberia?"

"Yes, and with it, man-made trouble."

"Dangers lurk everywhere, it seems." She shuddered, and he wrapped his arm around her. "As long as it stays over there."

"It's far from our home. To reach the base of these magnificent mountains you have to ride for at least another three to four days, depending on the weather."

"And how much trouble is on the other side?"

Beside her, Milo gave a harsh laugh. "The rulers – Visigoth and Saracen – switch their allegiances whenever the wind changes direction." He sent an apologetic glance to Bellon.

"You are right, Milo. Despite our joint efforts, they have dithered and turned traitor time and again. But King Charles has announced a new move across the mountains. As soon as it gets warmer and the snows melt, he will arrive here, and we will head south."

"And about time," Milo added.

"So soon again?" Hilda frowned.

Bellon nodded. "I'm afraid we must. Fortunately, our own boundaries are now fairly safe. You can rest assured that you will have a suitable amount of armed men for the defence of Carcassonne. But Lupo of Vasconia has been stirring up rebellions in the west – at the coast of a sea far greater than the Mare Mediterraneum – and he and his Vascones warriors keep attacking the borders of Aquitania."

He could not hide a shudder. Those Vascones had a reputation for being fierce fighters, and he had encountered them in many small skirmishes. Open battle was not for them.

Seeing Hilda's look of concern, he smiled swiftly and waved off the dark mood. "But that will be for the spring. Now, we will ride on a bit further, to the small settlement of Rhedae, which lies on the route south. This territory is called the Razès, and it's a strategic point for crossing east to west and north to south. Because of that, the settlement of Rhedae has recovered more quickly than other places, and is growing fast."

"It sounds intriguing. I've not seen any large settlements apart from Carcassonne."

"True, there are but a few, and many on the coast." He helped her back into the saddle before mounting his stallion. "Rhedae differs from our built-up fortresses. You will like it. Shall we?"

Hilda nodded and, together, they nudged their horses into a canter.

Chapter Thirteen

Early April, 2018

Maddie had barely put the key in the lock when Bertrand pulled the door open and beamed at her. She could swear he looked like an excited boy who had made an unusual discovery. Well, perhaps he had…

"Ahh, finally," he almost shouted. Then he glanced behind her before his gaze met hers again. "Where is Léon? Is he not with you?"

She nearly burst out laughing. Never mind that she was the owner of this house… "*Non, désolée.* He had a call from Gina. Something about a group and a missing key to the wine cellars." She shrugged apologetically and felt sorry for him when she saw the disappointment in his eyes. "Am I allowed to come in?" She smiled and pointed at the corridor.

"*Oh, bien sûr!*" Flushing a shade of crimson, Bertrand shuffled to the side to let her in. It was almost comical. His surprise didn't have the full audience he clearly expected, but at least she would find out what went on here.

"Léon will join us later, don't worry. *Salut,*" she called to Monsieur Marti who stood leaning against the kitchen doorframe. "*Ça va?*"

He laughed, nodding at Bertrand. "Well, I'm not allowed to continue just yet. *Monsieur le Maire* has forbidden me from continuing and informed the authorities."

"For what?"

"See for yourself." He moved out of her way and let her look over the mess that had been a kitchen floor earlier. They had removed two-thirds of the old tiles, together with the layer that had glued them to the base. Ah, now the tarpaulin-covered trailer outside her gate made sense. The builder must have taken all the rubble out.

The drop was several inches deep, to allow for proper levelling, as expected. But in the far corner the mud looked more disturbed than elsewhere. Small mounds of earth had been heaped up, leaving large holes.

"What's there?" She dropped her bag and coat on the bannister in the corridor and stepped gently into the kitchen. It resembled…

Her heart was beating faster, and she blinked.

"Bones," she whispered.

A shiver ran down her spine, and, almost on auto-pilot, she crouched at a safe distance, not wishing to step on anything interesting. Half-uncovered, one piece was clearly a bone, possibly human, and another seemed to be part of a skull. It was like being on a dig, only in her own home. What were the chances!

"Careful," Bertrand whispered from the door. "It may be a person."

Maddie nodded. "Indeed. The curvature here that shows above the earth could point to a human cranium. The bone you have revealed, Monsieur Marti, could be a tibia." She stood, facing them. "This is intriguing."

Both men nodded enthusiastically.

The remains of a human being in her kitchen. "Could there be more?"

Monsieur Marti shrugged. "I wasn't allowed to check…" He glared at Bertrand who ignored him.

"This is exciting, *Madeleine*, *non*?"

"Absolutely. Excuse me for a second." Her mind made up, Maddie headed past them to where she'd left her bag and began searching it. She hadn't brought any utensils for an archaeological dig – who would expect something like this when renovating their kitchen? – but she had a brush for her blusher in her make-up case. That would do.

"Ha!" She raised her hand, brandishing the cosmetic item. "There we are." She went to the sink and ran the brush through her fingers until no traces of make-up remained.

"But…Madame…Madeleine… Shouldn't we wait for the professionals? I called the history museum in Carcassonne, and they said they'd call us back…though they don't seem in a hurry."

Bertrand looked positively flustered, and for a moment Maddie worried he may be heading for a heart attack. On second glance, though, the look on his face resembled more a child waiting to open a Christmas present than a man close to cardiac arrest.

"Please don't worry, Bertrand, I have studied archaeology and have assisted at many digs…discoveries…across Europe and north-east America. This," she pointed at the brush, "will help me. Would you like to watch?"

"*Bien sûr.*" He nodded, delighted he had a front-row seat.

She smiled at his enthusiasm.

"Please stay outside the perimeter… Yes, it's fine by the door. Monsieur Marti, would you lend me a hand, please?"

The builder joined her. His eyes wide, he stared at the bones.

"There's nothing to worry about. Once we have uncovered these items and have checked the rest of the floor, your work can continue as planned. I hope…" She grinned.

The poor man didn't look reassured, but shrugged his shoulders.

She knelt at arm's length from the bone, which was half-uncovered, and gently pulled it up. "Monsieur, do you see the pack of kitchen towels over there, on the cupboard in the corridor? Yes? Please hand me one, so I can lay this bone somewhere safe, where it can't be damaged. Take two, as you'll need one as well."

Bertrand pulled two towels from the bundle and handed them to the builder, then sat down again in the doorframe.

It often surprised Maddie how the tallest and heaviest of men could walk gently and gingerly when needed. Monsieur Marti's heavy shoes barely touched the ground, and he immediately returned with the towels, handing them to her without coming near the find. A man of few words. Maddie nodded in thanks.

She laid out a towel on the churned-up ground beside her and placed the bone onto it. Then she brushed off the earth that stuck to it. It was definitely human, in her view. She held it against her forearm, then her thigh. Yes, too long for an arm bone; most likely a femur.

"Could you please move this over to the far wall and place it on a fresh towel, so we don't step on it by accident?"

"*Oui*." Again, Monsieur Marti did as bid, carrying bone and towel at arm's length. Maddie suppressed a smile. Perhaps he was superstitious.

"So, this bone… Is it human?" Bertrand's whispered words reached her.

She nodded and cast him a sideways glance. "I believe so, yes. But it'll be up to the laboratory to establish how old it is – and whether it's Visigoth, or later, or even earlier. So when the experts call you back, ask for someone to collect them for tests."

"I will. This is extraordinary!" His voice was still full of wonder. Then his brows knitted together. "When they come back from the lab, I'd like to keep them here. They're local history."

"I agree, Bertrand. These would be perfect for the Minervens History Museum."

He beamed. "You would let us have them? Many finds from the cemetery have gone to bigger museums in the region." His face fell, then his fighting spirit broke through. "But we shall keep these, in that case!"

"Indeed." Maddie smiled, then turned back to the corner and focused on the piece that looked like the top of a skull. The cosmetic brush was not ideal, but it was the best she could do. Soon, she'd removed enough of the earth surrounding the find to recognise the remains of a human cranium. Possibly a female, as it was smaller.

Gently, she touched it with her fingertips. A sense of sadness settled over her. A woman left like that? Far away from any others. It wasn't even a proper grave, unless someone had disturbed the bones in the past, perhaps without having known of them.

Maddie had taken part in too many graveyard digs to know that this was different. And Visigoth graveyards were of a certain type, that much she knew. The way these pieces lay here, with no evidence of a sarcophagus or burial shroud, sent alarm bells ringing in her head. It didn't have the sense of a proper grave.

Finally, after what seemed like ages, she had freed the fragment from its shallow grave. She cradled the partial cranium in her hand. Her fingers tingled, and she gently laid it onto the kitchen towel to rid herself of this electric sensation. Slowly, she began to brush off the dirt. As the small clumps became loose, the scent of lavender rose from them.

Maddie cocked her head, and a shiver ran down her spine. It had been a while since the last time. "Can you smell lavender, Monsieur Marti?"

The builder hovered beside her. "*Oui. C'est tellement bizarre.*" He scratched his head. "Where is it coming from?"

She pointed at the cranium. "From this, it seems."

He took a step back. "Maybe there are plant roots somewhere in the ground?"

"Under the floor? No, I don't think so."

Shrugging off the discomfort, she continued with her work. After a few minutes, tears stung her eyes, and she quickly wiped them off with the back of her hand. What was wrong with her? She'd uncovered many human remains over the years, yet this one brought up strange emotions in her.

It felt...personal. Close.

Must be because it happens in my kitchen, she thought. Just as well that Elizabeth didn't witness this.

Eventually, she brushed the last crumbs of mud from it and cocked her head, puzzled. Who was this person? She held out the cranium to the wide-eyed builder.

"Monsieur Marti, could you take this over to the other bone and then give me your trowel, please?" Again, he did as bid with minimum fuss, carrying the cranium reverentially to the towel. Within seconds, the trowel landed in her hand, no words spoken. He stood back again, almost as if in prayer.

The silence in the kitchen was only disrupted by sounds of scraping. Carefully, she loosened a second layer. After several minutes of digging, the trowel hit resistance. She put it aside and prised the mud apart with her fingers. It crept under her nails, but she didn't care.

It was as she thought. Another bone. This one shorter. A forearm, perhaps? She uncovered it gently and exposed it in full. After cleaning, it joined the femur and cranium on the towel. Then, getting into a routine, she dug on.

Now in her element, it didn't take her long to discover several slightly rounded pieces of bone. Ribs?

"Can I have a fresh towel, please?"

She handed Monsieur Marti the dirty dish cloth and received a clean one in return which she laid out beside her.

Maddie smiled at the serious faces of her audience. "It's quite something, isn't it?"

"*Absolument!*" Bertrand nodded. "What do you have there?"

"Likely her ribs. From the shape, the bones should be those of a woman."

She freed three of them and put them on the towel. When she lifted the third one, she startled. Much to her surprise, she found what must have been a diagonal break crossing it.

Like a cut.

Looking back at the spot where she pulled the last, shorter piece out, she prised the earth apart. Yes, there was the second half. She swallowed hard.

Now serious, she cleaned the four bones and checked them. "There's two ribs with a cut. See?"

Bertrand had come forward, and both men leaned over her. "What does that mean?" the maire asked.

"Broken ribs mean she could have had an accident or a fight. Perhaps she broke her back whilst horse-riding. Or someone injured her with a sword."

"*Mon Dieu!*" Monsieur Marti exclaimed.

Bertrand crossed himself. "*La pauvre fille.*"

"It might explain why there seem to be only one person's bones. If we could find the spine, that would tell us more, but yes, the poor woman…"

Something horrific had befallen her. Tears pricked her eyes again and her skin crawled.

But who had this person been? When did she live?

And had she died a brutal death?

Chapter Fourteen

15th August, AD 778
The pass at Roncevaux, western Pyrenaei

"Ware! Attack!"

"To arms!"

"Vascones!"

Spears came flying from both sides of the path. On their return to Francia after a brutal campaign in Iberia against the southern Vascones, the Franks had split from their allies again. The Lombards and the Burgundians had taken the easier road northwards along the east coast of the Mare Mediterraneum, but King Charles and his Frankish and Visigoth soldiers were crossing the western Pyrenaei. The pass at Roncevaux provided them with the most direct route back into Aquitania.

They thought it was safe…

Bellon ducked as yet another short spear whizzed past his head, almost scraping his ear. Beneath him, his stallion collapsed into a heap of mangled legs, its heavy body pierced by two lances. He pushed himself from the saddle and lay flat behind the bulky rump as the onslaught continued. He blinked hard. There was no time to mourn the loyal beast.

"Put your helmets on and grab your weapons!" he urged those men from Carcassonne who had survived the campaign. "Shelter in the shrubs!"

Surveying the area, he saw movement all over the woodland hillsides.

Where had the attackers come from? And why had there been no warning from the lookouts?

With little time to think, Bellon clumsily untied his helmet from the saddle and pulled it over his head, fastening the leather strap under his chin with shaky hands. Then he grabbed his shield. Glancing around, he realised the alarm cry had come too late for many of his fellow warriors. He took the hilt of his sword in a firm grip.

Appearing from the thick leaf cover of the forest, men were crawling closer over the rocks of the steep mountain pass. Soon, he spotted two fighters nearby squatting behind a large oak. They were whirling their slings in the air before they turned to face him and his fellow soldiers and let loose a hail of rocks. He raised his shield, and the stones thudded against it. When he next dared a glance, four other men had joined them, some throwing their short spears whilst some prepared another volley of stones.

He huddled behind his dead horse again, escaping another onslaught. Beside him, men were scrambling for their weapons and helmets, unprepared as they all were for such an attack.

We should have known better.

Then the Vascones overran them. His fellow soldiers did not have enough time to draw their weapons and fight back. Bellon had seen many skirmishes and battles, but this was no battle. It was a massacre!

He fought off two attackers who realised that he was too well-trained and uninjured to engage in direct combat. With a few scratches, they escaped into the undergrowth as quickly as they had appeared.

It was the perfect place for an ambush, and a small voice inside his head commended them for choosing it. Then, reality returned with another man, armed with a short sword and a dagger, facing him. He parried each stroke and kept an eye on the knife. The Vascones were hardy warriors, brutal and without mercy. As they circled each other, Bellon manoeuvred the man towards his fallen stallion, then pushed forward. Losing his footing in the blood-soaked ground, the warrior slipped, then stumbled over the horse's legs. With a swift move of his sword, Bellon dispatched his attacker to Hell, or whatever the man had believed in.

Huffing with exhaustion he looked around. Only a few of his men were still standing.

"Run!" The cries from the vanguard reached him. "Retreat!"

Had he heard correctly?

"What? The king is leaving us to these heathens?" A young Frankish lord huddling down beside him stared at the trees, his eyes wide with horror. A gash on his temple was oozing blood.

"It would seem so. Look!"

Bellon watched in astonishment as the Vascones merged back into the forest, heading south, towards where his group had come from.

"What is happening? Where are they going?"

Around him, men gathered, always scanning the trees, but the attackers had left.

The eerie silence was broken moments later when scores of cries rose at once.

Bellon's head shot up, and he stared at the deserted path behind them. "The rear guard!"

"God save them. The heathens are regrouping."

"Milo!" He nodded grimly. King Charles had tasked Milo, together with several Frankish lords, to maintain the safety of the baggage train.

The clashing of metal mingled with the increasingly urgent cries.

"We must help them. The bastards will be after the spoils." He took a step but a Visigoth warrior from his group stopped him.

"Wait! We have to tell the vanguard. We are but a few and can't face the Vascones alone."

Bellon hesitated, knowing the warrior was right. "Then send a man to let them know."

A messenger was dispatched to the vanguard whilst Bellon and the other survivors headed along the track, towards the growing noise. When they turned a corner, they halted.

He had not expected the sight that greeted him.

"Christ have mercy!" The Frankish soldier crossed himself.

"They're like ants," the Visigoth whispered hoarsely. "All over them."

"We need more men."

Desperate to join the melée and find Hilda's father, Bellon blinked back tears as he watched the carnage before him. Rarely was he stunned into silence, but even when the Franks had burned Pamplona before their return, the king had allowed a level of mercy.

Those wild heathens showed none.

"Retreat!" A voice called out behind them. "By the order of King Charles, retreat!"

"No!" Bellon pushed away. "You should go back," he told the soldiers around him. "I'm going down there."

"And be slaughtered like the rest of them?"

"I...must!" He drew his sword and stalked down the path soon strewn with bodies, horses and donkeys. He could not make out Milo, or any other men he knew, as most of the men were already lying on the blood-soaked ground. The heathens hacked into anyone moving without flinching.

"Bellon, you have a wife; you have duties..." He barely acknowledged the voice as one of his own entourage. "It is too late."

Tears brimmed in his eyes as he hesitated. Ahead of him lay the rearguard of Charles' army, dying and massacred by a frenzied horde, and all the treasures they had collected in Iberia.

A howl went up. The Vascones had spotted his little group. Some let go of their victims and began to rush up the hill. Instinct told Bellon to run, loyalty to Milo to fight.

"Bellon!" He recognised the voice calling from behind him to belong to one of Charles' closest advisers. "We must go. Retreat now or die!"

Three Vascones, their cries piercing the air, were coming closer, brandishing swings and swords, and others followed, sensing fresh blood.

"Milo..."

"He's likely dead, Bellon. We can return later, once the heathens have gone."

"I cannot—"

A horse approached him from behind, and the adviser pulled at his shoulder. "Come! This is an order from the king!"

He shrugged off the hand and turned to the lord. "Take my surviving men safely back to Carcassonne!"

Then he held up his shield and strode towards the approaching Vascones.

***

Early September, AD 778
Carcassonne

Hilda stood on the walkway and breathed in the warm air that came from the mountains to the south, barely visible in the darkening haze. For weeks, the undulating heat had been too much to go out during the day, and she had fretted over her herb garden. Keen to please, Lot had built a cover, which shaded the more sensitive plants from the glaring sunlight. Now, as dusk had fallen, she watched him water her small herb plot inside the recently reinforced walls of the settlement.

"Do not fret. He won't be drowning them!" Amalberga grinned at her critical observation, and Hilda knew she was right.

"I know. I just wish I could tend to them myself."

Her companion gave her well-rounded middle a pointed glance. "Of course, and you would end up rolling all over them," she quipped, with a smile. "But soon, so you will again continue the work that you started, caring for the infirm and sick. Mind you, this little one will probably keep you occupied for a while first..."

Hilda laughed and entwined her arm with Amalberga's, stroking her belly with the other hand. "I guess so. It's all so...overwhelming."

What if the birth goes wrong?

Truth was, doubts had plagued her these past few days as the time drew nearer. She was not afraid to face the pain herself – which Amalberga had told her could be something she had never experienced – but how could she ensure the child's health? Afraid of failing Bellon, she had prayed to the Goddess, and even her husband's God, for a living, breathing heir. For all the efforts Bellon made, and his long absence on warfare with Charles, he deserved a boy.

Although the Goddess would likely be very pleased with a girl. But girls were worth less, only of importance to forge alliances, like her marriage.

Hilda realised she was fortunate in that she and Bellon had truly come to love each other. Over recent months, she had met other ladies at Charles' court, and not all shared her situation.

She even wondered briefly if the Goddess was withdrawing from her, surrounded by so much male dominance...

"Look, Hilda! What could be the meaning of this?"

Amalberga's question drew her from her dark thoughts and she followed her gaze. A commotion near the gate drew cries of pain, and panic ensued in the yard. Men were dropping carts and women came running from their huts towards the growing crowd.

A sense of dread washed through her. "Something has happened, Amalberga. Quick, help me down the stairs."

They carefully descended the steep stone steps and hurried towards the crowd. The wailing of some women sent goosebumps down her back, but, as the countess of Carcassonne, she had to maintain calm.

Amalberga nudged people to the side, so Hilda could get to the centre. She halted beside Dagobert, the captain of her guard, who stood facing the strangers.

"They arrived from the west, lady, from Aquitania," he explained.

Her eyes widened. "What's this?" She asked of a ragged-looking group of men huddled on the ground, exhaustion etched into their faces. Their clothes were torn, and she noticed some had injuries wrapped rudimentarily with torn strips of blood-stained cloth. Their appearance marked them as Visigoths, but they were not from around here. Women handed out cups of water, and the men drank greedily.

"I am Nanthild, countess of Carcassonne. What has befallen you?"

A man, not much younger than her father, approached and bowed his head. "Lady, we have been ambushed. These men and I are from a village a day's ride to the north. We followed your lord husband."

"Ah. So, who ambushed you? How? And where?"

The man did not meet her gaze, but kept staring at the ground at her feet. "By those scheming Vascones, near the pass of Roncevaux which we were crossing on our return from Iberia. They waylaid us, then split our line in two. King Charles ordered a retreat, and we fled, but our rear guard was…" His voice trailed off.

"Your rear guard was what?" Her heart beat loudly in her ears.

"They were cut off, and…and…there were no survivors. We were the last to escape alive."

Numbness spread through her limbs, and she clung to Amalberga's hand. Around her, she saw the worried faces of women, old men and children. Bellon had taken all men of fighting age, who were not needed for the fields or vines, with him on campaign.

"And," she swallowed hard, "where is my husband?"

The man's lower lip trembled, and he sent her an apologetic glance. "Truth is, we do not know, Lady Nanthild. We waited several days at a marker stone fifteen miles from Tolosa, but he did not arrive. Count Bellon and our leader, Alric, who died by a spear during the attack, agreed the meeting place on our journey south. There are but a few of us left." His hand swept over the scruffy, deflated group behind him.

Hilda blinked back the black spots that had danced before her eyes. She must keep control over her emotions. Bellon could have chosen a different route, or perhaps he was with Charles and safe. Before she dissolved into tears in front of her people and these poor strangers, she had to ensure they were looked after.

"Lot, find Roderic and ask him to make sure that these men are fed, clothed and have a place where they can rest."

The lad sped off in search of the *majordomus*, and Hilda faced the arrivals again.

"You are welcome to stay for as long as you need, although I must ask that you leave your weapons with my guards. How do I address you?"

At her signal, two guards carrying a large empty vat stepped forward, and the warriors handed over their swords, axes and knives.

"That is very kind of you, Lady Nanthild." He nodded. "My name is Ervig. We are grateful for your accommodation. It has been a long, tiring walk, and some of my men are injured."

"We will keep your weapons secure in a tower, for you to take with you when you are ready to leave us. Please follow me to the hall where I will see to your injured men."

"Thank you." They slowly followed in her wake.

"Amalberga, can you fetch my basket of ointments, please, and a bowl of warm water and clean cloths? Lot shall help you carry it to the hall."

"Of course, my lady. Lot," Amalberga called to the lad who had just appeared at the door to the hall. "Stay where you are; you can help me." She took the steps up, slowly.

Dusk settled around them, but the air was still balmy. Yet still a shiver ran down her spine. What had happened? And where was Bellon?

"All is prepared, my lady." Roderic met her at the door to the hall and held it open until she and the Visigoths had entered. Then he turned to the strangers. "Please make yourselves comfortable by the hearth. We have ale and watered-down wine for you to refresh yourselves, and later some pottage and meat cuts. Later, I will show you to your quarters."

Ervig and his men settled on the benches and stretched. As it had been so hot, the hearth was bare, but the hall was warm enough for the men to feel comfortable, and they soon helped themselves to the ale with Roderic's help.

"Now, who is injured?" Hilda asked. She looked at Ervig for guidance.

"Are you a healer?" He raised an eyebrow.

She nodded. "I am, and your men have nothing to fear from me."

"Thank you, lady. It is good to be in knowledgeable hands." He nodded to a boy not much older than Lot. "Sisbert here took an axe blow to the thigh. He was in the cart for most of the way."

Sisbert's face was pale, and he sat with his leg propped up.

"Who else?"

"Wamba over there had a blade slice through his arm. I fear we're going to lose it."

The man in question, perhaps a score years older than her, was sitting in an awkward, bent-forward position, his injured arm in a sling tied close to his body.

Hilda met his gaze and saw fear and shame. "I will see what I can do. Any others?"

Ervig scanned the group. "We all have grazes and scratches, but nothing as serious as those two."

"Good. My maid can see to those."

At that moment, Amalberga and Lot arrived with her large basket and a bundle of cloths.

"I'll fetch the water now," Lot said and left again.

Spreading the contents of her basket on an empty trestle table, Hilda waved Amalberga to her side. "Most men appear to have only superficial scrapes, which you can tend for me, but two are more gravely wounded." Facing the wall, she pulled an old, oversized kirtle over her gown and tied the belt loosely.

"Yes, I will see to the cuts and bruises, but are you certain you are in the right state for the serious work? You should be resting." Her tone had turned forceful, and Hilda knew only too well her companion's mind.

"I shall rest once I have cared for these brave men. I'm not ready to face my thoughts alone yet." She grimaced and knew Amalberga understood. If these men had made it here on foot, Bellon would have made the journey easily on horseback. Had he been alive…

Hilda swallowed her gloomy thoughts and opened jars and flacons just as Lot burst through the door carrying a large bowl of steaming water.

"Thank you. Can you place it by the hearth, please?" She poured a few drops of lavender tincture into her hands and rubbed them firmly.

Facing the two injured men, she said, "Please remove your bandages, so we can see who needs treatment first."

Roderic helped with Sisbert, who flinched as she unwound the fabric from his wound. His hose was torn, but someone had made sure the frayed ends did not enter the gash. And whilst the skin looked red and puckered, it relieved Hilda to see there was no pus. She gave the young man an encouraging nod.

"You will be well again, Sisbert."

Meanwhile, Amalberga helped Ervig with untying Wamba's arm. The man groaned and drifted to the side. "Quick, a chair," Amalberga urged, and two warriors grabbed Hilda's chaise, and together they eased Wamba, who was only partly aware of what was happening, into it. One man kept hold of his shoulders.

Wamba's left arm was almost severed above the elbow, and Ervig held it in place. It was one of the most serious injuries she had dealt with in her life.

"He needs us first. Roderic? Please help Ervig hold Wamba whilst I check the arm. Amalberga, bring the *aqua vitae* and pour the man a generous cupful."

Then she faced the warrior, who blinked at her with unfocussed eyes, and held up a short stick covered in bite marks. "Wamba, drink the spirit. It will dull the pain."

She watched as Amalberga held the cup at his lips, and he took a few sips and coughed. Immediately, Wamba's eyes were streaming from the strong liquid. Ervig gently patted his back, and they waited until his breathing had steadied.

"Now, bite on this. It will hurt."

Chapter Fifteen

Early April, 2018

A knock on the door made Maddie jump, and she sat back on her heels.

Bertrand was already heading down the corridor. "Ah, Léon. Finally…"

"*Salut.*" Léon followed him inside. "You're still here?"

The *maire* ushered him past Monsieur Marti into the kitchen. "Come, come. We've been waiting for you."

Léon raised an eyebrow in question, and Maddie waved at him, laughing. "Hello, stranger!" He looked from one to the other.

"You see," Bertrand said, wiggling his index finger at her, "this is all very exciting, if a little macabre…"

"Yes, look at what we found!"

Léon stopped just inside the doorframe, staring around the room.

Maddie changed position before her legs gave way. Kneeling again on an old cushion, she brushed off another piece she'd uncovered. Flashing him a smile, she said, "We've been busy here."

His eyes widened. "Are these all bones?"

"Yup."

"Human?"

She nodded. "Yes, a woman most likely, given the frame. We have half a cranium, a thigh bone and a forearm, several ribs – some of them cracked – and part of her spine." Picking up the largest piece of rib, she showed it to him, pointing at the serrated edge with her finger. "She had a broken back. Here, see?"

"I hope Elizabeth didn't murder anyone…"

Maddie grinned. "No, I can safely exonerate my mother. This lady here is much older than any of us. We're going to send the pieces for analysis to identify just how old she is."

"It's sad, though, isn't it?" He sobered. "Something that was once a flesh-and blood person. A person who had lived; perhaps had a family. Then she died of a broken back?"

'I fought for my life…'

"What? Did you hear that?" Maddie looked around. Had the men heard the voice, too?

Bertrand cocked his head. "Hear what?"

She stared at the bone in her hand. "Like someone was saying she fought for her life."

Monsieur Marti glanced over his shoulder and stepped backwards into the corridor, joining Bertrand. "I didn't hear anything."

"Nor did I," said Léon, "but perhaps she only speaks to you. You mentioned before that a voice seemed to speak to you here in the house."

"Yes, but I thought we agreed that that was just my imagination. I was tired."

"And the moving ground?" His gaze roamed the bones.

"What are you thinking?" She gently put the backbone on a towel, then stood to face him.

"Well, perhaps the woman is trying to communicate with you." He shuffled his feet.

"You mean a ghost?" Bertrand's eyes lit up.

Maddie shook her head. "There are no ghosts."

"Are you sure?" Léon sent her a questioning glance.

"I am, actually. Now," she was keen to change the topic, "I'm going to dig a little more here until the experts from the museum arrive. If you want to make yourselves useful, please take these finds – carefully – into the corridor and lay them out on the dresser."

"Yes, ma'am." Léon approached the cloth bearing the cranium and several ribs and studied them. "Some of these snapped cleanly."

"They did. I've been wondering if she fell off a horse. But why leave her. It wouldn't have killed her instantly, unless the neck was broken, too. Which we haven't found."

"The poor woman."

"Indeed." She knelt on the cushion again and continued to trowel through the mud.

Twenty minutes later, she gave up. "Nothing in that corner. I'll try on the other side."

"Is that strange?" Bertrand asked.

"Yes, it is. If this was a grave, all her bones would be here. They were deep enough in the earth. That is…unless an animal got there first." She shuddered. "But what we have here means something disturbed the body. Or the hole was too shallow…" Working on settlement and graveyards was one thing, but this was different. It wasn't a burial site.

"A shallow grave? So something happened to her unexpectedly."

The mood turned serious. Too much so for Bertrand.

"It's not like you to shudder at the sight of old bones, Léon, eh?" The *maire* slapped him on the back.

"True enough," he conceded, laughing. "It's just bizarre watching Maddie dig out bits of a human being, a once flesh-and-blood person who lived here."

"It is different to other sites, yes. But not unusual. Let's try over there." Maddie shuffled to the other side of the hole and began anew.

Léon stepped forward and crouched next to her. "Can I help?"

She nodded and handed him a small penknife. "Here, I found this in a drawer. But first, get your hands dirty in there." And she showed him how to rake through the earth.

Having someone join her made it far more focused. Together they uncovered further fragments of bones and placed them on a fresh cloth that Monsieur Marti put between them. They worked in companionable silence, only occasionally commenting on an interesting piece.

To her surprise, she forgot the two older men watching them. Instead, she relished Léon's closeness, his keen interest in what they found. She'd imagined him to be the impeccable businessman, but then she remembered that he told her he'd do much of the work on their vines himself. A man who got his hands dirty. She smiled to herself.

"I'm just keeping the history group updated on our finds," Bertrand said from his perch by the door. "I'll be back in a moment. Jean, come with me!"

"*D'accord.*"

She heard Bertrand dial a number on his mobile as their footsteps receded.

Minervens would soon get its own archaeological exhibition. She wasn't joking. Not about an ancient cemetery, of which there were quite a few in the area, but an intriguing case of one lonely body.

Oh, but what had befallen the poor woman? Glancing at the latest piece, a fragile finger bone, she shuddered.

I wonder what you suffered. Are you at peace?

'*Non!*'

Léon withdrew his hand and toppled backwards, dropping the knife. "*Putain!*"

Maddie sat up. "You can say that out loud. Jeez, so you heard her this time?" She turned her head to see him sit behind her, his face pale. Reaching out, she touched his arm. "Are you OK?"

He ran a hand through his hair. "Yes, I think so. Was that…"

"…the woman?" She looked at the bone. "I wonder. I've been hearing a female voice ever since I arrived, but I thought until now that it was only in my head. But you definitely heard her too?"

"Loud and clear."

She lowered her voice. "Just as if she waited for Bertrand and Monsieur Marti to leave."

Léon nodded. "A good point. She sounded cross. Were you thinking of her?"

"Yes, I was wondering whether she was at peace."

Heat shot through her fingers, as if she'd touched a hot oven tray. "Ouch!" She dropped the bone onto the loose mud and sat back.

"Let me see." He knelt beside her and took her hand, studying it. "Did it hurt?"

"Yes, as if it was burning."

A small weal formed on her skin where the bone had lain.

"This is serious, Maddie. I...I think you might need a doctor – and an exorcist!"

She laughed out loud, but it sounded hollow to her ears. "For what? The poor woman is in bits, literally." Squeezing his hand, she reluctantly retrieved hers. It felt good to be cared for. "Thank you."

Gently, she picked up the bone again, cool to the touch now, with her other hand and put it on the towel.

"We need to find the rest of her, if we can. Then she deserves a proper burial."

"I agree. Shall we go on for another hour?"

Casting a glance outside, she saw that dusk was settling fast. Soon, there wouldn't be any daylight left, and the kitchen lamp only cast a meagre light.

"Yes, let's continue for a little while, then start again tomorrow morning." She knelt on the cushion again and started to dig close to where she'd found the finger bone.

Léon cleared his throat. "And dinner later?"

Her eyes widened. With all the excitement, she had forgotten about their date. Well, not a date – a meal out.

She sent him a sheepish glance. "Of course. But I'll need a shower after this first."

The look he gave her made her head spin. Was he reading her thoughts? He smirked. "So do I. At home..."

And he picked up his knife again and bent over the corner he was working on, a smile playing on his lips.

A date, then...

Chapter Sixteen

Early September, AD 778
The border between Vasconia and Aquitania

Bellon held his breath, sinking deeper into the undergrowth until it fully covered him. The voices rang loudly through the forest. Vascones warriors. Had they found his trail?

He thought he had been careful, crossing the rugged mountains mostly at night to avoid detection by Lupo's cunning followers. Despite his anger, he had to admire the daring of the Vascones. They knew even the narrowest path in this large forest. And they knew how to hide.

Unable to understand their strange dialect, he stayed calm. After what seemed like ages, the voices finally grew fainter. Relief flooded through him. Perhaps it was just a patrol, tracking Aquitanians.

Closing his eyes, he waited until he heard no more sounds other than birds singing, then carefully prised the branches and leaves apart. Only the forest greeted him. He sat up and squinted at the early morning sunshine. Yet another hot day lay ahead. He could handle the heat – it was even hotter on the plain – but the humidity here tired him out.

But he was so close to the route to Tolosa, and once he had left the mountains behind, it would be easier to travel. He brushed off the dirt and winced as he put pressure on his injured leg. When did he last change the bindings?

Looking around, he found two clean large leaves and wiped the dew off them. Then he unwound the bindings and removed the old, grimy leaves he had put on the wound the day before. The gash still looked red, but it appeared to be healing a little. He wished he had Hilda's knowledge of herbs and flowers. Alone, he was at a loss of which to use, so he simply rinsed it regularly, then clapped on some clean leaves to cover it before securing them.

Eventually, he was ready to move on. Around him, birds were singing, and he even spotted a deer grazing in the distance. His stomach growled, and he took some berries he had collected the evening before from his pouch and chewed on the remaining handful.

If his bearings were right, he would be in the plain – and in the relative safety of Aquitania – before noon. Risking another day in hiding when he was so close was no option. He had wasted enough time, and God only knew what news had reached Hilda. Before he departed, she had told him she was with child, and the thought had kept him going until the moment he had heard of the danger Milo had found himself in. Never had he wanted to give his wife the sad news of her father's death in her condition. What sad timing!

But then, after he had killed the three Vascones warriors that attacked him, he disappeared from sight and melted into the forest, cursing his injured leg. He had slowly approached the place of the attack on the rearguard, aware of potential men sneaking up on him from behind. But the path was still swarming with Vascones plundering the carts and stealing from the dead. From his hiding place, he saw Milo's body lying on the path, unmoving. Rage tore through him when a man took Milo's boots and cloak, rolling the body over uncaringly in his greed. Over the distance of thirty yards, Bellon, unable to challenge the thief without being killed, stared into Milo's open, unblinking eyes, and he turned away in grief. Nothing he could do would bring back the man who had been like a father to him, who had entrusted his daughter to him. He could avenge his death now – and promptly die with him. Or he could live, for Hilda and their child. He knew what Milo would have wanted him to do, but never in his life had he had to make such a heartbreaking choice. Resigned, he disappeared into the undergrowth.

The pain in his heart was still raw, and Bellon had used several opportunities on his journey to kill Vascones outposts. After their victory, the fools had considered themselves safe, certain that Charles' army had moved on swiftly. Plunging his sword into their bodies had briefly brought a sense of satisfaction, but the sadness and anger remained.

As he continued his walk downhill, his thoughts morose, he looked for settlements, for a chance to borrow a horse, but any huts he came across stood abandoned. He used the half-derelict buildings to pause, to rest his sore feet and to light a small fire to roast a few morsels of meat, mostly hares he caught by setting traps – and waiting. Not much else he could do during the daytime, when Vascones could still pounce on any unsuspecting travellers.

Apart from wild berries and some apples from trees in abandoned, overgrown fields he found no nourishment of worth. Crops had been burnt, and the people who had fled must have taken their livestock with them.

He gazed around the plain opening up below him. Only the water of the Garona river, its levels low from the long, dry summer season, showed signs of life. Glad to leave the hills, and their treacherous tribe, behind him, he could finally head towards Tolosa in broad daylight. This would increase his chances of seeing traders who he could ask for a lift.

A new sense of urgency surged through him. By now, Hilda would have heard the tidings of Roncevaux. Even King Charles might have stopped off, knowing that she had lost her father, and possibly her husband, in battle. And knowing the Frankish king, Bellon knew Charles would plan for the future of the stronghold.

Eventually, much to his relief, he reached the route that followed the Garona towards Tolosa. After the last few days of hiding, walking in the dark and staying out of sight during the day, finding himself on a well-travelled road made him feel like he had finally returned to civilisation.

Early that evening, he hailed a passing peasant, his cart full of apples and pears for the great market in the big town, and asked if he could join him. When the man, after eyeing him up, agreed with a grunt, he took a seat beside him.

"Put your sword in the back," the peasant said, his words revealing a broad Visigoth dialect.

Relieved to have found a connection, Bellon placed his sword and shield on top of a large vat behind him.

"Thank you. I'm grateful to you," he said, aware of his blood-soaked look, then turned serious.

"I don't normally take strangers, but," the peasant met Bellon's gaze, "you look lost."

Grimly, Bellon nodded. "Yes, I suppose you're right. I'm from Carcassonne, but have just come from the mountains. There was a battle…"

***

Mid-September, AD 778
Carcassonne

Hilda leaned into the soft cushions of her chair and placed her bare feet on a footstool, grateful for the breeze entering through the narrow window. The days were warm, but, thankfully, the nights had cooled. Coming from the north, she suffered from the relentless heat. Even the residents of the fortress, though used to it, breathed a collective sigh of relief. Pruning of the vines had begun in the still intense early autumn sunshine, but Amalberga had ordered her to stay indoors and rest. Perhaps she was right.

This evening, she had retired to her chamber early. Looking after Ervig's group for the past week had tired her, and she found it hard to forgive herself for being unable to save Wamba's arm. They had to cut it off just below the shoulder joint, and an infection had set in. For days, she had sat by this stranger's side, tending to the inflamed stump. It was perhaps a small mercy that he slept through much of the time, with only rare, brief glimpses into the horror that awaited him on waking.

Sisbert's wound was healing well, and she had taught him how to cleanse the gash without help. He had also spent the nights watching over Wamba, as had Ervig. The group lodged in an unused room in an eastern tower, at Ervig's behest. He did not wish to be a burden and occupy the hall.

Hilda was grateful for their support, and a little voice inside her head kept nagging her. Wamba's arm had been severed so much, with sinew and muscles exposed, they had had no choice. It was impossible to reattach it. Ervig agreed, with a heavy heart, his eyes full of guilt, even though it had not been his fault.

Drained by pain and the heat from the fire, Wamba had gulped down several cups of *aqua vitae* and had promptly fallen asleep. Roderic had taken a sharp blade, heated on a fire, to the arm whilst Ervig and three of his men held the poor man down.

But his life still hung in the balance.

Hilda picked up a cup of wine chilled with cold spring water and cradled it in her hands resting on her bump. Relishing the strong scent of grapes and berries, she closed her eyes and let the silence engulf her.

Only in solitude did she allow for her thoughts to return to her husband. There had been no further arrivals since Ervig and his men had showed up, nor had there been any word of the Neustrian army. Her worries grew stronger each day, and only the occasional kicks from her unborn baby kept her spirits up.

What had happened in the mountains?

She had no wish to become a widow after such a short time, and before the birth of her first child, and she held onto a certain belief that Bellon was still alive.

But she knew her father, responsible for the spoils of war, had often travelled with the rear guard. Surely, he would have come to her immediately, to let her know he was well. That no message reached her of both men sent shivers down her spine. Yet, all she could do was wait. It was a wife's lot.

With her pregnancy advancing, Amalberga had forbidden her to tend to any sick, something she had taken up after Bellon had left in early spring. Whilst she could, she had ridden out and discovered new plants and herbs, the effects of which she had tested. Sitting still had never been her strong point, and she had grown impatient of resting.

Tomorrow, she would send a messenger westwards to Tolosa. Cursing, she berated herself for not having thought of this earlier. He could find King Charles.

And Bellon and Father...

She sighed.

Lifting her cup to her mouth, she nearly spilt wine on her gown when the door flew open and a flustered Amalberga rushed in.

"Hilda, come quickly! The king is approaching." Gasping her breath, her companion held her hand on her chest to steady her breathing. "He is due to arrive within the hour."

Hilda put the cup aside and rose. How curious timing! She had just thought of him, and here he was.

"So soon? Why did he not give us more notice?"

"I do not know, but the kitchen are preparing the wild boar that Dagobert's men caught this morn munching the vines. That's all we can offer him."

"And his men? We can't feed an army!"

"We shall see how many will appear. It sounded like it was just a small group." Having recovered her composure, Amalberga ran her hands through Hilda gowns hanging on a peg. "This one, yes."

She stood, untying her laces, and let Amalberga help her change into the fresh tunic. It felt tight around her belly. Looking down, she quipped, "This will have to do for tonight. I don't feel like eating, anyway. Oh, Amalberga," she took her companion's clammy hands in hers, "he might bear tidings from Father, or from Bellon."

Her companion nodded. "I sincerely hope so. This cannot continue, this state of not knowing."

Hilda stretched her sore back. "How do I look?"

"Fit to receive a king."

The hall was a flurry of activity. Roderic co-ordinated helpers who moved tables into a square around the central hearth, now clear of all debris as it had been too hot to light a fire. They draped large linen cloths over the table on the dais, on the northern side of the hearth, and a kitchen maid placed baskets with fresh loaves of bread, still steaming from the oven, on each table. Two young women brushed the stone floor and scattered cut sheaves of lavender on the ground, the scent already turning the room cosy.

Hilda beamed at the result. How quickly it all came together when everyone lent a hand!

"I will not have to feel ashamed of our household, Roderic. Thank you."

The *majordomus* blushed, then picked an imaginary bit of fluff from a cloth. "It does not match the king's palace at Aix-la-Chapelle, but it is the best we can do given such short notice." He huffed, making Amalberga smirk.

"I agree. And the food?"

"I went first to the kitchen. They are roasting the boar, and the meat of two deer killed last night is now cooking in a stew, spiced with wine, rosemary and blackberries."

Despite her lack of appetite, Hilda stomach growled. "It sounds wonderful. Please ensure that the king will want for nothing. We must offer him my chamber for the night, too. I will move into the small tower, with you, Amalberga."

"That makes sense. I will see to the rooms," Amalberga said. "But you sit down and rest until he arrives."

"Thank you, I shall. Roderic, please speak with Dagobert about space for their horses and whatever else they are bringing."

He nodded. "Dagobert has already prepared part of our stables and hay for the beasts. I was just on my way to check. Will you stay in the hall?"

"Yes, I shall. Don't fret about me."

"Lady." The *majordomus* guided her to her chair, ensured she was comfortable with a large cushion in her back and her wine, her feet propped up on a footstool, then left.

"They're here! The king is here!" Lot held open the door to the bailey, shouting in.

Hilda joined him, her eyes searching for Milo and Bellon in the darkness. Torchlight showed tired, drawn faces of strangers, and it took her a while to identify the king. He stood talking to Dagobert, handing over the reins of his stallion to a stable boy. Clovis stood close by him, barking at the lad. She shuddered, his words at Easter and the leer in his eyes still etched into her memory.

Brushing aside the brief thought of regret that this obnoxious man had survived an ambush where many other good warriors had not, she let her gaze roam the group of around three score men. Recognising many faces from Carcassonne filled her with relief. So some of their people had survived. She watched as they reunited with their families.

It was not quite the big army she had expected, but perhaps Charles had left them outside on the plain. With a sense of dread, she realised she could not see Bellon or Father. Why was Bellon not with his men? Goosebumps rose on her skin. Was that what Charles was here for? To bring her bad tidings?

She swallowed hard as the king walked towards her, his tunic dirty with dust from the road. Deep grooves lined his strong face, and his eyes held a hint of sadness.

Of loss.

He took the few stone steps up to meet her at the door to the hall.

"Good evening, Sire." She curtseyed before he gently pulled her up and embraced her.

"Dear Countess," he whispered coarsely and drew away, still holding on to her arms. "Thank you for your hospitality. I know we did not give you much time to prepare."

Her mind was whirling, not expecting to talk of food and welcome. "'Tis not a problem, Sire." She took a sideways step and glanced over his shoulder. "You and your men will be well cared for."

He nodded. "Of that, I have no doubt. Thank you. Now—"

Straightening her back, she crossed her arms above her belly and looked at him, no longer caring about royal protocol. "Where are my husband and father, Sire?"

He sighed, then led her into the hall. Her heart beat a steady drum in her ears, and all of a sudden, she was grateful for his arm.

"That is the reason I'm here, Nanthild. You may wish to sit, especially given your...condition."

She took a deep breath. Her worst fears had come to pass. "Are they dead?"

The pain in his eyes was too strong to miss, and she turned away.

"Let me take you to your chair," he said, signalling for Roderic to come over, and together, they settled her in her seat.

Her mind numb, she let them fret over her. "I am well, thank you." She waved off Roderic's offer of a cup of wine, and he stood beside her, a welcome comfort.

Charles drew a stool close. He would not meet her gaze; instead, he stared at the wall behind her.

"What happened to them?" she whispered.

"I fear the worst, child. I am so sorry. Milo was a good ally and a friend of many—"

"What happened?" she repeated, blinking at him, all pretensions forgotten.

"As often in our campaigns, Milo was in charge of the rear guard—"

"And your spoils of war?" Hilda could not hide the bitter taste in her mouth.

"Yes," he nodded, "that also. The rear guard was..."

"...attacked. Yes, I know this already. A group of Visigoth warriors from the mountains to the north has been staying with us for a few days."

He looked down at their entwined hands. "So you know that we found no one alive when we returned to the site of the ambush?"

She drew in a sharp breath as tears trickled down her face. "No, I didn't know that. Ervig and his men moved on before you went back. So...there were no survivors?" Her voice turned to a croak.

"No. I am sorry. We buried the dead and headed back."

"You buried Father?"

He nodded. "Yes. It was one of the saddest moments in my life. Milo was a good man. Reliable. Loyal. I will miss him and his dry sense of humour."

Hilda shuddered. "And now he lies in a hole in the mountains somewhere?"

"Y…yes. Like many of my noble men. We could not take their bodies with us in this heat. They would have begun to rot."

Blinking hard, she did not dare imagine.

"And Bellon?" She held her breath.

"Bellon was, well, as you would expect… Well, on hearing of the attack, he went to search for Milo, disobeying my orders to follow us. We could not risk more men to die. Vascones were swarming all over the place. It was not safe."

"He went back to help Father?" Staring at her hands in her lap, she ignored his reasoning.

The king nodded.

"So you have buried him as well?"

"No."

Her head shot up. "You did not?" Her heart was pounding in her ribs, and dizziness overcame her. "Why ever not?"

"We could not find his body."

She closed her eyes as the pain shot into her belly, and she pressed it with both hands. "Amalberga!"

Then her world went black.

Chapter Seventeen

Early April, 2018

Maddie was nervous as she stared with growing panic at the clothes she'd brought with her. What do you wear to a dinner out in this part of the world? Do you dress up – or down?

Léon had invited her to a top restaurant in a village on the shore of the Canal du Midi. Was it a date, or just a meal amongst 'friends'?

Heat crept into her cheeks.

Agreed, they had become a little closer over the recent weeks. It wasn't only to do with their discovery, although, to her surprise, he had shared her keen interest in the find. Excitement coursed through her veins every time she saw him. The warning signs were all there.

For now, she pushed away all thought of the bones and the woman's voice they'd both heard. This was important. Scary. French ladies dressed up when on a nice night out, and she wanted to look good for him. Hell, was the dating game back on?

She threw aside her jeans, and another two pairs, as she combed through her meagre belongings. With the works in her kitchen, she hadn't had a chance to return to York again to collect more items, and all she had with her were practical tops and jeans!

Maddie eyed her mother's solid oak wardrobe. I have no choice. She hadn't got around to removing any of Elizabeth's clothes yet. Their styles were very different; her mother's very much the hippie that she'd always been. Opening the doors, she peeked inside. Patchwork skirts nestled against flowing tops. Her mother had kept her figure, so anything she had should fit Maddie, but still, she hesitated. It seemed wrong.

"To hell! If someone picks these up in a charity shop and wears them, so can I."

There it was, what looked like a long, black skirt. Maddie pulled it out and held it against her waist. It was the right length, A-line, ending above her ankles. Perfect. She threw it on the bed and wove her hands through the tops. The purple colour of one caught her eye. Very brash. Was this her? Maddie wasn't sure, but still took the top off the hanger. It lay nicely around the hips, and a V-neckline would expose just enough flesh but not too much!

She changed into her mother's garments and looked at her reflection in the mirror. It was like Elizabeth stood there, and it catapulted Maddie back to her childhood. She blinked. No, this was distinctly her, just wearing different clothes than what she was used to.

Quickly, she gathered her hair in a loose bun, and chose a pair of large hoop earrings. This would do. Picking up a black silk scarf from a shelf in the wardrobe, she glanced at her image again. It wasn't her own usual self that looked back at her, but a new, more feminine Maddie.

"Hmm." She didn't feel entirely uncomfortable, but it would have to do.

Happy with her choice, she put on her black, heeled boots and went downstairs, giggling. She was turning into a girlie yet…

A knock alerted her to Léon's arrival. She glanced at her watch. 8.32 pm. A polite two minutes late. Grinning, she opened the door.

"*Bonsoir*," he said, holding out a bunch of flowers.

She'd seen the brand on the plastic wrapper in the local supermarket and smiled, taking them off him. "Hello and thank you. That's very kind. Come in whilst I put them in water." Typical man. But it was the thought that counted…

"*Merci*."

He closed the door behind him as she stepped carefully over the uneven kitchen ground. Busying herself with finding a vase and unwrapping the flowers, she felt his gaze and turned to catch him out.

Instead of looking embarrassed, he grinned. "You look good."

Heat rose into her cheeks and she quickly added water and put the vase in the sink. Instead of responding to his comment, she merely said, "These can wait here until I get back."

Then Maddie ushered him towards the door, grabbing her clutch bag from the dresser still blocking half the corridor. Being in this narrow space, winding their way between kitchen cupboard and sideboard, made her feel…what?

Her breath hitched as he turned before the closed door. "Ready?"

She nodded and stepped forward, fully expecting him to open it for them, but he simply stood, then took her free hand and pulled her towards him. Her heart beat faster by the second, but after a brief sense of apprehension – she'd been single for too long – something clicked inside her head.

"*Oui*?" she whispered.

When his mouth met hers for a tentative kiss, it suddenly felt right. The house…their discovery…his presence… France. She responded with the same gentleness. Too late did she realise that the scent of lavender hung in the air again. Goosebumps rose on her skin and she slowly extracted herself from his embrace.

"Shall we?"

He smiled, then opened the door for her. "*Certainement*. After you."

Two hours later, Maddie was sure she couldn't eat another morsel. She leaned back in her chair and glanced out of the large French doors that led to the empty terrace. Darkness had settled, but she still made out the water of the Canal du Midi glistening in the light of the street lamp. Soon, boats would head up and down the waterway again, something she was looking forward to seeing.

After a shared starter of *charcuterie* from a local butcher with crunchy fresh bread, she had enjoyed her perfectly steamed lemon sole with its accompaniment of crushed potatoes and green beans.

"I could get used to this." She smiled at Léon over the rim of her glass of rosé – Château de Minervens, of course.

He cocked his head and turned serious. "That's what I'm hoping for…"

So far tonight, they had avoided to talk about their growing attraction, focusing instead on the discovery and their work. But with her innocuous comment, she seemed to have triggered something she wasn't sure she was ready for.

Her smile wavered, and he quickly held up a hand. "Hear me out, Maddie."

Desperate to wet her suddenly dry throat, she took a sip and merely nodded.

Léon put his glass down and, folding his hands, leaned forward. "I think – and please correct me if I'm wrong – that we have something special here. From the first moment I saw you, I felt drawn to you. You're a fascinating woman, Maddie, with your intriguing working life, your research, and your interest in all things historic."

Deflecting his comments with a wave of her hand, she said, "It's just old stuff for some. Nowadays, my head's more in books. I'd say it's rather boring."

"And I say it's intriguing. So there!" He grinned, before turning serious again. "I'd love it if you stayed here."

"I am already, as you know."

"For longer than the year your mother demanded…"

Maddie swallowed hard. "It's only been a couple of months, but…"

Her eyes locked with his and she held out her hand. He took it and covered it with a soft kiss.

"But?"

At last, realisation hit her. She had fallen for this quiet yet confident guy. A vineyard owner of all things! And a volunteer *pompier* – a firefighter. Léon was a man of many talents.

"No but." She blinked back the tears and quickly sipped her wine. "Shall we see how this year goes before I decide fully?"

He nodded. "Fair's fair. But let me tell you – I can be pretty persuasive when I have to."

She laughed out loud. "I bet. You're selling wine to restaurants and then drink it yourself!"

A cough from the waiter brought them back to the here and now. "*Umm, êtes-vous prets pour un dessert?*"

"I'm sure I am," she said, allowing the giddiness in her head to show. "Are you, Léon?"

His mouth quivered as he held her gaze. "Bien sûr, Maddie."

Chapter Eighteen

Mid-September, AD 778
Carcassonne

Hilda woke as if from deep yet disturbed sleep, confused. Bellon had haunted her, as had Milo. Even her mother had appeared. She had been a child when Alda died, but in her dreams, her mother's warmth and gentleness had seemed real.

Now, her skin crawled at the memory. Or was it because she felt so cold? Shivering, she blinked. Beside her, Amalberga was breathing deeply, her eyes closed and mouth wide open.

She smiled and started to rise until she spotted him. Between her and her companion lay her son, wrapped in swaddling clothes, also asleep.

As calmly as she could, she reclined, her gaze not leaving the tiny face. It was a miracle.

Watching him, she tried to remember what happened since she collapsed on her chair in the hall, in front of the king!

Hilda closed her eyes. It was just as well she had lost consciousness, or her embarrassment would have been her undoing. How could she possibly meet him again?

Memories started to come back: of pain, of blood and screams. And of heat and cold. During more lucid moments, she thought she would die, but Amalberga would have none of it. Even the king had hovered over her bed. She remembered his deep voice penetrating the fog in her head, but could not recall his words. Or had he been in her dream as well? Reality and dreams had blurred.

Except for Bellon. More than anything, he had dominated her vivid dreams. His laughing face; his confidence; his hand stretched towards hers; his anger at his inability to reach her.

Could it be real? Was he reaching out to her from the dead?

Tears pricked her eyes. So much death. At the moment of her triumph, when she had given birth to a living boy, she had lost those dearest to her.

Father. Bellon.

She opened her damp eyes and stared at her baby's calm face. "Why?" she whispered. Had the Goddess deserted her? Or was her husband's God punishing her?

Through all her life, she had hidden her real beliefs from everyone. She had not dared set up an altar to honour the Goddess, but kept all items safely locked in a small casket. Only the knife she carried on her belt. But Hilda still prayed to her, and the healing she did with her herbs and hands was dedicated to her, proof she had never forgotten her.

But perhaps the Great One did not like secrecy. The stark reality was that, as a daughter of a Frankish count, with the Franks fervently serving the Church, she could not dare show her real leanings.

Amalberga shifted in her sleep, and the little boy grimaced. Hilda smiled. Her companion had looked after him well whilst she had been unwell.

A smacking of lips, then his mouth tightened. She watched in wonder as his cheeks turned puce, and he let out a howling scream.

Amalberga stirred and sat up, cooing over him, before she realised Hilda was awake.

"You keep resting, Sweeting. I'll look after your boy." She pushed herself from the bed and adjusted her shift. "With a voice like that you shall be commanding armies soon!"

"Is he hungry, do you think? I can..." Heat shot into Hilda's cheeks.

"You are too tired. A kitchen girl gave birth a few weeks ago. She has helped us feed him after his birth. Although she is below your station, we had no choice if we wanted to keep him alive."

"I know, and I'm grateful. But I'm awake now…and my chest hurts." Until he screamed, she had not noticed the pressure on her breasts, but her son was hungry, so it made sense. She sat up, leaning into the soft cushions and pulled her shift up. "Give him to me."

Amalberga tutted, then placed the infant on her front, skin on skin. Hilda wrapped the blanket over him, then winced in pain when the boy began to suckle. Soon, a feeling of contentment washed over her, despite the discomfort, and she gently stroked his head.

"He's beautiful!" Tears shimmered in her eyes.

Amalberga nodded and sat by the bedside. "That he is. And strong."

"His father's son." Her voice wobbled, and Amalberga put her hand over hers.

"Bellon would be proud."

"Yes, he would be." After watching her son drink greedily, she looked up. "Oh, what am I to do now?"

Her companion fidgeted with her girdle. "The king has left his instructions, and a trusted man to ensure they are being adhered to." Amalberga's voice had turned sharp, and she coughed. "For the moment, you are to remain here in Carcassonne with your son."

"For the moment?" She knitted her brows. "What does he mean? This boy is Bellon's heir to the county. Is he not?"

"Well, Sweeting." Amalberga began to fold up a small pile of dried swaddling cloths.

Hilda straightened, adjusting the suckling baby so she could sit up straight. "Is he not?" she repeated.

"He is but a newborn, and King Charles knows very well how precarious children's lives can be. He said…" Another sigh, and Amalberga put the folded items away.

"What?" Her mind whirled. "That I might lose my son? Like I lost his father and grandfather?" She bit back the tears as fury tore through her.

Just as her life had become settled, secure in this southern stronghold with a man who cared for her, the Gods had deprived her of him. But she would never give up her child!

"He said Carcassonne required a strong ruler, and you, in time," she added in haste, "needed a step-father for your son."

"He will be soon." She took a sharp breath. "By the Goddess, we don't even know for certain if Bellon is dead, and Charles is already busy planning his next alliance? No!" Her fist hit the bedcover. "I shall not agree to it."

Having slaked his thirst, milk was dribbling from her son's mouth, and Amalberga gently took him off her. She placed a smudged cloth over her shoulder and lifted him up, softly patting his back.

Hilda adjusted her shift, then threw the covers aside and put her feet on the cold stone floor. "I have to speak to him."

"You should not get up so quickly, Hilda. Besides, the king departed yesterday for Neustria."

"He has gone?"

Amalberga shuffled her feet, her eyes not meeting hers. "Yes, and...as I said...he has left a man in charge of our defence."

A cold shiver ran down Hilda spine. With the Carcassonne men returned, Dagobert would be perfectly capable of dealing with any issues.

An unbidden memory returned from the moment of Charles' arrival. And of the knight who stood beside him when they handed over their horses to the stable boy.

Clovis.

"Not that rude oaf from Carisiacum, is it?"

Amalberga pulled a face and nodded. "Yes, it is him. And he has made himself right at home in the hall." She snorted in disgust. "He's pushing Roderic around like a hearth boy. We're all appalled."

"Does he? The more reason for me to go downstairs. We need to show him who is in control! I will just get dressed, then I will expel this braggart from my hearth."

A short while later, Hilda – wearing a gown of loosely-woven green wool over a fresh shift, her hair brushed and tied back in a thick braid – left her chamber and, followed by Amalberga and the baby, made her way down the steep steps. Her heart was beating in her ears, and she still felt the after-effects of the last few days. Her body was screaming for rest, but with Bellon's fate unknown and her son's future in danger, she had to be strong.

The cool breeze helped her senses, and she took deep breaths.

Raucous laughter sounded from the hall, and she paused outside the sturdy door for a moment. Something was going on. Slowly, she opened it and peeked inside. Rage tore through her when she saw the merry gathering: men were gathered around tables, playing dice, clearly drunk. Two women she did not recognise drifted from bench to bench, hopping on laps and allowing men to paw them like the harlots they were.

Eventually, she spotted Clovis. Sitting at her table in Bellon's chair, he was deep in conversation with another man she did not know, a draughts board abandoned beside a pitcher.

Ushering Amalberga inside, she pulled the door closed with a bang.

All heads turned to her, and she swallowed hard before crossing the room.

Clovis' eyes did not leave her, and she noticed a smug grin forming. How could Charles think she was safe with this man? She would send a messenger when she had returned to her chamber.

"What is going on here?" The sharpness in her voice earned her a few open sniggers. Looking around, she was certain some warriors had known her father. Yet now she faced nothing but…what? Ridicule? Lust? She focused her gaze on Clovis.

"Ah, the lady has risen. Are you feeling better?" He did not bother to get up from the chair nor offer her a seat. What was he playing at in her own home?

"I wasn't sluggish, if that is what you're referring to. I have given birth."

"So I see." He stared behind her at Amalberga who was cooing the grumbling infant. "This is no place for a child."

"Pardon? What is not?"

"The hall. You can see the boy disturbs the men. I bet he'll start screaming any moment."

"I'll scream any moment if you and this lot," her hands waved around the room in a sweeping gesture, "haven't left by tonight."

Clovis glared at her. "I'm here on the king's behalf, to look after a strategic stronghold of our kingdom. You are merely a woman who lives here – for now."

"What do you mean by 'for now'? Regardless of what befell Bellon, I am still Countess of Carcassonne, and—"

He sneered. "You are nothing but a spoilt daughter of a dead count and widow of another. The king is considering what to do with you, by the way." Clovis rose and slowly walked around the table. He stopped bare inches before her, and his eyes wandered up and down her body, making her feel exposed and vulnerable. Perhaps she should have brought Dagobert along for protection?

She tried to keep her voice calm. "Carcassonne is my home and my son's inheritance."

"You hold lands off your father in the north. Valuable, I hear." He raised an eyebrow. "And the boy won't live out his first year, anyway. They rarely do. Hell, even his father couldn't stay around for long."

At this moment, her son gave a lusty cry which stopped her from slapping Clovis' smug face. The men around them looked away, whether in embarrassment or simply uncaring she could not tell.

Hilda clenched her fists. "I will send a messenger to King Charles. With Dagobert looking after our defence and my son the next count of Carcassonne, we will be able to hold this place for him without your interference."

"There will be an appointment for who is in charge here, ultimately. For the foreseeable time, however, it is under my command…as are you, Nanthild. Come to think of it, you're still occupying *my* chamber." He gripped her wrist. "Although I could consider an…agreement to allow you to stay there…"

Revulsion tore through her, and she tried to back away, but he seized her arms, his fingers boring into her flesh. The room went silent.

"Let me—"

"Oh, how the mighty have fallen." He chuckled then pulled her towards him. "Look where you are now: a lonely widow in need of a strong man."

She beat her fists against his chest, but he held her in an iron grip.

"Clovis, I don't think King Charles would approve…" Amalberga berated him.

"Don't chide me, woman! The king is far away by now, and always open for…strategic alliances." His eyes raked over Hilda's chest. "And this alliance is already in hand." He chuckled at his joke. "A mere administrative delay."

Hilda blinked hard not to lose consciousness. Behind her, she heard Amalberga whispering to her wailing son. The whole moment felt strange, as if Clovis were talking about another woman, not her.

But his hands on her body brought her back. One dirty paw was moving up her neck, then down her front. Keeping her breathing shallow, she did not want to give him the satisfaction of her chest heaving.

"That is better. We will continue this…arrangement… tonight. But don't forget who's in charge now." A calloused thumb flicked the nipple of her left breast, and she pushed back again, but it only spurred him on. Pulling her to lean into him, his mouth crushed hers.

"No!" She bit on his lip, and he slapped her face.

"Witch!"

"You're going to pay for this."

She vaguely heard benches and chairs scraping, and Clovis stiffened. Had these men finally seen enough?

A sword appeared from over her right shoulder, settling at the base of Clovis' throat, and a strong arm encircled her waist, pulling her away.

"I must reiterate to Charles that you are nothing but a self-seeking rogue, Clovis."

"Bellon!" She leaned back and fell into her husband's arm, relieved. Tears stung in her eyes as she stared at his tired face. He gave her a brief, encouraging wink.

All would be well.

Clovis stepped to the side, and his hand reached for his sword, but he found it missing. "So the whelp has returned?" He stepped out of reach of Bellon's blade.

Bellon did not drop his sword but kept it pointed at the despised man. "Yes, and just in time, it appears. Now pack your bags and be gone!"

"Just as the lady has said," Amalberga piped up from behind her, and Hilda turned and took her son off her companion before glaring at the knight again.

"Charles has left me in charge—"

"Charles is not here, to repeat your own words." Bellon took a step towards him. "Carcassonne is mine, as is Nanthild. Now leave!"

Chapter Nineteen

Late April, 2018

"Are you sure it's OK?" Maddie eyed the rickety ladder that led to the attic and tried to spot Léon.

So far, her damned fear of big spiders had stopped her from exploring the top of the house. She didn't even know if there was anything up there. She hadn't accompanied the roofer three days earlier when he replaced the fallen tiles, so when Léon had suggested they have a look together, she reluctantly agreed. Who knew what her mother had kept up there – if anything!

A sense of normality had returned after the discovery of the bones, which she had sent to the laboratory for checks. Likely, she'd donate them to the village to which they, in her view, belonged. Perhaps she would keep the cranium and bury it somewhere. With no more fragments found, Monsieur Marti had finished the kitchen floor which was now covered in beautiful – and even – tiles. She had cleaned and repainted the Welsh dresser, bought a new sink and gas cooker with her mother's bank card, and put the other pieces of furniture back in. Later in the spring, she was planning to paint the table and chairs and the sideboard.

There had been no further occurrences of moving floors or female voices, nor had she noticed the scent of lavender lately. Not since their first kiss…

Room by room, the old house came together, but as her mother's savings dwindled, she paused any further work and focused on her writing. When Léon left her for the winery in the mornings, she poured herself another coffee and sat by the kitchen table with her laptop and a pile of books. Photographs lay spread out across the surfaces. Until she had turned a spare bedroom as an office, this would do. So far, she had added 3,729 words to her book as her inspiration had returned. A positive result.

Léon appeared at the hole to the attic. "Yes, it's perfectly safe. Come up!" He knelt and held out a hand.

She blinked as dust fell into her face, still unsure. "If you say so…"

Carefully, she took the ladder rung by rung until she joined him. The walls were high, and she found she could stand up fully.

Crouching as he moved under the eaves, Léon held a torch aloft and pointed into various corners.

"There is no insulation here, so I'd suggest you get some…eventually. It'll be more energy-efficient and convenient against the heat in the summer and the cold in the winter."

"A good point." Maddie nodded and stared where the light hit. "It looks like she didn't really use this space."

"No. There are a few ancient travelling cases over on that side stacked against the chimney," he pointed at the far end, "but otherwise there's nothing here. I've never seen such an empty, tidy attic." He grinned.

"Nor have I." She laughed, then stared at the three 1950s suitcases stacked on top of each other. "I wonder why she kept them. There's a newer case with wheels on her wardrobe downstairs, so she'd have no need of those."

"Maybe we'll find something in them."

Maddie grinned. "Yeah, old curtains most likely."

"Let's have a look, shall we?" Léon ducked under the broad wooden support beams that criss-crossed the attic and she followed, avoiding the ancient cobwebs. "Hold this!"

She took the offered torch off him and focused the beam on the cases while he knelt in front of them, brushing off dust. Then he picked up the top one. It was the size of a children's case, a muted red in colour after decades in a dark, musty place. A faint flicker of recognition hit her, but she couldn't put her mind to it.

"It seems almost empty." He rattled it, but only a slight whooshing sound emerged.

"It could just be paper. Why would she keep them?"

Léon half-turned towards her. "Perhaps she'd forgotten she had them? Here."

"Good point." Maddie nodded and took it off him. Staring at it, her memories returned.

"This was mine. When I was little, we would sometimes go away for a weekend. And she used the black case in the middle – yes, the one you're pulling off now."

"*Putain*, this is full!" He slid it off the biggest one and tried the metal locks, but they stayed unmoving.

Intrigued, Maddie stepped forward and picked it up. "Jeez, it weighs a ton. It barely rattles, it's so packed. And yes, this was definitely Mum's." She put it down beside hers. "But I don't recognise that large case. It's almost a trunk."

"You've never seen it before?"

"No. Look! The leather is of excellent quality and that pattern is exceptional." She touched the brown surface, her hand following the intricate grooves. "We wouldn't have been able to afford such a beautiful item."

"Perhaps a man's?" Léon pulled it away from the chimney, and Maddie stepped back as a large huntsmen spider scurried off into the darkness.

"Yuck!" She shuddered.

He laughed. "It'll eat your flies and mosquitoes, don't forget!"

"I know," she said sheepishly. "So you think this is a man's case? Why? I can't remember Mum ever inviting men in long enough for them to need a suitcase."

"The style isn't feminine, though you never know. It's lighter than the last one, but it also won't open."

"Hmm. Intriguing."

Léon brushed off the remaining dust with his hand, then stood. "Shall we take them outside to see what Elisa kept in them?"

"A good idea. But how?"

"I'll go down first, then you can pass them to me; push them over the edge. How about that?"

Maddie high-fived him. "Sounds like a plan!"

A few minutes later, cases wiped down with a damp cloth, they stood on the terrace, staring at their treasure.

"Do you have a hairpin?"

"Hmm, no. Would a small screwdriver do? I don't care if the locks break as I don't really need them."

"You might change your mind, so I'll try to open them carefully. You're sure you haven't seen any old small keys anywhere?"

Maddie laughed. "I've not gone through all of Mum's drawers yet, and I don't think I'll manage in the next week or two. Let's just break the locks. I'll get a screwdriver."

But the locks wouldn't budge. "That's quality workmanship, that!"

"I know. What—?"

"*Bonjour*!"

Maddie's head shot up, and she waved to Bernadette who stood leaning over her fence. "*Bonjour, ça va?*"

"*Oh, ça va.*" Her neighbour brushed off her question. "Have you found more interesting stuff? You look as if you explored a cave." She pointed at their dusty clothes.

"Yes, something like that." Léon laughed.

"We were up in the attic."

"Ah, a good idea. Did Elisa have it insulated?"

"No, she didn't. I'll get that sorted."

"You should. It makes such a difference, especially in the heat."

"I'll make sure she does, Bernadette." Léon winked at her and the old lady beamed, then turned her attention to the suitcases.

"What do we have here? Did you find those in the attic?"

"Yes. Have you ever seen Mother using them?"

Bernadette shook her head. "No. Only a modern case with wheels."

"Then they must've been upstairs all those years. You see, we can't open them, and I have no idea where to look for the keys in Mum's hundreds of drawers, but..." She eyed up her neighbour's hair – it was kept in a bun at the back of her head. "You wouldn't have a spare hairpin or two, by chance?"

"*Bien sûr!*" Bernadette loosened her knot and handed over three pins whilst shaking her long grey hair out. "I hope it works."

"*Merci.*" Léon took them and sat in front of the little red case.

Maddie held her breath as he tried to manipulate the old lock. After several minutes that seemed like hours, the metal bar opened.

"Yay!" She peered into it. It was empty except a now crumpled bundle wrapped in musty off-white paper.

"You want to see what it is?" Léon moved aside to let her pull the paper off.

"It's a garment of sorts." She pulled it out and held it up.

"A baptism gown!" Bernadette exclaimed, her hands flying to her cheeks. "It's beautiful."

"I've never seen it before."

"Well, you wouldn't really remember, would you?" Léon prompted.

Puzzled, Maddie stared at the delicate lace gown the train of which flowed twice as long as your usual baby dress. The once white fabric had turned a shade of sepia over time, but the fine stitching, inlaid with pearls forming shapes of little flowers, proved it to have been an expensive item. Not something Elizabeth could have afforded.

"No, you're right. But the weird thing is... I was never baptised. My mother was a Pagan. She didn't believe in the Church, even though she's now buried in a churchyard."

"How strange that she would then have – and keep – such a beautiful item," Bernadette said, her voice hushed in awe. "May I see it? It looks like it could come from Caudry or Calais."

175

Léon stared at it. "The best French lace on the market comes from Caudry."

"Does it?" Maddie handed it to Bernadette who gingerly held it in her hands. Not in a million years could Elizabeth have afforded something like that – especially for an occasion she'd never use it for.

"Oh yes, it is. Look here, this pattern is typical of Caudry. There is no label, but then, not every item had one. Lace made for the big stars, and for nobility, didn't require the same type of label you see in clothes in the normal stores."

"But why would my mother even have such a piece?"

"That, I don't know, I'm afraid. She never mentioned it to me." With a wistful glance at the delicate dress, Bernadette handed it back to her. "But I have a sense it was very special."

Maddie folded the delicate item back into the white paper and put it on top of the otherwise empty red case. Her mother's actions hadn't always made sense, but an expensive baptism gown?

It baffled her. The rattling of metal drew her back to the present time.

"Ha!" The locks of the black suitcase unlatched and Léon pulled up the lid.

"What the—?" Maddie stepped closer. The middle-sized case was full of notebooks, some wrapped in faded rubber bands to stop them from disintegrating.

"Looks like your mother was a writer too." Léon picked up a couple of journals and handed them to her. "You have a look. It's probably personal."

"Oh, how intriguing. I never saw your mother write, dear." Bernadette smiled. "But I could well imagine her doing it."

"Keep a diary, you mean?" Maddie leafed through the first pad. "You're right. This is from 1971." She flicked through the pages. "February… April… August… Well, I never…"

Tears welled in her eyes as she scanned a few paragraphs. "I wonder if Mother wrote something at the time she met my father." A faint flicker of hope formed inside her. Would she finally find out where she belonged?" Léon looked at the first page of a small bundle. "It could be. These range from the 1960s to the late 1970s, from what I can see, and there are more underneath." He gently put them back. "Looks like you have quite a bit of family history to catch up on." He smiled encouragingly. "Now, let's see what's in this baby." He turned to the big brown case with the imprinted pattern.

"Now, that's a posh suitcase," Bernadette remarked.

"Yes, and Maddie doesn't know whose it is."

"Oh la la! I love a good intrigue."

Maddie was still staring at the journals. "I'll have a look through these later to see if I can find the ones for the time I'm looking for."

"That's a great idea. I hope you'll get some answers. Now…" Léon wriggled the hair pins inside the lock until it, too, sprung open. "Voilà!" He opened the heavy lid.

Maddie put the journals she'd been browsing back into the black case and came over. "What's that?"

He dug a little in the fabrics inside, then held up a jumper. "It's full of men's clothes. As in 'old'… No offence, Bernadette!" He winked.

The neighbour laughed. "None taken. But I've never seen a man friend visiting Elisa here."

"Nor do I know of any she was seriously interested in." Maddie searched through the items. Several shirts in 1970s/1980s style lay neatly folded on top of two pairs of jeans and three pairs of trousers. Below those, she found three thick woollen jumpers and, at the bottom, wrapped in plastic, lay two full formal suits with wide shoulder pads.

"God, the plaits on those!" Léon grinned as he half-pulled out a pair of chinos. "I'm so glad fashions have changed. Could these be your father's?"

A dizziness overcame her, and she sat down on the tiles. "Perhaps. The age of the clothes matches. But I don't understand…"

She could not stop her voice from shaking, and Léon crouched beside her, wrapped an arm around her and pulled her close. He softly kissed her temple and wiped away a stray tear. From the corner of her eye, Maddie saw Bernadette disappear to somewhere in her garden, giving them privacy.

"It's a lot to take in, isn't it?" he asked.

Maddie nodded, letting the tears of decades of frustration fall. "Why could she never talk to me about this…stuff?" She sniffed. "Mum always deflected my questions, yet she kept all this in the attic for years. Why?"

He pushed back a strand of hair that had fallen over her face and tucked it behind her ear.

"Perhaps she wanted to, but was too stubborn to take the first step. Or too embarrassed…"

"But I'm her daughter, her only relative."

"I know." He sighed. "Look, do you want to dig out some of these books tonight to see if you can find any hints? If so, I can leave you to it."

Maddie swallowed hard, then smiled. "Yes…if you don't mind."

"Not at all, *chérie*. And I'm always at the end of the phone if you need me."

"Thank you." She kissed him, grateful for having found someone so understanding.

Tonight, Maddie would browse the journals. With a little luck, she'd finally find out where her father had come from – and who he was.

Chapter Twenty

November, AD 782
Carcassonne

The sun stood low over the plain as Hilda, accompanied by Amalberga and a well-armed Lot, returned from a hamlet two hours' ride west of Carcassonne where she had assisted in a complicated birth. Her tincture had brought calm and assurance to a scared girl, a few years younger than she had been at her own wedding. Together, they had helped the girl's mother in delivering a healthy, if quiet, baby. Much to their relief, the little boy had soon voiced his unhappiness at being thrown into a cold, dark world. She smiled at the memory.

The autumn wind, coming in from the sea, whipped at her cloak, and she tucked it back in place. It had been unusually warm, despite the beginning of Advent being only five days away, and she had sweated in her thick woollen kirtle. Sweat covered her shift. But now, the welcome breeze made her take deep breaths.

With Bellon in Iberia, seeking new treaties with the Saracens, she had had more time to spend helping her people. But each day, she was glad to return home, to be with her boys before they had to go to bed. At just four years old, Guisclafred was discovering the world of knights – and wrestling. She indulged him in it, as she knew he needed playtime to rid himself of his excessive energy. The sons of her retainers let him join them, and, despite some setbacks and major tantrums, Guisclafred had already learnt the important lesson of being part of a team to be successful.

But her second pregnancy, too soon after his birth, had left her exhausted, and she had taken certain herbs to pause her from conceiving – without Bellon's knowledge. She swallowed back the guilt that overcame her every so often, and she swore again that she would stop after the holy days had passed.

"Ooh, this is getting silly," Amalberga complained, as the wind lifted her cloak and kirtle high around her.

Lot snorted and averted his gaze towards the nearest tower. Hilda laughed.

"We'll soon be home, where you don't have to concern yourself over showing off your legs to anyone."

"Humph! The youth of today – no respect for your elders."

"Umm, I'll ride ahead and alert them to our arrival." Lot briefly scanned the route for an ambush, but around them, the land lay deserted. They would be safe. Unable to stifle a grin, he waited for her to nod, then kicked his horse into a gallop.

"He doesn't want to be caught up in our banter, Amalberga." Hilda smirked and helped pull her companion's garments back into place.

"Humph!" came the response from the older lady.

She was still sulking. Hilda looked ahead, seeing the gate opening on Lot's shouted demand.

Soon, she would hold her sons again.

Despite Guisclafred's insistence that he was grown-up enough to eat in the hall, Hilda requested him to take his meals in their bedchamber. He had not given up trying, and only Bellon's stern orders kept the boy quiet for several days. But her oldest son had clearly inherited his father's stubbornness.

Remembering fondly the first year of her marriage, where she and Bellon had the room to themselves, she watched as Rotlinde spoon-fed little Oliba whilst his brother pushed the small cuts of meat around his bowl. A partition divided their cots, and the little table and chairs at which they took their meals, from Hilda's own large bed. Bellon had insisted the boys sleep separately straight away, and Hilda had given in, albeit reluctantly. But whenever Bellon was away, which was often, she allowed them to join her in bed in the mornings.

A squeal distracted her from her thoughts, and Oliba burst into tears. She raised her eyebrows at her oldest who had picked up his brother's bowl still half full with warm mashed carrot and parsnip and began to scrape the food out with his fingers. "Guisclafred! Eat your own meal, not your brother's!"

"But I don't like rabbit! Or parsnips."

Rotlinde smiled, then gently but firmly extracted the bowl from his grip. "But there are parsnips in here." She pointed at the orange mash whilst shifting Oliba from her right leg to her left. Immediately, his hand went out towards Guisclafred's food. "That is not for you, Sweeting. You can't have it yet." And she picked up a filled spoon, and Oliba gulped down his mash eagerly.

"Blurgh, parsnips!" Guisclafred exclaimed noisily, wiping his fingers on his hose.

"Stop this right now, my little lord!" Hilda took his hand and cleaned it with a cloth. "You don't steal from your brother. Is that clear?" She put his bowl back in front of him. "Eat!"

"But Mother, I—"

Hilda tilted her head. "You do want to play wrestling with Liuva in the morn, don't you?"

He nodded.

"So you better make sure you're strong enough to beat him. Therefore…" She pointed at the stew.

With a heavy sigh, Guisclafred stabbed a small cut of rabbit and, smacking his lips, he began to chew.

"Quietly."

Eventually, he obliged, and she exchanged a nod with Rotlinde.

"Thank you," the young woman whispered, then focused her attention back to feeding Oliba.

"I'll be in the hall if there are any more such antics."

Wrapped in her cloak, she descended the steps to the hall. Darkness had settled for the night, and the winds had gained in force. She stayed close to the wall and took each step carefully.

A sudden commotion caught her eye. In the noise of the storm, she had not heard the horses' hooves on the ground. Now, a group of riders, some carrying torches, approached the stables. Voices reached her, and laughter.

Just as she arrived at the door to the hall, it opened, and Roderic emerged.

"It's Bellon. He has returned." Hilda recognised her husband's familiar shape, and his stallion. "And he brought a visitor."

"I shall inform the kitchen, lady. My lord will want feeding." His moustache quivered over a hidden smirk, and Hilda grinned.

"Yes, without doubt. Who knows what diet he had to endure in Iberia this time."

"Lady." The *majordomus* descended the stair to the yard, then turned towards the kitchen built at the side of the keep.

"Hilda!" Striding across the yard, Bellon waved at her, then he spoke quietly to a tall, broad man beside him. A Frankish lord, it seemed. He looked familiar, though she could not remember where from.

Bellon took the steps two at a time and embraced her in a fierce hug. She savoured the scent of him, dust and grime. Then he held her at arms' length.

"I have missed you, my love. Has everything been well?" His eyes searched her for any signs of distress.

She smiled and stroked his cheek covered in stubble. "Yes, Bellon. All is in order here. Dagobert and his men have kept us safe, as always."

"And the boys?" A shadow crossed his brow.

"They are fine, although…" A smirk played on her lips.

"Although?" He held his breath.

"Guisclafred has decided he doesn't like rabbit."

Bellon laughed. "Ah, all normal, then." He wrapped an arm around her, then turned towards their visitor who had slowly climbed the steps. "Hilda, do you remember Count Guillaume of Autun?"

Recognition dawned and Hilda took the knight's hands in hers. "Of course. Welcome to Carcassonne, my lord. If we had known of your arrival, we may have been better prepared."

"I thank you, lady. I'm certain that whatever your hearth has to offer, it will be sufficient for me."

Retracting her hands, she gestured to the door to the hall. "Then please come within."

***

Bellon lifted his cup and raised it to his visitor. "Carcassonne welcomes you, Guillaume. It was fortunate that our paths crossed outside Narbonne." Turning to Hilda sitting between them, he explained, "The king wants him to join us in our forays into Iberia, to gain a better picture of the situation there."

"Which is, as always, delicate…" Guillaume added.

Bellon grinned, then took a draught. "It is indeed."

Hilda nodded, but the look in her eyes told him she could not go against her nature. "There are too many ladles stirring the pot for it to be calm."

Their guest raised an eyebrow.

Bellon's grin widened. Her forthright manners – manners that had developed deeper since the birth of their sons – often took Frankish visitors by surprise.

"My wife is an astute judge of politics, Guillaume. She follows all reports of events in the kingdom of the Franks, and in Aquitania and Iberia."

Guillaume's face turned puce, and he nearly choked on his wine. Hilda gently patted his back until he wiped his mouth on his sleeve.

"Does this help, lord?" Her voice sweet, she looked at him with concern. "Our wine may be too strong to those unused to it. It's unlike like that watered-down Rhenish fare we always had in the north."

Bellon laughed, proud of his wife's knowledge, then sobered. "I do apologise. As you can see, we're far away from the Frankish court."

Guillaume nodded and took a deep breath. Then he smiled. "Yes, so we are. And thank you, Lady Nanthild. I'm much better thanks to your…um…intervention." He sent her an admiring glance. "Your lord father would be proud of you."

A shadow fell on Hilda's face, and Bellon grew serious. It had been over four years since the battle at Roncevaux, and he knew she still missed her father very much. It also tore his heart that Milo had never met his grandsons. He would have been so proud. But thus was life in times of war, and Milo had seen – and survived – many of Charles' campaigns.

After the meal, with the tables moved away from the hearth, they settled into more comfortable chairs by the side of the fire. Whilst the days were still warm, the nights had grown cold, with a threat of frost hanging in the air. On his return journey, he had seen the first snow cover the highest peaks of the Pyrenaei.

Stretching his legs towards the warmth, Bellon, content at last, cradled a cup of wine in his hands. Guillaume was leaning back into the cushions, his gaze on the flames. Rotlinde and Amalberga had briefly brought the children to the hall, to bid them goodnight. Both boys had run towards him, Guisclafred faster than his small brother who was still uncertain on his feet but firmly supported by their nurse. Much to their joy, he had raised each squealing boy in the air and hugged them close before sending them to their mother. Hilda had gently kissed them, then Rotlinde picked up Oliba and Amalberga took Guisclafred by the hand, returning them to the bedchamber. Oliba let out a loud wail when a retainer opened the door to the yard.

Bellon smiled. Both boys had grown so much since he had left for Iberia, and they were quickly developing into intriguing little characters. His eyes met Hilda's, and he knew she thought the same.

At his signal, Lot, who was hovering by a trestle table in a corner, came forward and refilled their cups, before he withdrew again.

"You can be proud of your sons," Guillaume said. "They are well-cared for."

Hilda nodded. "Yes, but like all children, they keep pushing their boundaries..."

"That's lads for you."

"You know much about raising children. Do you have any?"

"Yes, I have two sons; possibly three by the time I return."

Guillaume winked, and Bellon burst out laughing.

"Then we have to make sure that our forays won't take too long."

"I drink to that!" Guillaume took a deep draught.

"I assume your lady wife has help with the children?" Hilda asked, her head cocked to the side. She was clearly appraising their visitor, and Bellon could not read her mind.

"Oh yes. We have a large household compared to some, perhaps a few more people than you have here. Cunégonda has several women helping her, so she has plenty of time to worry about my well-being." He laughed out loud, the warmth in his eyes revealing his respect and admiration for his wife. "Some would argue, too much!"

Bellon smiled. "Your home is in safe hands with her."

"Oh yes, it is. But when she hears tidings like the recent news from Saxony, she becomes overly concerned."

"Not without cause," Bellon said grimly.

Guillaume had told him about the king's actions against the Saxon rebels, but on seeing Hilda curious glance, Bellon wished his visitor had not mentioned it.

"What happened in Saxony?" she asked promptly.

At certain times, he preferred it if his wife was not interested in what went on outside their county. He sighed, then exchanged a glance with Guillaume.

"King Charles has finally quashed the resistance of those blasted Saxons," Guillaume said.

Hilda nodded. "I remember Father joined several expeditions into Saxony. It wasn't too far a journey to make from our home. The king wanted them to convert to Christianity."

"That's correct," Guillaume confirmed. "And now, many have done so. But not without the rebels making sacrifices."

Bellon drew in a sharp breath. "They made the ultimate sacrifice."

"And they will burn in hell for all eternity." Guillaume's mouth contorted into a tight line, and he crossed himself. "They could have simply—"

"The king could have shown mercy."

"Not to those treacherous heathens," Guillaume snapped. "You don't know what those Saxons are like: wild, unchristian, uncontrollable. They killed many of our nobles during their pointless rebellions."

"Father agreed that they were wild, yes, but also loyal to their leaders. Isn't loyalty a trait that is usually rewarded?"

"That particular loyalty cost them their lives, whilst their coward of a leader, Widukind, fled to Nordmannia."

"Then he wasn't worthy of their allegiance. But what happened to them?" Hilda looked from Bellon to Guillaume and back to him.

"They were all executed," Bellon said quietly, maintaining their eye contact.

Hilda flinched, then she regained control quickly, sending their guest an inquisitive glance. "That does not surprise me, although the king could have found other means of punishment."

"They were pagans," Guillaume spat. "We have to teach them the way of Christ. And now, finally, Christianity can spread across Saxony." A look of contentment on his face, he took a sip.

"Amen," Hilda whispered, her voice hoarse.

Guillaume nodded approvingly, clearly unaware of her underlying cynicism which Bellon recognised only too well.

He watched his wife closely. Hilda had gone pale at Guillaume's clear hatred of pagans. For a long time, Bellon had suspected her of using ancient practices, her demeanour often aligned with that of other pagan Visigoths he knew. If so, it was imperative that they kept the situation secret. It was too dangerous to reveal even the slightest bit of sympathy.

"But what a price to pay," she said. "How many were… executed?"

Bellon groaned inwardly. He wanted to change the subject, but his mind had gone empty. Regretting bringing this visitor to his home hearth, he shrugged his shoulders.

Guillaume straightened his back, his eyes full of religious fervour. "We beheaded everyone who rebelled against Charles at the battle of Süntel – over four thousand men!"

Late that night, Bellon and Hilda sat in silence. Lot had just refilled their cups for a last time and left them alone in the hall. The fire had burned down, and only a warm orange glow illuminated the room. Holding her hand, he was bereft of words. But if he had ever needed proof of his wife's real leanings, it had been delivered to him in the bluntest way possible. It was only fortunate that Guillaume had not recognised it, or she would face serious questioning.

Her attendance at Church was like anyone else's. She prayed and seemed a devoted follower. Lot had told him about her forays into the hamlets, tending to the injured and sick with the help of her herbs. It was something he was proud of – his wife, the healer. Another sign of where her calling lay. But although he had kept his knowledge to himself, he would not push her to reveal her true faith, but wanted her to tell him of her own will. If not tonight, then he hoped one day she would trust him enough to reveal her secret.

"Thank you," she whispered.

Surprised, he looked at her. "Why? What did I do?"

She squeezed his hand and smiled. "You shielded me. It… was a shock. I always knew warfare involved deaths, but apart from Father's, it never touched me. Of course, I worry and pray for your safety whenever you're away, but… but…" Her words trailed off, and she shuddered.

He waited quietly, stroking her palm, until she had recovered her composure.

"How can someone be so kind, yet so cruel at the same time?"

"You mean Charles?"

Hilda nodded. "Yes. I always admired him, even though I heard tales of retribution and punishment. I guess Father kept the worst tidings from me."

"And rightly so." Bellon agreed with Milo's assessment.

Her eyes blazing, she stared at him. "But I would have wanted to know. How can I cling on to my respect for Charles if he kills thousands of men at one strike? And all because of religion!"

"Don't forget that many of us now follow Christianity."

Her gaze moved to the fire, and he quickly added, "But I agree with you. I was shocked, too, when Guillaume first told me."

"It makes you wonder…"

He signed. "It does. And whilst I won't rescind my allegiance to Charles," he whispered, "which would have disastrous consequences for Septimania, I'm making sure we don't persecute Visigoths of different beliefs, at least not under my rule."

She let out a long breath, then kissed his hand, sending him a long look. "Thank you."

This was as close to an admission as he would get. It was enough.

Chapter Twenty-One

Early May, 2018

After over a week of Léon staying every night, the house seemed empty after he left. Too quiet.

Maddie wondered if she'd gone in too fast, but the tingling sensations she felt every time she saw him made her banish her doubts. As her colleagues in York would have said – he was a keeper.

Hell, she couldn't even remember how long it had been since she last spoke to Brian. That in itself was revealing. Oh well...

Sitting on the edge of the sofa, she stared into the open case at her feet. Piles of notebooks waiting to be explored. But was she not prying into Elizabeth's deepest secrets?

"Nonsense," she said out loud. "She's dead."

Maddie waited for the echo, for the scent of lavender, but all stayed as normal. Had the...ghost...moved on with her bones after all?

Shrugging off her suspicions, she took out some journals and checked the dates in the front of each. Often, they contained gaps of several months, but her mother had always continued, eventually. Then, she found the relevant years. She put them on the sofa beside her. Delving deeper into the pile, she pulled out a book from the bottom and flicked through the pages.

July 1992... September 1992... December 1992...

These where from when they lived in Normandy. Maddie smiled as her memories returned. Monsieur, the big grey semi-feral cat they had taken in. Bruno, the starving, neglected *Fauve de Bretagne* hunting dog Elizabeth had saved – or rather, abducted – from a local *chasseur* who had sent the gendarmes after her. Only her mother's charms and her threat of contacting the Brigitte Bardot Foundation about the injuries poor Bruno had received at the hands of his owner had convinced them that the dog was better off with her. Yes, Maddie remembered that year well. She had been so proud of her.

There would be plenty of time to catch up on her childhood memories. For now, she wanted to focus on the years from 1982 to 1984 when she was born. She put the journal from 1992 back into the case.

After she'd closed all the shutters and locked the front door, she filled a large glass of red wine from a box, grabbed a packet of waffles and picked up the books she'd left on the sofa.

Upstairs, she plumped up the spare pillow and changed into a t-shirt and leggings. Though the nights were getting warmer, she dove under the duvet. Temperatures could still plummet.

Finally, she was ready. Or was she?

Her hand shook when she took the first notebook. 1982. She remembered her mother telling her about the time she back-packed through France. That must have been it.

Swallowing hard, Maddie opened the journal and began to read...

Two hours later, and she had a better idea of Elizabeth's adventures during her early years in France. Her mother had helped on farms in the Ardennes, then headed west towards Nantes and south to La Rochelle from where she had joined a sailing crew going to Bordeaux.

Elizabeth had gone sailing? "Why, I never..."

Maddie took a large sip of the wine and pulled a waffle from the pack. Her youthful mother's feisty nature and courage intrigued her.

Mother sailed down the coast of France on a boat. Not free, mind you, but working on it.

Tears welled up as she thought of her mother later in life, just content to be at home. What a free spirit Elizabeth had been before she was born!

She skipped several references to men 'courting her', as her mother had put it in her flowery handwriting, but none of the relationships seemed serious. 1982 had been a year full of journeys, of meeting people and enjoying life. But not one reference to a special man.

With shaking hands, Maddie opened the notebook entitled 1983. It had to contain some details about her father. Fortifying herself with yet another long draught of wine, she began to read…

2nd February, 1983

Still in Cauterets, helping Micheline with the *chambre d'hôte*. In the end, things worked out OK, despite Gaston's absence, so I was happy to stay on. Nevertheless, I feel sad about causing their split, but I just couldn't keep knowledge of his disgusting behaviour to myself. The man's a cheat!
Micheline has become such a good friend, so when I walked in on the bastard in bed with that American woman, Grace, I had to tell her. At first, it was a little awkward, but now she puts on a brave face. We're running a busy B&B!

24th February, 1983

This season is mad! Skiers, hikers, spa visitors, they all descended on our little place. It has been non-stop, and Micheline and I have had barely time to breathe. But that's great news as it means more income for her. Gaston has come over to convince her to give him another chance, but she sent him away. Brave girl, that!

12th March, 1983

We've been working our little socks off, but boy, is the place heaving. Being a small B&B, we were lucky that not every type of guest wants to stay in the big hotels. Some prefer the more cosy comforts we are providing. Neat, clean and warm.

Oh, I almost forgot. A lovely group from Burgundy stayed for nearly a week. There was one guy who kept watching me. Not in a creepy way, but friendly. We started chatting in the evenings, after I'd finished my work. In the daytime, they went skiing, but after two nights he left his mates to themselves and invited me out for a drink, and that's what we did every night until they left.

His name was Jérôme de…something. I can't remember his surname. Very French, though. I enjoyed his attention, but I was too tired to agree to anything more than a few drinks and long conversations well into the night. I got far less sleep than usual. But then, today, they had to leave unexpectedly, and in the hurry we forgot to exchange details. Stupid, I know. They drove off before I could give him a note.

Though perhaps Jérôme was just happy to chat to a chambre d'hôte cleaner on his holidays, but didn't really want more…

Maddie gulped. Was this Jérôme possibly her dad? But the dates didn't match, and he couldn't have been. Besides, nothing happened, according to her mother. But it sounded like Elizabeth had truly fallen for him.

Her throat parched, she picked up her wine glass and read on.

13th March, 1983
What a bloody mess! This afternoon, Gaston came back with Micheline's father. Why on earth did the old man stick to the liar's side and not stand up for his daughter? She was the wronged party here.

So Micheline told me I had to pack my bags and leave. Her eyes were puffy and red. When I asked her if she'd taken him back, she nodded.

'It's for the best,' she said. I wonder for whose best!

So I packed my belongings, collected my pay and said my farewells to Micheline and a smirking Gaston. Oh, I wanted to punch him, and the Goddess was egging me on, but I behaved like an adult. I was lucky to find a bed in the youth hostel dormitory for the night. But where to go next? The season isn't over yet, but nobody will employ anyone at the end of the season. They'll be winding down instead. Oh, decisions…

28th March, 1983
Lourdes
Oh God! Yes, you! Did you ever expect this selling-out of your teachings? I'm so glad to be out of here after just two days. There's no way I can stand this any longer. Goddess, please help me calm down!

3rd April, 1983
Toulouse
What a difference a week makes! I just LOVE Toulouse. A little like Bordeaux, but also very different. As Micheline had given me a written reference, I found a job in a small hotel near the Garonne river. I'm dealing with enquiries over the phone and take bookings. Quite a change, but as I did all that at Micheline's as well as cleaning, Cheryl gave me a chance. It helps that I'm fluent in French, and she can talk to me in English. Her French isn't that great, so I might end up teaching her a little.
Onwards to new adventures.

Maddie smiled. Elizabeth sounded excited after her shock dismissal, rather than down. Her mother always believed in opportunities arising when you needed them, and it would appear that that was exactly what happened.

But still no mention of her father. She skim-read the next few pages, all about Elizabeth's new life in Toulouse. Springtime there sounded lovely.

She was just about to give up and go to sleep when her eyes spotted a name: Jérôme!

Could this be…?

29th July, 1983

You wouldn't believe it! Today, a visitor arrived looking for a room without a reservation. When he walked through the door, my heart nearly stopped. Luckily, the small reception area was otherwise empty, or other guests may have just witnessed two people staring at each other for yonks before bursting into mad laughter. Then, he reserved a room for the night.

Yes, Jérôme is in Toulouse! My hands are shaking, and I have little time to write. My shift over for today, and I'll need to get ready to meet him. He's taking me out for dinner. Oh, the Goddess must be smiling on me.

Chapter Twenty-Two

September, AD 793
Carcassonne

"Open the gate!" Bellon waved wildly at the sentries above the entrance to the fortress from half a mile away, but he need not have worried. Already, the guards he had left behind opened the heavy gates.

Beside him, Guillaume of Autun, who had replaced the duplicitous Torson as duke of Tolosa under the king's order, urged his stallion forward. "I hope your defences are solid, Bellon," he cried, his voice hoarse, "in case the infidels launch an assault."

"Carcassonne will hold out against any attack."

Guillaume's doubtful expression irked him. After all, it was under the new duke's command that had seen them lose this battle against the Saracens in the hills just to the north of Carcassonne, too close to home for his liking.

His mind was whirling. What had gone wrong? Their small army knew the area well. At least, his own men did. But Guillaume had ignored some of his suggestions about the lay of the land and an advantage they would have held had they crossed to the north of the stream and awaited the enemy there.

The high opinion Guillaume has of himself doesn't help.

Approaching his home, he gritted his teeth. Today, he had lost several men – good warriors he could scarcely spare, especially now that the Saracens had returned with frequent attacks. So far, they had steered clear of Carcassonne, likely due to her ancient defensive walls. But after defeating the Frankish army, would they dare an attempt?

Time would tell.

He rode through the narrow gate into the yard. Already, a couple of stable lads awaited their arrival, and he dismounted and threw the reins of his stallion to one, nodding his thanks. Around him, his own warriors and Guillaume and his men from Tolosa came through in small groups. Leaving the duke, Bellon took the wooden steps to the allure, the upper stone walkway inside the solid walls, and joined Dagobert who had stayed above the gate. He looked through the merlins and saw the last of their party ride through, then his captain gave the signal to drop the grate and close the heavy doors.

Dagobert raised his eyebrow. "What happened?"

Bellon leaned against the wall, slowly regaining his breath. "There was a battle. The Saracens caught up with us."

"The Saracens? This far inland?" Dagobert glanced across the deserted plain. "I heard they stayed near the coast and in the mountains?"

"Yes, they ventured farther than we'd thought. We fought a battle up there," he pointed towards the northern hills, "where the Orbiel river flows."

Dagobert shook his head. "That makes little sense. It's far from the route to Tolosa, and there is no major settlement in that area."

"You're right. That's what I've been wondering ever since we left. We lost fourteen men today." He clenched his fists and closed his eyes briefly, taking a deep breath.

"Christ's blood!" The captain crossed himself, a shadow forming on his brow.

"I know. Keep a good watch! The curs might feel brave enough to attack us here."

"I shall. I'll call up any men fit to join us on the wall, so we appear well-defended," Dagobert said, his voice heavy but full of purpose. "We could still fend off an army, even with a small amount of men."

Bellon nodded. "I know. And get Duke Guillaume's men, too. He owes me that much!" He clenched and released his fists.

"Duke? Count Guillaume of Autun? I thought I recognised him. He's rising fast in the king's favour."

Bellon gave a harsh laugh. "He is. Though his stubborn ignorance of our region cost us dearly today. Not that he'll lose his new title for that…"

Together, they turned to watch the mayhem in the yard. Guillaume, clearly in a foul mood, was barking orders, then marched in the direction of the hall.

Bellon straightened. "And now we must host him, too. Pah! Never mind, I have to fetch Hilda to care for the injured, and then give the families of our lost brothers the sad tidings." It was not a prospect he cherished, but he was honour-bound to take care of them.

"If there is anything I can do…"

He slapped the captain's shoulder. "Thank you, Dagobert, there is. Send out a sentry to discover where those curs are heading to. Then we'll know more about their plans."

"I shall."

Bellon descended the stairs and walked across to the hall into which Guillaume had just disappeared. He did not want the man to talk to Hilda before he did. But to his relief, his wife emerged from their chamber above, alone. Weaving through the throng of horses and men, he waved.

When he reached the bottom of the steps, she spotted him, her expression one of surprise and concern. They met outside the door to the hall, and she took him in a firm embrace.

"Bellon, what is going on?"

For an instant, he forgot the loss, the chaos, and relished the scent and calm of his wife. Then he took a step back.

"Are you hurt?" Hilda looked him up and down, but found nothing worse than a few scrapes on his arms and rips in his tunic and hose.

He smiled. "I'm fine. Only some minor scratches." Turning towards the yard, he added, "But some men have more severe injuries."

Her critical eye assessed the situation swiftly, and within moments, she had recognised those in need of help. "I'll see to them. But what happened?"

"There was a battle, just north, on the banks of the Orbiel."

197

"The Orbiel? Why on earth would there be a battle? There is nothing to gain." Facing the crowds, she called out, "Everyone who is hurt, come into the hall now. I will see to your wounds."

Proud of his wife, he waved over a few of Guillaume's men who were hesitating. Some of their own also urged them forward.

Hilda held the door open. "Bellon, could you fetch Amalberga, please? I ordered the boys to stay up there on penalty of being grounded, but they'll be right glad to see you."

He grinned as the last of the injured warriors filed past. "And I've been wondering why the scoundrels haven't come out yet."

"Well, I didn't know what had happened. I don't want them to mingle with strangers."

"Wise as always. And then I must inform the families of our killed men of their loss…" He kissed her cheek, then took the stairs to their private quarter two at a time, silently thanking God for his family.

***

Late that evening, Hilda sat by the fire, a cup of red wine in hand and her thoughts wandering. She had tended to the injured warriors for several hours before they had eaten a hurried meal of meats and vegetables. Bellon had given orders that nobody was permitted to leave, not even to hunt. With the Saracens prowling the vicinity, the danger was too great.

It hurt her that she had lost two men whose injuries were too severe, and she could not save them. Before her eyes, they had bled to death. Silently, she had intoned the God and Goddess to welcome them. Outwardly, she had joined Bellon and Guillaume in prayers.

With the casualties settled for the night in another tower, Amalberga had gone to bed, exhausted. Hilda could not blame her. At over three score years, her companion needed more rest than before. And with her sons growing fast into young men, they had no need of an elderly maid. Now being educated to read and write by Peter, the priest at the fortress, it would soon be time for Guisclafred to join his father. She shuddered.

At least her daughter, Alda – named after Hilda's mother – would stay with her for longer. Safe in Rotlinde's capable hands, her now eight-year-old daughter knew already how to wrap the knights of Carcassonne around her little finger.

She's one to watch!

Smiling, it comforted Hilda that none of her children had to face any battles yet. But the day was approaching fast. Bellon wanted to take Guisclafred with him, but the lad's recent injury to his leg incurred in training – barely more than a scrape, truth be told – had seen her win the argument. Thinking of all the men they had lost this day, a shiver ran down her spine.

It could have been my son.

"We must attack them before they arrive outside your gate." Guillaume's raised voice reached through her musings.

She briefly closed her eyes. The duke had been in a bellicose mood ever since their arrival, and she feared that Bellon would soon lose his temper. It took much to rile him up, but the pompous fool who Charles had put in charge of the duchy of Tolosa was getting close.

She looked up. "Perhaps that is what they're expecting of you? To rush out to meet them, leaving Carcassonne open to attack?"

Guillaume glared at her. "That's all you care about, eh?! Your little fortress here, in the middle of nowhere."

Bellon sent him a sharp glance, and she laid a hand on his arm.

"Our *little fortress*, as you call it, is a vital stronghold halfway between Narbonne and Tolosa – which is now yours to defend, is it not? So if," she held up a hand to stop him from interrupting her. "So if Carcassonne fell, what would be their next target, do you think?" She returned his stare defiantly.

"You're talking nonsense, woman. Know your place!"

"Hilda place is at my side, Guillaume." Bellon's voice was suspiciously calm, and she pressed his arm lightly. "Besides, her skills helped many of your men tonight."

The duke grunted. Did he always insist on being right?

"A woman's focus is on her home. She should leave the politics to us."

"My perception of your political games is as astute as any man's. Don't forget that my father taught me."

"A big mistake."

"I do not wish to seem unwelcoming, but it's time for my wife and me to retire. We have a long day ahead, and there may be trouble during the night. I trust you will find your way to your lodgings?"

Bellon stood and took her hand.

At that point, the door opened and Dagobert entered, deep lines etched into his face. "Lord?"

Guillaume had risen, too. "Are we under attack?"

"No, lord duke." Dagobert shook his head, then turned to Bellon. "But our scout has returned."

"Did he see where the Saracens are going?" He gripped Hilda's hand tighter, and she sensed his inner tension. Even though he did not wish to show his concerns in front of their visitor, she could read him easily.

To their surprise, Dagobert grinned. "He did indeed. They have taken the road to Narbonne."

"Narbonne?" Guillaume's voice was full of doubt. "Why would they go back whence they came?"

Bellon nodded. "Simply to see what's here. They've beaten us, and now they are spreading word of our defeat. That will worry the people of Narbonne."

"Then we must go to their aid."

Hilda stepped forward. "I would not do anything in a rush."

"I'm inclined to agree. Could the curs have spotted our scout?"

Dagobert shook his head. "No. Alric was certain they had not seen him."

"So we stay tonight, and in the morn we shall ride to Narbonne."

The duke agreed. "It sounds sensible. But you are keeping watch?"

Dagobert bristled, and Hilda bit her tongue. "Of course, lord duke. We always do."

"Thank you," Bellon said. "I will join you later."

The captain nodded and left.

"Tell your men to prepare for an early departure, Guillaume, and then get some sleep. We'll leave at sunrise."

Hilda climbed the stairs to their room, with Bellon following closely. She quietly opened the sturdy door and slid in, not wishing to wake the children. Bellon took off his boots by the door, then tiptoed behind the screen where Guisclafred and Oliba slept soundly.

She smiled when she looked at their bed where Alda lay stretched across the covers. Gently pulling the blankets from beneath her daughter, Hilda shifted her towards the edge, tucked her in, then sat on the other side. A moment later, Bellon joined her.

She stroked his face, looking worn and tired after a long day, and he wrapped her into a tight embrace.

"You will be keeping watch tonight?"

Extracting himself, he nodded. "Yes, but only later. I will rest awhile with you and this one..." He pointed at Alda, grinning. "She takes liberties already, stealing our bed!"

Hilda suppressed a giggle. "I know. Let me help you get out of these sodden clothes."

The fact that he let her help remove his tunic and hose without a dry retort worried her. Bellon was more exhausted than she had thought. But then, battles were no games...

She took a small cloth from a shelf and dipped it into a bowl of water by the narrow window. Then she quietly washed him down. After she had rinsed his back, he lay down and let her wipe the water off his arms and torso.

Then she quickly undressed, and they slid under the cover, moving slowly as not to wake Alda. He pulled her close, and she wrapped her arms around him. Nestling her head onto his shoulder, she whispered, "Why are you going with Guillaume to Narbonne?"

"I have to."

She sighed. "But it could lead you into a trap."

"Yes, it could." His voice sounded resigned. "But we have to know where our enemies are."

"Of course, you do. We shall be safe here. Dagobert is a capable captain."

"He is. I trust him with my life – and my family." He turned his face to her and stroked her cheek with his thumb. "But you have to promise me something."

She furrowed her brows. "Me? What?"

"That you do not venture outside the fortress until we are certain that all Saracens have truly left the area."

Hilda swallowed. "But hasn't Dagobert said they did?" Confinement to her home was not what she had envisaged. If there was an emergency in one of the villages…

"Yes, but it could be a ruse. Promise me. No visits outside these walls for now. I want to know you're safe."

"But I am—"

"At home. I shall have your word!" He sat up.

Resigned, she sighed, avoiding his imploring gaze. "Yes, Bellon. I promise."

But in her heart, she knew she would always follow a call for help.

Chapter Twenty-Three

Early May, 2018

So Jérôme had returned, and he clearly meant a lot to Elizabeth. Maddie set the wine glass down and took a deep breath. Her hands were shaking, and she blinked away the tears before reading on.

Over the following two weeks, Elizabeth and Jérôme met every day. He'd wisely moved into another hotel, so she wouldn't risk losing her job as things started to become more…serious.

"So that's it! He must be my father," Maddie whispered, her heart pounding in her ears, as she turned the page. A feeling of elation surged through her. "But why had Mum never mentioned him?"

To her surprise – or perhaps not, given how much time they spent together – the gaps between entries grew wider. But still Elizabeth's love story continued. Until…

14th August, 1983

Oh, it's tough. Business is heaving, with August being THE month for family holidays in France. Fortunately, the heat of July has passed a little, but we've been rushed off our feet all day.

Just as well that Jérôme had to return home after an amazing fortnight here. We speak on the phone every evening, but it's not the same. I miss him terribly, but he has to work, too. His family own a large vineyard in Burgundy, and they soon start their *vendanges* – harvesting the grapes ready for turning them into wine. He might be able to sneak off for a couple of days here and there, but it's such a long journey by train he wouldn't have long to stay.

Oh, the phone rings!

2nd September, 1983

I've taken three days off to meet Jérôme in Nîmes, roughly halfway. He kindly paid for my train journey, even though I can afford it, but he wouldn't hear of it.

What an incredible place this is! So full of history. Our time will just fly by.

4th September, 1983

As much as I adore Nîmes, the fact that they have bull-fights here disgusts me. Jérôme too. He told me he wanted to become a vet, looking after animals, but his family decided he should join the business, even though he's their second son. His parents are retired now, but they sound very old-fashioned, not brokering any opposition, and his brother is the head of the vineyard. Apparently, the family is French nobility.

So now, instead of healing pets, he's supporting local animal charities. Can I just love him a little more for that?

As nice as Nîmes is, we agreed next time we'd meet somewhere else. Now I'm on the train back to Toulouse, and I'm missing him already.

Maddie yawned and looked at her watch. Five after midnight. Part of her felt like an intruder, reading about her mother's romance, but if Elizabeth hadn't wanted her to see these journals, she'd have destroyed them before she fell ill.

"Time for a coffee." She slid out of bed and, taking the empty wine glass with her, went downstairs to the kitchen. The new ceiling light shone a touch too brightly for her tired eyes, but as she looked around, she was pleased with the changes. Maddie put the wine glass into the sink and switched the kettle on. Then she filled her cafetière with ground coffee and waited.

For some inexplicable reason, she missed the bones below the old tiles. And whilst the new surface was beautiful and modern, something was different. The scent of lavender hadn't returned in recent weeks, and she felt like she had lost a friend. Had she set the poor woman free by excavating what was left of her? The thought of the cracked ribs and spine made her shudder. Tomorrow, she would enquire when the lab would send the bones back.

"I'm going to keep the cranium," she said, more to the dead woman than herself. "I hope you can hear me." Looking around, the room stayed silent apart from the water boiling in the kettle. No lavender, no moving ground. Nothing. "I'll bring you home and give you a lovely funeral."

Five minutes later, she was back in her bed with a fresh mug of coffee. Was Princess Leia admonishing her for waking her in the middle of the night? She grinned at the space heroine's pointed look. "Cheers!" And she took a few sips before picking up the next journal.

15th October, 1983
Toulouse
I'm bored. The visitors have gone, and the city is quieter again. Still a lovely place to be, but I'll need to think of where to go for the winter. I might head to the Alps, to seek some work in the chalets. They're always looking for English-speakers – or cleaners. I'll then also be much closer to Jérôme who I haven't seen in three weeks, and then only for two short nights. He asked me to move to Beaune, to be closer to him. We could even live together. But as his family were so abrasive when he suggested they'd meet me, I'm not sure. Clearly, they think I'm a gold digger. Plus, Beaune is a small place. How would I earn money? I don't share Jérôme's optimism that 'something comes up'. Hmm.

2nd December, 1983
Chamonix
I've arrived in the French Alps, and what a beautiful sight the mountains are! Such dramatic scenery. This morning, sleet greeted me, beating against my window shutters. How exciting! And after living in a city for months, it feels wonderful to breathe in the fresh air.

I have a job at a local hotel reception. We work shifts, which I'm used to, but I won't need to do any cleaning. That suits me fine, as I'll be happy dealing with people. And I only work four days out of seven. I can then set aside time to meet Jérôme. He finally accepted that I didn't want to be near his home – yet. His mother threw a tantrum when he told her of his plans to rent a small house he'd spotted in Beaune. It appears she has her own ideas and keeps introducing him to eligible young ladies. I have to laugh. He looked so fed up when he told me about this last week and said he would find a way. But for now, he's going to visit me in a fortnight. We'll go hiking on my time off. I can't wait!

18th December, 1983

I'm exhausted! Two full days of trekking in the mountains have proved to me that I'm definitely not the fittest. Jérôme is! And whilst he has no problem covering sharp inclines, I'm gasping for breath after a few hundred yards. We laughed so much! But it's hard to describe the beauty of the scenery here, the sharp, snow-capped peaks in the distance, and the serene calm. I'm shattered and would love nothing but lie in bed, but we're going to try a Swiss meal tonight: *raclette*! I've seen it served, but never had it. So cheesy, I won't be able to move afterwards. But we deserve it!

Maddie smiled. She remembered having *raclette* in the winter in Normandy. The perfect hearty meal for cold, damp nights. They had been inventive with the accompaniments to the melted cheese: apart from crusty bread they had cauliflower, potatoes, salami and cut-up sausages, even Brussels sprouts! It was always a fun meal that lasted for hours. Perhaps she could look for a raclette set and enjoy it with Léon…

She skipped through the next few pages with Elizabeth's tales of working in a bustling ski resort. They met regularly, but still his parents' refusal to meet her hung like a cloud over their relationship.

Then her eyes caught a word: 'accident'. What had happened? The handwriting looked unsteady. Had her mother had been in shock.

14th March, 1984

Just a quick note before I get up. I can't wait to see Jérôme later. He's arriving in two hours, and we're going to have three wonderful days exploring again. But I also have news, and I'm sure he'll be thrilled. I'm going to share them over dinner tonight, to make it special…

News? Maddie wondered and counted back the months from her birthday in early October. Could it be? She read on quickly.

15th March, 1984

If only I'd have gone with him! Dear Goddess, why? I can barely hold my pen, but write about yesterday's events I must. I just don't know what to do, or where to go from here. Jeanne has been very supportive and drafted in another colleague from her break. She has sent me home to my small flat and made sure I had tea and cookies. She'd also made an appointment for me for tomorrow with her doctor.

Yesterday, Jérôme and I had planned to head for the hills again. But because a colleague was sick, I had to go into work after all, so Jérôme left for a hike on his own. We know the slopes up in the mountains are slippery with melting snow and recent rain, and he never veered off the path. He should have been safe!

So…how can it be that my Jérôme fell down a ravine which is several yards away from the track? He wouldn't have risked coming down that way; he's far too experienced. I don't understand it. It makes little sense.

Now my wonderful boyfriend, the kindest man I've ever known, lies cold in the mortuary with a broken neck. The mountain rescue said he must have died immediately. Died!

I can't believe he's gone.

Maddie blinked back the tears and put the journal down beside her. There was the answer to her question: her father was dead. Deeply sad about the fact that she would never meet him, she let the tears flow. Tears she'd held back for decades; for the chances that never were. Eventually, she wiped her face with the back of her hand, then took a few sips of coffee to steady herself.

After a deep breath, she picked up the journal again.

16th March, 1984
What have I done? Why are things that started off so beautifully now going wrong?

Jérôme's family have claimed his body, and they have barred the mortuary staff from telling me anything else about him. All I want is to be able to say goodbye, so I'll be calling them tomorrow to speak to his brother.

And I must tell them the news that Jérôme never knew about. A test at the doctor's confirmed it. I'm pregnant.

"Oh Mum!" Maddie gasped. Why had Elizabeth never told her? Surely, when she'd grown up, there was no reason to keep all this a secret? Blinking hard, she read on.

18th March, 1984
What a rude bunch the de Montceau family are! All hoity-toity with their noses up in the air. When I called them to convey my condolences, it started off fairly civilised. Marie-Pierre, Jérôme's older brother, was polite and sounded almost supportive, but then his mother took the phone off him. Seriously, why does a man of thirty years of age let his mother treat him like a child?

The countess left me in no doubt of her low opinion of me. I was not to come to Jérôme's funeral, nor was I allowed to visit the family crypt in the old cemetery in Beaune. She reminded me of their noble lineage – a family of counts, no less, whose roots dated back to the days of Charlemagne – and that she never supported Jérôme's 'obsession' with me.

But the worst thing was when I told her of the pregnancy, she offered me money – to get rid of the child! Dear Goddess, what a vile harpy the woman is. She insisted I have an abortion, and that no support for any child forthcoming. Hell, she even hinted that it could've been

208

anyone's baby. 'There is no proof,' she said. How cold does your heart have to be?

So I'll continue to work in this hotel over the summer. Jeanne has promised to help me until I know what I wanted to do when the time came.

But all this pales into insignificance now. I've lost my love. The one man I'd have followed around the world. Nothing will ever bring him back.

24th September, 1984
Beaune, Burgundy

I made it, regardless of what Old Harpy said. They can kick me out of the cemetery for all they like.

But I have to admit the de Montceau crypt is stark but beautiful, almost Romanesque in style. Minimalist. I had to give them that. I cried again when I read Jérôme's name carved in stone. He has gone too soon. I miss him so much.

From here, I'll be making my way north, to Normandy. A friend from England, Sylvia, lives there. She will help me look after my child when he or she arrives next month.

So this is farewell, Jérôme de Montceau, kind and caring man that you were. We'll meet again in the next life. Blessed be.

Goosebumps rose on Maddie's skin. Jérôme de Montceau. Beaune. Burgundy. She finally had the information she'd wanted to know all her adult life.

Her eyes flicked to the next entry, a date she knew well.

4th October, 1984

It's a girl! Oh, she's beautiful, but I'll never have another, I swear. I had to have an emergency caesarian, and I'm glad I did after twenty-six hours of pain. The good doctors likely saved both our lives. I'll name her Madeleine.

Oh, and a surprise parcel has arrived in the post. It contained the most delicate baptism gown I've ever seen. Too beautiful to keep unwrapped! I don't think I've ever had such a precious gift, well, apart from my daughter.

Such a shame the gown will never be used, as I won't take Madeleine to be dunked by a priest. I suspect it came from Jérôme's brother, but there was no address or note attached.

But now I must sleep. I'm tired…

Chapter Twenty-Four

Early October, AD 793
The hills north of Carcassonne

"We should have left earlier," Amalberga mumbled and wrapped herself closer into her cloak. The wind had increased during the afternoon, and thick grey clouds began to gather.

The air smelt of rain, and the trees around them shook off their leaves as the branches swayed in the strong breeze. The path they were following, parallel to the river, became less clear as darkness descended.

"We couldn't. I had to make sure Gunda had delivered her child safely. And as you know, children can take their time."

"Then we should have stayed." Amalberga huffed, staring straight ahead.

Hilda looked to Lot for support, but he merely shook his head.

"Amalberga is right, lady. 'Tis not safe outside, and dusk is settling too fast. On this uneven ground, our horses can only trot, not run, or we'd risk them losing their footing."

She gritted her teeth and urged Roma forward, ignoring the gusts tearing at her hood.

"Lady, don't! We are far away from the villages, and a storm is coming in from the west. You have seen the dark clouds. It might catch us before we reach Carcassonne."

"So we must hurry." She sent him a challenging glance.

"'Tis unsafe to rush here in the forest." Panic crossed his face, and he raised his voice in a plea. "Please slow down."

"Once we are through this narrow valley, we're out in the plain. Then we can go faster."

"But we'll be exposed to the elements." Amalberga's tone held a hint of fear, and Hilda slowed down.

"And potentially to enemies," Lot added. "I didn't like the look of the men who were hiding on that hill behind the village earlier."

Puzzled, Hilda turned in the saddle to stare at him. "True. I have forgotten about them. I hope they won't attack Gunda and her family."

"There seemed to be only three of them, lady, but we don't know. Come to think of it, 'tis curious that we saw no trace of them later."

"Perhaps they moved on."

"Or they are ahead of us…" Amalberga crossed herself. "We should have left earlier," she repeated.

Hilda felt a sense of dread. She should have listened to her companions. After all, they were her responsibility, and it was her duty to get them back home safely. And whilst Lot was well-armed, and she also carried a sword on her hip and a dagger in her boot, they were no match for three grown men like those watchers.

Thinking back to when Lot pointed them out to her, she thought that the bearings of one seemed familiar, but they had been too far away, and she could not recognise them. Saracens they were not – they had dressed in the Frankish way. Soldiers.

Or mercenaries.

She shuddered. "We'll be home soon, before the sun sets fully."

A few yards ahead, the path narrowed, and she clicked her tongue at her mare.

"Lady, wait!" Lot called out. "Let me go first."

"You watch our back, Lot," she ordered and veered into the centre of the lane. Looking over her shoulder, she saw that Amalberga followed at a short distance, and Lot, sword in hand, behind her.

"I don't like this one bit." Amalberga's voice reached her, and goosebumps rose on her arm. She should not have asked her companion to join her on such an arduous journey.

"Let's get through this chasm quickly." She set Roma off into a run. "Then, we'll be—"

A scream escaped her as her mare stumbled over an obstacle, and she fell over the beast's long neck.

When Hilda came to, she was lying on the ground. Beside her, Roma was whimpering.

Black spots danced before her eyes, and she blinked repeatedly to rid herself of them. Taking a deep breath, she propped herself up onto her elbows, but the fall had winded her and she breathed in deeply. A shard of pain shot into her shoulder blades. She tried to move her legs, but it was as if they no longer belonged to her.

What had happened? Had a snake slithered across the trail? Unlikely at this time of year.

She turned her head and saw Roma's panicked eyes. The front legs lay sprawled at an ugly angle, both broken. Her beloved mare whinnied pitifully.

Tears welled up, and she wiped them away. "Lot? Amalberga?"

Roma blocked the view of the path behind her. She heard horses neigh, but from her companions came no answer. The silence unnerved her.

"Lot? Where are you?" Fear gripped her as a suspicion dawned on her.

Amalberga would be fretting over her, and Lot would be rushing to her side. But with neither responding, had something befallen them? Her breath caught in her throat.

Eventually, she heard voices. Male.

Had Lot found help?

Listening intently, she could not identify the young man's accent. Instead, she recognised the language of her father, of the Franks.

The scrape of a sword drawn reached her, followed by a gurgling sound. What was that?

Her heart pounded loudly, and her hands began to shake. She balled them into fists; her nails digging into the flesh, to calm herself.

"He won't pose a danger anymore." A harsh laugh echoed through the forest.

Who was *he*? Lot? She shuddered, and tried to turn onto her side, but her lower body did not budge.

I must have broken my back.

Tears stung in her eyes. Knowing what fate awaited her as a cripple, she swallowed hard. If she survived the day, that was. Perhaps the men were robbers. She had nothing of worth on her other than a few small coins.

"Ah, there we are. The lady Nanthild has need of us, Pepin."

Her skin crawled as she recognised the voice, and the man it belonged to.

"Clovis," she whispered.

What was he doing in this remote part of Septimania, far away from Charles' campaigns? Should he not be with the forces fighting the Saracens?

She glared at him, annoyed with herself for not being able to move. All was suddenly clear. He had waylaid her.

Eventually, he bent over her, his face a grimace of hate... and lust.

"I have waited a long time for this moment, Hilda. At least now you can't escape me." He sent her a pitiful glance.

"How...how did you know where I was?"

He trailed a hand down her legs. She felt nothing. "Oh, I was close to Carcassonne when I saw you leave this morn. So I thought..." Slowly, he pushed up her gown. "Well, why not follow the lady and surprise her? When the lord is far away..."

"Damned cur!" She could not even kick at him. Desperately, she tried to punch his face, but his superior strength made all her feeble attempts futile. Easily, he pinned her down by the wrists. She turned her head, only to look into Roma's sad eyes.

"You...will pay for this," she whispered, her voice hoarse with strain. "Bellon will—"

He smacked her across the face and pulled her up by the shoulders. As he lifted up her body, a fierce pain shot through her back, then stopped at her hips.

"My horse!" Clovis bellowed.

Within an instant, Hilda found herself thrown over the saddle, like a sack of wheat. She pushed her arms against the stallion's frame, but a firm hand pinned her down as Clovis sat behind her.

"Get rid of the bodies, Pepin, and take the guy's weapons," he shouted. "Then shove them into the undergrowth. Bero should help you. You'll find me where we stopped on the way up."

A dead calm descended on her as she looked at nothing but the beaten earth of the path. He rode for a mile or two, then veered off the route along a narrow lane. When he finally paused, she raised her head and saw several derelict, roofless huts. A hamlet deserted decades earlier.

He picked her up roughly and walked her into the nearest hut. There, he lay her on the bare floor. Stones and branches cut into her back, but she kept her gaze firmly directed at his face.

How could she have known this man would stoop so low as to injure and abduct the daughter of a count, and wife of another!

Realisation of what he wanted with her had become clear.

"Don't stare at me like that, witch! Oh yes, I heard of your healing skills. And look how much they help you now!" Then he fumbled with the belt that held his leggings in place. "And don't fret! No-one will ever know of our little…tryst." He laughed, the harsh sound grating in her ears.

"You call the abduction of a countess a tryst?"

"Oh, don't be so high-and-mighty, Hilda. You women are all the same. Now, be a good girl and spread your legs for me."

"I would rather die."

"That can be arranged," he said calmly. "Afterwards. Now, as you seem unable to move them, let me do it for you."

Fear swept through her at the glimmer in his eyes as he pushed her thighs apart. He would never take her home. Her mind spat out the obvious: he would use her, then leave her for dead.

Never again would she hold her children, or Bellon. Tears began to flow, and she let them run.

Filled with desperation, she pummelled against him with her hands, but each movement sent waves of excruciating pain through her upper body.

"Damned witch! Lie still!"

Her nails drew blood from his cheek, and he smacked her again. This time, her temple hit a rock. Dizziness overcame her, and her arms went limp. She moaned.

"That is better," he muttered as he pulled up her gown. In her pained haze, she felt anger stirring, but her body would no longer react to her will.

Suddenly, he halted. The sound of voices and horses' hooves drifted their way. Someone was nearing.

A small glimmer of hope rose in her chest, and she opened her mouth to cry for help. But a grimy palm covered it immediately, and he pinned her down with his weight. She tried to breathe in, but found it impossible. His big hand covered her nose too. It smelled of dirt. She could not inhale. Feeling the blackness threatening, she wriggled beneath him, but to no avail. The voices receded, but still he held her down. Before the blackness won, she sensed his fear. He would be afraid of her husband's revenge. So he should be. Bellon would kill him.

Finally, he lifted his hand. She took a deep, ragged breath and forced her eyelids open to stare into his. Then, with the last of her strength, she whispered, "Clovis, I curse you and your offspring in perpetuity, in the name of the God and the Goddess. Their wrath will be absolute."

The alarm in his eyes told her that her words had an effect. Christians still feared the old religions, and this man was no exception. A sense of peace descended on her. She trusted the Goddess. And Bellon's revenge.

Later, as Clovis covered her with layers of damp earth too heavy to shift, she let herself drift in and out of consciousness, repeating the curse in her mind. There was no air, no escape. She would become one with the earth…

***

His mood dark, Bellon had ridden late into the night, oblivious to the storm around him. As he finally approached the walls of Carcassonne, he tried to shake off a lingering sense of foreboding.

Dagobert had sent a man earlier this day to where the Franks had set up camp, to the east of Narbonne, which remained in the hands of the Saracens. The messenger told him that Hilda had gone missing, together with Lot and Amalberga.

Throughout his hurried journey home, Bellon prayed fervently that they had returned safely in the meantime. In his despair, he addressed not only his Christian god in prayers but also Hilda's pagan gods, feeling no guilt at invoking ancient beliefs. One of them might listen. He hoped…

The heavy rain had drenched him, and his wet cloak was not enough to keep the chilly winds at bay. Yet, none of this mattered if he had lost Hilda.

Dagobert awaited him inside the gate, his mouth in a thin like.

"Have they come back?" Bellon dismounted and passed the reins to a stable boy.

The captain shook his head. "No, lord. We have searched the north for miles, as far as the hills, and found no trace. I am sorry," he added.

"Let's go within," Bellon grabbed his arm. "I know my wife well. 'Tis not your fault she has ventured out."

"Still…" Dagobert opened the door to the hall and followed Bellon.

The warmth inside engulfed him, but he could not shake off the chill in his heart.

"Lord." Roderic came forward and took his sodden cloak off him. "There is mulled wine waiting for you. Rest yourself."

"Father!" Guisclafred hovered by the hearth, rubbing his hands over the fire. His son's tunic and hose were almost as soaked as his own. "We searched for hours, but found no trace of Mother."

"Here, Father. Dagobert." Oliba approached them from a trestle table with two full cups. His clothes were equally wet, and tears welled in his eyes. Swiftly, he blinked them back.

Bellon took the cups off Oliba's trembling hands and passed one to Dagobert. Then they joined Guisclafred by the fire.

With a sigh, he dropped into his chair, aware that he would make the cushions damp. Hilda would tell him off...and he felt her absence strongly. Whenever he returned from a campaign, she had been there. Solid. Quietly supportive. A presence. Now, the hall was an empty shell.

Dagobert sat on a bench opposite and took a draught. "She insisted on leaving early this morn upon hearing of a woman's plight. Apparently, there were difficulties with her labour."

Bellon nodded. Leaning forward, he cradled his cup in his hands, breathing in the strong scent of berries and grapes. "And did she tell you where that woman lives?"

"No, lord. I should have asked…"

"Yes, you should. Only Lot always knew where she was going. For some reason, she seemed to find the secrecy necessary."

"But telling us would have been for her protection," Guisclafred pointed out. "So we would learn where she was."

Bellon snorted. "You know your mother. No amount of pointing out to her that safety was important would ever move her to share her whereabouts. She's over-protective of the people she treats, and perhaps rightly so." He did not want to state the obvious – that her methods could get everyone into danger if the Church heard about them.

"I wish I'd asked her anyway," Oliba whispered. He sat beside Dagobert and stared into the fire. "There aren't that many villages up there."

"The only thing I remember the man saying is that the village was on the shores of the Orbiel river," Roderic said, then looked up. "Oh, and he gave the woman's name as Gunda."

"And that's where you searched, northwards along the river?"

Dagobert and Guisclafred nodded in unison.

"Then we'll leave again at first light. If she's out there, we will find her." He glanced at his oldest. "Is Alda asleep?"

"Yes, finally. It took all Rotlinde's soothing skills to get her to bed and rest."

"Good. Sleep will help her. Now," he turned to Dagobert, pushing away his tiredness, "tell me where you searched, and then we can plan for the morrow."

After reaching the base of the northern hillsides, their group had split into two. Dagobert, Guisclafred and a few men would follow the route close to the banks of the Orbiel river, whilst he, Oliba and the remaining men-at-arms would scour the surrounding forests. They had agreed a meeting place where their paths crossed, deep in the hills.

But as he rode along the narrow, winding route, his hopes faded. They had passed through two hamlets close to the main route, but neither had seen Hilda or her companions. Scouts searched abandoned huts to see if she had sought shelter from the storm the previous night, but they had found no trace.

"There's another hamlet ahead, Father." Oliba, riding in front, pointed at a clearing not far ahead.

Bellon looked up, but his brief sense of hope was fading fast. Only half a dozen hovels stood in a small circle. What were the chances?

Nudging his horse to level up with his son, he approached the settlement with trepidation.

As they neared it, a young lad of Guisclafred's age bearing an axe emerged from the largest hut, stopping at a safe distance from them. "What do you want?" He eyed them suspiciously.

Bellon raised a hand. "Greetings. I'm Count Bellon of Carcassonne. We have no intention to harm you or your family. Instead, we wish to ask you whether you have seen a lady travelling past here, with her two companions."

The man lowered his axe, though did not let him out of his sight. "A lady, you say? When was that supposed to have happened?"

"Yesterday." Did this stranger know something? He seemed to mull over something. "My wife travelled with a guard and her companion."

Bellon's hope soared when the man turned his head and called, "Mother, come out! These people might be looking for the woman."

The woman? His heart was pounding loudly. "Have you seen them?"

"Yes, we saw them, first in the morn, then later again. The sun was setting already when they passed us – your lady, an armed man and an older maid."

A woman of around Bellon's own age emerged from the hut.

"Mother, this is Bellon, the count of Carcassonne. He's looking for his wife."

"And her companions," Oliba added.

Her eyes grew large. "The… Show your respect, boy," she slapped her son softly on the head before kneeling on the bare ground. "I'm Svinthila and this is Ardo. Welcome, lord."

Her son was swiftly following her example, sending him an apologetic grin.

Bellon dismounted and handed his reins to Oliba. Then he approached the two. "Thank you. Please rise. It is important that we find them."

The woman's eyes filled with tears. She stood, nodding. "Yes, lord. As Ardo said, they passed us. But later, when my son went out," she looked away furtively and Bellon guessed he had been hunting.

"Your son went out…and what?" He prompted her, unconcerned about the reasons. Like these folk, he followed some of the stricter Frankish rules only loosely, so he did not pursue poor people for wanting to feed their families. People needed to eat and keep warm, and there was plenty of game in the forests.

She took a deep breath. "Tell him, Ardo." She nudged the young man who swallowed hard.

"I…I came across the guard, lord. He was dead," he said. "It looked as if he'd been killed by a spear, then had his throat cut. There was blood everywhere." His voice shook.

"Our men went out and buried the wretched soul beside our own departed," Svinthila added solemnly.

Bellon took a shaky breath and crossed himself, as did Oliba beside him. Ever since he had rescued Lot, he had felt responsible for his welfare. Lot had been like a son to him, and now some cur had cut his life short.

"Thank you and your men for your kindness, Svinthila. I shall not forget it."

"Poor Lot. He didn't deserve this," Oliba whispered.

"No, he did not. We'll avenge his cowardly murder, do not doubt it!" He looked back at Ardo. "Did you see the women?"

"The older one, yes."

His heart sank. "Was she dead, too?"

"No," Svinthila said. "She's within, but gravely injured, and I don't know how long she'll remain with us."

"Amalberga is alive?" A small glimmer of hope. She may know what had befallen Hilda. "May I see her? Did she wake?"

Hilda shook her head. "No, she hasn't come to since we brought her here. Her attackers had thrown her into a ditch near the man you called Lot, but Ardo heard her whimper." She waved him over. "Please enter, lord."

He bent low through the entrance and entered the hut which was separated into three sections by curtains. A lit fire in the centre spread warmth across the room, and the beaten earth was covered in dried lavender branches, which let off a fine scent with each step. A few clean pots hung on hooks in a corner.

"This way, lord." She pushed aside a curtain, and he entered what must be her sleeping area.

Bellon blinked back tears when he saw Amalberga. Her face pale, she lay on the pallet, covered by a blanket and a warming fur – the origins of which he did not wish to know. Kneeling beside her, he took her hand. The coolness of her fingers, despite the heat, worried him.

"You have done well in looking after Amalberga, Svinthila. I'm in your debt."

The woman shuffled her feet, a faint smile on her lips. "I wouldn't leave an injured soul out there." She sobered. "I'm only sad we didn't find your wife. You know, after Ardo came across your man and then this woman – Amalberga – our men went to look for the lady, but all they found were tracks of horses' hooves. The attackers must have taken her."

He nodded, his mind made up. "Yes, I believe that is what happened. We need to build a litter so we can carry Amalberga back to Carcassonne."

Voices rose outside, and he stood, listening.

Svinthila tilted her head. "My husband and brother-in-law are returning. They will help."

It did not take long to find the right branches, and with Oliba and the men-at-arms helping, they put together a solid litter. Bellon also dispatched a man to meet Dagobert further up in the valley, to tell the captain that they were returning to Carcassonne forthwith.

In the meantime, Ardo took him to where he had discovered Lot's body.

A sense of dread hit him when he inspected the scene. *The perfect place for an ambush.* Bellon stared up and down the narrow path, his skin prickling. *Someone knew what they were doing.*

"This is where I found your man, lord." Ardo pointed at a discoloured patch of leaves. Matted blood stuck to the earth.

Bellon shuddered. He patted the youth on his back. "It was brave of you to approach a mutilated body."

"He could have been alive. As was the horse, a little further up where we just passed. The attackers left the poor mare to die, so—"

"A mare?" Both Hilda and Amalberga rode mares. "Of what colour?"

"Light brown, with a white spot on her chest. Both her front legs were broken." He fidgeted, avoiding Bellon's gaze "We had no choice but to…release her."

Roma. So Hilda was taken here. A planned ambush. "You did right, Ardo."

And you'll have some food to tide you over the autumn.

They took another close look around, but found no clues as to Hilda's whereabouts. Eventually, his heart heavy, they returned to the hamlet.

A short while later, they took their leave from a teary Svinthila.

"Thank you. I won't forget what you've done for us. You are always welcome at the fortress should you need to go to a safe place. I will send someone to return the blankets to you and bring you more furs."

"Thank you, lord. That is kind of you. We were glad to be of help. I have given Amalberga a calming tisane so she won't feel the bumpy journey. And our men will keep scouring the forest for your lady wife. I pray she is alive and well."

He nodded, and their little procession went on its way south again, though more slowly this time. Amalberga lay cocooned in blankets, tied to the litter which was carried securely between two horses.

A little later, they spotted yet another long-abandoned hut several dozen yards from their path.

"Let's have a look at this one. How did we miss it on the way up?"

"It's hidden from sight by those shrubs, Father." Oliba pointed at the thick undergrowth on the side of the path.

Only a few crumbling walls remained from what appeared to have been a Roman home many years ago. A shudder ran down Bellon's back as they searched the remnants. The ground was churned up, but there was no sign of any lit fires, likely meaning nobody had stayed there overnight in a long time.

Still, he took steps into the dense undergrowth around the sad ruin, but apart from a few cracked branches, nothing stood out. Yet he could not shake off a growing sense of unease. He stared into the gloom of the trees when a deer broke out of the thicket and rushed past him.

"Ah. The likely cause of the broken shrubs. Wild animals." He swallowed hard. "Hilda wasn't here."

"Then let us head home, shall we?" Oliba lay a heavy hand on his shoulder.

Bellon nodded, then mounted his horse. "Agreed, son. Keep watch, though! I feel like we've missed something."

"Yes, Father." Oliba followed him, his voice shaking.

They returned to the path where their men-at-arms waited with Amalberga and turned southwards again.

Hilda hovered above a mound of earth covered in branches and leaves only a few yards into the undergrowth. She reached out her hand but knew they could not see her. Oliba's sadness tore at her heart. Oh, once more to touch her family, to hold them in her arms.

Stretching as far as she could, she kept her gaze firmly on Bellon, savouring this final chance to look at him. Then he was gone. And she was alone...

Chapter Twenty-Five

Mid-May, 2018

A knock on the front door brought Maddie out from the kitchen where she had nursed her coffee whilst reading three notes from the dig in Yorkshire. All useful material for her book, so she had annotated several passages for reference.

She opened the door to a man hidden behind a large parcel labelled '*fragile*' in large print. "Madame Winters?"

"*Oui, c'est moi.*"

He was about to drop the box on her doorstep when she caught it and gently put it on the floor in the corridor.

"*C'est fragile*, Monsieur!"

She glared when he shrugged and held out an electronic pad for her to sign without another word. Then she shut the door in his face.

"Delivery people aren't what they used to be," she mumbled as she carried the box into the kitchen where she carefully set it down on the table and fetched the scissors from a drawer. Gently slicing through the sticky tape that kept the lids in place, she prised it open. The laboratory had wrapped the bones individually, and she discovered to her relief that every item was almost as she found it – minus the small pieces they'd taken out for analysis, but the cuts were barely visible.

She picked up the written report that accompanied the items. So the bones were definitely over 1,000 years old, belonging to a female, with the ribs and backbone broken in a way that implied an accident. Had someone left the poor woman to die? A horrific suggestion, but realistic enough as in times of warfare nobody was safe.

Maddie laid out the pieces on the table, aware of a slight current between them and her hands. The bones were vibrating, clearly happy to be back home. She cradled the cranium and whispered soothing words. "Don't worry. I'll see you receive the respect you were denied in death."

A horse neighed, and she shook her head. Was it her imagination again? She gently placed the cranium beside the bones and looked out of the window, but no horses passed by. Yes, she was being silly.

What am I going to do with you? Maddie sat down and looked over her small hoard. Bertrand would take some pieces to keep them in the small museum beside the *mairie*. But now she had to decide which pieces would go and which she would keep. She felt bad having to split up the bones, like tearing apart a real person.

'Rest.'

Maddie's head shot up. So she was still here, the woman whose bones now lay on her kitchen table.

"You wish to rest? I can lay you to rest here, in Minervens. We'll find a beautiful spot for you. But I promised Bertrand a few bones for his collection. I'm so sorry."

'Home.'

Not for the first time did she wonder what had happened to this woman who had lived over a millennium ago.

"I have to do the right thing."

Her mobile phone vibrated on the kitchen cupboard where she had left it to charge. She grabbed it and smiled at the message.

Fancy dinner by the canal? My treat x

Why not? She'd not seen Léon for two days as his winery held a special promotional weekend, but it would be lovely to catch up with him.

She had told him about her father, and he recognised the name de Montceau. Apparently, it was a highly respected wine-growing family business.

Only Maddie couldn't see anything worthy of respect in a family that rejected one of their own – her!

Still, dinner sounded good, so she agreed for him to pick her up at 7 pm.

"I'd like you to meet my parents, Maddie."

She choked on her Aperol Spritz and pinched her nose where the fizzy liquid had tickled her. "What?" Was their relationship gone that far already? "Umm…"

Léon back-pedalled quickly. "There's no rush. They're just curious about you. My father spoke to Bertrand, so they know about the bones and the renovations. And, I guess, they're wondering why I'm hiding you." He smirked behind a large glass of blueberry gin and tonic.

Maddie laughed out loud. "Well, that's fair enough, I suppose. It's just…after what I've read in Mum's journal, I wonder if I need to be on my guard."

He took her hand and stroked it. "My folks don't bite. They're intrigued by your work – my mother is a member of a regional history society – and she is curious about the bones. And your plans."

"My plans? What about them? After the renovations, I want to…"

What did she want? She stared at him, fully aware of his thumb stroking the inside of her hand, a sensation that addled her brain.

Her original aim had been to sell Elizabeth's house as soon as the year was up. But she hadn't counted on meeting Léon or finding the bones. In recent weeks, the house, this village had started to feel like her home. People welcomed her. Would she still want to swap this warmth for the coldness of a small, empty flat in York?

"Maddie?"

She met his querying glance straight on. "Yes. Umm…"

He nodded. "I understand. If you'd rather—"

"No, I'd love to meet your folks. And to tell them about my plans." She grabbed his hand. "Things have changed. Unexpectedly."

Léon smiled. "Then you're cordially invited round for dinner on Friday. Oh, and I have other news, too."

She swallowed. "Oh, do you?"

"Yes." He pulled a sheet of paper from the inside pocket of his jacket and handed it to her. "I wanted to wait until after we've eaten, but I'm too curious know what you think."

"What's this?" She unfolded the A4-sized sheet. "An email from…what?"

Had she read correctly? She checked the name at the bottom of the message again.

Marie-Pierre de Montceau.

"What is this?" Tears shot into her eyes, stopping her from reading it. She blinked.

Léon took the sheet from her and tucked it away. "It's an invitation to the Château de Montceau. My mother reminded me that I'd met the owner at a wine show in Paris two or three years ago, so I got in touch with him. I hope you don't mind. I haven't told him about you, but he's welcoming me and my girlfriend to stay at their *domaine*."

"Wow!" Maddie took a large gulp of her apéritif. "But we should tell him about me before we meet him, shouldn't we?"

"Yes, it would only be fair. So, I guess you're ready to see your family?"

So much to take in, she simply nodded. "Unless he tells us to go to hell, like his mother did…"

Léon laughed out loud. "He should try!" The glint in his eyes was unmistakable. He'd not accept a rejection lightly.

She grabbed his hand and kissed it. "Thank you."

Stroking her cheek, he smiled. "You're very welcome. Here, to us!" He raised his glass.

"To us!"

Chapter Twenty-Six

Early October, AD 793
Carcassonne

It was late at night when Bellon and his retinue finally arrived at home. The litter had hampered their pace, and Amalberga's occasional, incoherent whispers worried them. None of the words she mumbled made any coherent sense, though.

Roderic emerged from the hall just as he dismounted. "Welcome back, lord. Any tidings?"

"Yes, but not ones you'd wish for." He pointed to Amalberga. "Can you ensure she's gently taken upstairs and put into my bed? It's the most comfortable. Ask Rotlinde to care for her."

"Of course."

"And there's more," he added, ruffling a hand through his hair. "Lot is dead."

Roderic crossed himself and bit his lip. "Lot dead? He was so young. I will see his family. What in God's name has happened?"

"Their group was ambushed. Someone attacked him with a spear, and he had his throat cut. And they shoved Amalberga into the undergrowth and left her to die there." He took a deep breath and turned to the hall.

"Sweet Mother!" Roderic's hand clutched his arm. "And what about the lady Nanthild?"

Bellon met his gaze. "No sign of her. Now—"

"We have a guest," the *majordomus* blurted out.

Irritated, Bellon dropped the latch. "Ged rid of them. They can entertain themselves in the west tower."

"I'm afraid it's not that easy, although I tried. You see…
It's the lord Clovis."

"Clovis? Of all people… Christ's Blood!"

"He and his men arrived in the early afternoon, and he's
made himself at home since."

Bellon groaned. The last thing he wanted to do today was
entertain that oaf. He needed time to think, not spar with that
obnoxious knight. He took a deep breath, then grabbed the
door latch.

"Thank you for the warning, Roderic. Please get
Amalberga settled with Rotlinde and Alda, then join us in the
hall. Dagobert should arrive soon too, I hope."

"Father," Oliba appeared at his side. "Is that the man who
insulted Mother?"

Bellon nodded. "He is. You don't have to meet him…"

Oliba squared his shoulders and set his jaw. "But I want to.
You shouldn't have to face him alone, not after what we
discovered today."

Bellon smiled, recognising Hilda's stubbornness in his
younger son. He pulled the door to the hall open and entered
with Oliba by his side.

Clovis hailed him across the room. "Ah, there he is!
Where have you been, Bellon?" The Frank had settled
himself in a comfortable chair beside the hearth, his feet
propped up on a stool. Two other men, mercenaries by the
look of them, sat either side of him.

"Away," came his short response. He sent Oliba a sharp
glance, hoping his son understood not to reveal today's
events.

"The duke of Tolosa missed you at Narbonne, I heard. If I
hadn't been otherwise occupied, I'd have joined him in his
attempt at ousting the Saracens from our lands."

Our lands? Bellon bit back a retort, his irritation rising.
Why had God – whichever God – deigned to punish him with
the presence of this…fool, and today of all days? He was
tired and worried; angry and disheartened, and not in the
mood for Clovis' manipulations.

Oliba fetched two cups of spiced wine and handed one to him. His throat parched, he drank greedily, then set the empty cup aside. He could not risk getting drunk, however much he wanted to escape reality, if only for a short time.

Venturing towards the hearth, he glared at one of Clovis' men who was sitting in Hilda's chair. After a nod from Clovis, the soldier stood and sauntered to a bench. Bellon sat, leaning forward, and folded his hands.

"Why are you here?"

Clovis laughed. "Ha! That's what I like about you, Bellon. You always get straight to the point."

You do not like me at all, Clovis.

"You haven't answered Father's question!"

Bellon drew comfort when Oliba stood behind him.

Clovis pulled a face. "Ha! The son is as rude as the father. No sense of hospitality. Goths!"

"I'm afraid I don't have time to be hospitable. Septimania is under attack, so you will forgive me for being a little... irritable."

Chuckling, Clovis leaned back. "And your...irritation... has nothing to do with the disappearance of the lady Nanthild?"

Bellon glared at him, his mind whirling. How could the cur know? "What disappearance?"

A smile played on Clovis' thin lips. "The message I received from Narbonne mentioned her going missing as being the reason for your early departure. Duke Guillaume is most put out, apparently."

"I've left enough men to compensate him for my absence. And my wife has nothing to do with you."

Clovis' smile vanished. "So it's true, she's gone? Well, I heard rumours about her religious...inclinations, Bellon. You might be better off—"

Bellon jumped to his feet and pulled Clovis up. "Don't think I won't throw you out, simply because the king relies on your strong arm more than he needs to!"

231

Clovis' men drew their swords and surrounded him. Then Dagobert's voice reached them from the door. "Drop your weapons! You're outnumbered."

"Dagobert! Good to see you returned in time." Bellon pushed Clovis away. "Retreat with your men to the west tower where you can stay until the morn. By sunrise, I want you gone from Carcassonne."

Clovis adjusted his tunic. "I'll report you to King Charles. Your insubordination will cost you."

Bellon gritted his teeth, clenching and unclenching his fists. "The king will hear about your behaviour tonight. And of the other times when you insulted my family. Now leave, or I'll lock you up. Our dungeons are less comfortable than the west tower."

"You will regret this, Goth!" Bristling, Clovis ushered his men past Dagobert and four of his men-at-arms into the yard. Bellon and Oliba followed them.

At that moment, Alda came rushing down the stairs. "Father!"

Clovis' eyes bulged, and the hairs on Bellon's neck stood on end. Alda was the image of her mother.

She stopped a few steps up from them. "Amalberga regained consciousness."

"So she is awake?"

Alda shook her head. "Not anymore. She drifted back into sleep, but Rotlinde thinks she will wake again soon."

"We shall be gone by the morn, Bellon." Clovis stalked away without another word, his men following.

"Come here, Sweeting." Bellon took his daughter in a firm embrace. "You shouldn't be up and about this late at night. Not with strange men around."

"But," she pouted, "I was excited and thought you wanted to hear."

He smiled and kissed her forehead. "I know, my love. Now, to bed with you. Don't take advantage of Rotlinde having to care for Amalberga!" he chided gently. "Oliba, accompany your sister to my chamber, please."

His son nodded and climbed the steps.

"Good night, Father." She beamed.

He blew her a kiss. "Good night. And no more escapades!"

The girl was turning into her mother.

"Dagobert, call two men to stand guard outside the door to my chamber. If anyone approaches the steps, they must raise the alarm. Then fetch my sons and join me in the hall."

Dagobert met his gaze. "Yes, lord."

Moments later, Bellon sat by the fire, a cup of wine in hand.

"Are you certain you don't want any food? You need to eat, lord." Roderic's concern touched him, but appetite was the last thing on his mind.

Something was puzzling him. He waited until Dagobert, Guisclafred and Oliba had joined them.

"Did you find anything during your search?" He looked at his captain across the fire.

"Nothing at all. We reached our meeting point, and then returned, as you requested. Perhaps I should go further into the mountains. The lady Nanthild must have been up there somewhere."

"I agree. But for tonight, I prefer you here. I do not trust Clovis."

"Nor do I," Dagobert agreed.

His sons nodded.

"He barged in here like he was in command," Roderic said.

Bellon grinned. "Yes, I think he imagined being lord of Carcassonne, and he was bitterly disappointed when Charles chose me instead. But there's something else that I don't understand."

"What, Father?" Guisclafred asked.

"Did any of you notice his reaction to Alda's appearance? Before we left the hall, he was all belligerent. Then, when Alda arrived and spoke of Amalberga, he first stared at her as if he'd seen a ghost, then he couldn't get away fast enough."

"Yes, I noticed that too," Dagobert said. "He was suddenly more concerned with leaving. You do not think he has anything to do with the lady Nanthild's disappearance, do you?"

"He knew about it even though no one here told him," Oliba mused. "In fact, he was baiting Father when you appeared, Dagobert."

Bellon took a deep breath. "These are serious accusations, yet I can't find a reasonable answer. His reaction was simply too…"

"…predictive, as if he was guilty," Oliba finished his sentence.

"So we allow them to stay tonight?" Roderic raised his eyebrows and looked from one to another. "I certainly never mentioned the lady Nanthild to him."

"Yes, we let him stay. But we shall be keeping watch, out of his sight."

Dagobert nodded. "The guards we took with us today are eating at the moment, but others are ready. I'll allocate some men to hide in the stables and in the towers near where Clovis is staying. And three guards are at the top of the stairs outside, outside your chamber."

"That's a good plan. I'll be heading upstairs myself soon. I know every creaky step that leads up. Oliba, you come with me. Guisclafred, you will stay here in the hall for the night, with Roderic. And someone needs to watch the kitchen."

Dagobert stood. "Agreed. I'll be doing the rounds in the night. Do not fret, lord. Our visitors won't realise I'm watching."

"Wait a moment, Dagobert! Can you spare a man who is rested to head to Duke Guillaume in Narbonne? I must know how Clovis would have heard about my wife's disappearance. If the news is all over the camp, then it's clear. But if not…"

"Certainly. I know just the man to send. He'll be ready at a moment's notice."

"Great. He needs to be circumspect, though."

"He will be. And with your permission, I'll return to the hills in the morn, once Clovis has left. We'll identify the village where the lady Nanthild travelled to, I'm certain."

Bellon sighed. "Thank you. She is somewhere out there, and we're going to find her."

Five days later, Bellon's mind whirled as he rode at speed along the route to Narbonne, fervently hoping Clovis was still there. If necessary, he would chase him across the length and breadth of Francia!

Behind him, Dagobert, his sons and a small contingency of men-at-arms followed in grim silence.

His instinct had been right, and now he would seek justice. As count, it was his to give. And as an aggrieved husband, he was also within his rights.

Dagobert caught up with him. "How will you approach Clovis? Without doubt, he will try to draw away from it with his lies."

"Oh, let him! I'll speak to the duke first. Fortunately, he doesn't hold Clovis in high favour either. We shall take advantage of that."

"And then we take him with us to Carcassonne?"

"Yes, forthwith. We can't allow him any chance to warn his men or appeal to the king."

"It's a risky game, lord."

"A game I will win, Dagobert." Bellon gritted his teeth.

As they approached the large encampment of Franks outside the walls of Narbonne, they slowed down, not wishing to raise an alarm. Bellon waved a greeting to several men he recognised and eventually came to a halt at Duke Guillaume's tent. Tense voices sounded from within. A loud discussion was in progress. Then he heard Clovis laugh, a harsh grating sound to his ears.

"We have to change tactics, Dagobert." He kept his own voice low. "It appears our prey is awaiting us."

He dismounted and gave the reins too Oliba. "Wait here. Don't let him pass!"

"What if he tries?"

"Hold him, by my orders and by all means necessary."

The meaning was not lost on his son. "Yes, Father."

Leaving his men in position, Bellon nodded at an armed foot soldier outside the entrance who opened a tent flap and let him enter.

Guillaume sat on a chair near a small fire, with Clovis and two other soldiers facing him. "Ah, Bellon." He rose and clasped his arm. "Have you concluded your urgent issue?"

Bellon inclined his head briefly. "Not quite, lord duke. But I'm close." His gaze went to Clovis, who glared at him.

Guillaume gestured to the benches. "Join us. We were just discussing our latest attempt at breaching the impasse."

"Thank you, but…I'd rather have a word in private if I may."

"Now?" The duke cocked his head. "As you wish." He turned to his visitors. "If you could leave us. We shall pick up our discussion later."

"Lord duke."

Bellon nodded at the two commanders as they passed him, then held Clovis by the arm. To Guillaume, he said, "Clovis can stay. He might as well hear what I have to say."

He ignored the duke's raised eyebrows and pushed Clovis back to the bench. "Sit down!"

The warrior wriggled from his grip. "You can't order me around, Bellon. I have to leave. I've a fair journey ahead of me."

"So soon? I thought you haven't heard all about the siege yet." Keeping one hand on his sword hilt, he positioned himself in front of the entrance, blocking Clovis' escape.

Guillaume reclined in his chair, watching him. He pursed his fingers. "King Charles wants Clovis to join him in his northern campaign."

"The king will have to wait. A long time."

"What do you mean?" Clovis blustered, facing him. "You can't ignore a royal order."

"Unless you have good reason," Guillaume added sharply. "Do you, Bellon?"

"Yes, I do, lord duke. I must take Clovis back to Carcassonne to face a trial." He crossed his arms in front of his chest, his gaze firmly on the knight.

"A trial?" Clovis scoffed. "On what grounds?"

Bellon took a deep breath. "On suspicion of abduction and murder of my wife, the countess Nanthild, and the murders of my servant Lot and my wife's elderly companion, Amalberga."

Clovis snorted. "Now Amalberga is dead? So she couldn't have—"

"You don't seem surprised, Clovis." Guillaume's quiet voice barely reached them.

"Amalberga died this morn; it's true," Bellon said. "But before she passed, she spoke…"

"What could the old hag possibly say? Nothing of worth."

Bellon shifted his weight to his right leg. His heart raged, and he would have liked nothing more than rip the man in front of him to pieces. But he knew it was the wrong thing to do. The Franks had laws – laws he had agreed to uphold, as hard as it was. "Oh, but she's not the only one who spoke. We have witnesses. You were seen up in the Orbiel valley."

"Nonsense." Clovis turned to Guillaume. "How much longer do you allow this upstart to insult me? I'm the king's man."

"You're a cold-blooded murderer, Clovis. And you will face punishment for your actions."

Clovis stepped up to mere inches from Bellon. "That would suit you, wouldn't it? So you'd be the one dispensing so-called justice?"

"The deeds happened in my county. So, yes, I will sit in judgement of you on the morrow."

"That's ridiculous. I did nothing."

"The villagers identified you. They're already waiting for you in my keep. You were watching from a distance until Nanthild left, then you overtook her to set a trap. Only someone aware of strategic warfare would know of the advantages of the spot where they were attacked. Besides, you were always leering after my wife."

Clovis snarled. "She was a pagan harlot."

237

Bellon's fist connected with the Frank's jaw before the man could evade it. He staggered backwards, nearly tripping over a bench.

"You'll regret this, Goth!" He straightened.

Guillaume's hand pressed down on Clovis' shoulder, and he spun round. "Surely, you don't believe him, lord duke? He's a liar; not even of Frankish blood!"

"Your sword, Clovis," Guillaume ordered. "I've heard enough. The evidence against you appears to be strong."

"But...he has made it all up. It must have been mercenaries."

Bellon snorted. "There are no mercenaries in those woods. Only ordinary people. People who saw you. And don't forget – I spoke to Amalberga before she died."

Clovis paled. "She couldn't have."

"No," Guillaume enquired. "How so?"

"I—"

"Your sword, Clovis." The duke's voice sharp, his free hand outstretched. "I will have that, and any other weapons you carry."

"'Tis not just." Clovis unsheathed his sword and held it aloft for a moment.

Guillaume swiftly moved behind him, his dirk at the soldier's throat. "I won't repeat myself."

Bellon stepped forward and took Clovis' sword, throwing it behind the chairs. Then he removed the dagger from the man's waist. "Any other weapons?"

"I will kill you," Clovis whispered hoarsely.

Bellon went around him until they stood nearly nose to nose. Looking down at the bristling knight, he said, "Try, and you shall die. It would be my pleasure." He stepped back and called out, "Dagobert, take him!"

His captain entered and tied up Clovis' hands, then looked to Bellon. "We are leaving right away?"

"Yes; before he can alert his men."

Dagobert nodded and dragged Clovis outside.

"I'll accompany you, Bellon. As your overlord, I will sit in judgment with you."

Bellon suppressed a smidgeon of doubt. Guillaume would not stab him in the back, would he? King Charles would find many other suitable fighting men. He did not need this one.

But I do.

"As you wish, lord duke. But we must hurry."

Chapter Twenty-Seven

Early June, 2018

Her nerves were getting the better of Maddie as she kept folding and unfolding her hands in her lap. Travelling in Léon's business car, a black Audi A5, instead of her old Golf, had made the journey comfortable, but it couldn't help soothe her agitated thoughts.

She preferred when it was her turn to drive, as she focused on the traffic, and she loved how the luxury car purred beneath her. But now, as they neared Beaune after over six hours on the road, she was glad Léon had taken over again. She felt sick with anticipation.

Grateful for Léon's presence and help, Maddie shot him a sideways glance. He smiled.

"Thank you for speaking with the count. I'm surprised that – despite the obvious shock – he was still happy for us to visit him."

"Well, he sounded more curious than annoyed. Perhaps a little apprehensive, but you can understand his reasons."

"Oh, absolutely. I'm the same." She fidgeted with her moonstone ring.

"But also excited?"

"Ha! I'm a nervous wreck. What if they don't like me? Mum described the count's mother as an old harpy!"

"That was over thirty years ago…"

She laughed. "True. So she must be positively ancient now. She is a widow, isn't she?"

He nodded. "Yes. As you know, your uncle is the current count."

"Of course, yes." *My uncle.* Maddie still found the thought bizarre. "I still can't get over that. I have proper French blue blood."

"Just be glad the family survived the Revolution, or you wouldn't be here now. I wonder how…"

"They must have given up something."

"Not the château. That stayed in their hands. I'm sure we'll find out tonight."

"Gulp!" she joked, and he squeezed her hand.

"It'll be all right. He seemed like a nice man when I met him, and he was positively surprised when I we spoke."

"I'm so glad you did that for me. I couldn't have uttered a word." Maddie shuddered. "And what would I have said? '*Bonjour*, I'm your niece, and I want to meet you.'"

"Something along those lines."

"His mother would've stopped him."

"Maybe he's finally grown up…"

Maddie laughed. *Here's hoping!*

Tall beech trees lined the drive to the Château de Montceau on both sides, their branches reaching out to each other above the lane like a canopy. Gaps in the foliage allowed the faint spring sunshine through.

Léon whistled. "Impressive!"

She stared straight ahead. "Wow!"

Before them, the castle loomed large, with a central section flanked by smaller wings on either side. Though the word 'small' did not quite apply here. At three floors high, with columns flanking the main entrance and all corners, and two resting lion statues at the top of the stairs, it was the epitome of a French palace.

"No surprise the old dowager thought your mother was a gold digger. It makes my home look like a hut." He grinned.

"I prefer yours to this, though." She winked. "This is too…grand."

"You could say that, yes. Should we seek the servants' entrance?"

She punched his arm. "No! I want to meet the lady of the house head-on."

"So the front door it is, Madame..." His mouth twitched as he slowly drove up to the main door and stopped his Audi beside other cars parked in the large yard: a new Land Rover, a beautifully-restored CV5, and a sparkling silver Mercedes estate.

"Now I'm glad we didn't take my old, dirty Rover." Léon grinned.

"Or my Golf!"

Her heart was pumping in her ears and her gaze flashed across to the door through which several people emerged.

"That must be them. Are you ready?"

Deep breath. "*Ouais*."

"Stay. I'll let you out."

Léon skirted the car, opened the passenger door and pulled her as gracefully as possible from her seat. "Chin up, they won't eat you!"

He kept hold of her hand as they walked up to the steps where a well-dressed man in his early sixties stepped forward with a warm smile. "*Bienvenue*, Madeleine!"

"*Merci...*" She wasn't sure how to address him, so she left her response hanging in the air.

Marie-Pierre, *comte* de Montceau, took her hands in his and gave her three *bises* on the cheeks. "Enchanté! I'm so pleased to meet you. I'm your Uncle Pierre."

"Thank you. You're very kind...Uncle Pierre." She nodded to Léon. "I gather you have met Monsieur Cabrol before?"

The men shook hands. "Yes, I do remember. From Château de Minervens. Welcome!"

"Thank you," Léon replied. "It's good to see you again. You're very kind to invite us." He put his hand in the small of Maddie's back, and she was grateful for his calm support.

"It is a long-overdue pleasure. Please come!" Uncle Pierre turned halfway, then waved them to follow him.

Just outside the door stood two women who couldn't have been any more different: one likely in her fifties, her skin a darker, southern European shade, dressed in a floral skirt and wide, flowing top, her long black hair falling softly over her shoulders; the other in her eighties, wearing an immaculately-fitting trouser suit, her hair scooped back in a tight *chignon*. Very French.

"May I introduce Eleana, my wife of twenty-nine years…"

"*Bienvenue*, Madeleine."

Maddie exchanged greetings and *bises* with the countess, surprised to recognise a Spanish lilt. She immediately warmed to her.

"…and my mother, the Dowager Countess Florence de Montceau – your grandmother!"

The old lady's eyebrow twitched, but she gracefully allowed Maddie to greet her in the same manner as her aunt. Then she found herself at the receiving end of the woman's scrutiny and felt herself lacking.

"So we finally meet you, Madeleine," the dowager said, her mouth set in a thin line. "Marie-Pierre is very sympathetic."

"Madeleine has your nose and chin, *Mère*. You can't deny the link." Her son spoke calmly but firmly, and the old lady bristled.

"Fear not, Madame. I only wish to know about my father." Maddie smiled at her, ignoring the shivers down her spine. How stressful it must have been for her mother.

"Come!"

She was grateful when the countess took her arm and led her inside as Léon introduced himself to the dowager.

"Don't worry about my mother-in-law, Madeleine," Countess Eleana whispered with a conspiratorial wink. "I have been together with my husband for over thirty years, yet she still hasn't quite gotten over the shock of him marrying a foreigner. I'm Spanish, you may have guessed. Just like your father likely would have done had he known of you and not gone hiking that fateful day." She sighed. "I'll show you to your rooms, then we'll gather for coffee. Dinner tonight will be a bigger affair, with our two sons Patrice and Jean, our daughter Felicia – with their other halves – and our five grandchildren. They're so excited to meet you, their long-lost cousin and aunt."

An hour later, Maddie and Léon were lying on the large bed in her room, resting. They had been given adjoining bedrooms – most likely to spare the dowager any blushes – but linked with a door, so they could do as they pleased.

Léon stroked her hand. "How are you feeling?"

"I don't know, to be honest. It's a lot to take in."

Her mind was whirling. Finally, she'd not only discovered who her father was but also met his family. Her uncle and aunt had been welcoming, asking her questions, and keen to learn about her life. Her grandmother, however, was still very much the aloof woman Elizabeth had encountered. Maddie felt sorry for Eleana, who had to live with the 'old harpy' every day. This could have been her own mother's fate, and a small part of her was relieved that it had never been the case.

"I'm sure. But you've been desperate to find out about your father for so many years, and now you can ask them anything you like. It's like fast-tracking your past."

She nodded. "Yes, at the speed of a roller coaster!"

He turned on his side to face her, propping his head on his hand. "Are you disappointed?"

"No, it's just…weird." Maddie snuggled into his embrace, and her ragged breathing calmed. "Your parents aren't snooty at all, but very warm, even though they'd never met me before – and I'm some stranger from northern England. Such a difference to the dowager." She could not bring herself to call her 'grandmother' yet.

"She's old-school French where status is everything. My parents have worked hard in the vines, getting their hands dirty. And they like you, which is a bonus." He chuckled. "I can't see Madame ever having done that, though her son seems to be more hands-on."

"That's the impression I got, too. Uncle Pierre and Aunt Eleana – calling them like that still sounds bizarre to my ears – appear more down to earth."

"Do you want to freshen up soon? We can then take up the countess's offer of a walk in the grounds. From what I've seen, this old pile of rocks needs money."

Maddie drew back. "Old *châteaux* cost a fortune to maintain, and Montceau isn't open for visitors, from what I can see. OK, I'm off to have a quick shower." She slid off the bed and selected a fresh top and trousers – not jeans! – from her small case.

"Me too." Léon grinned, blowing her a kiss. "In my very own bathroom!" And he stalked from the room, laughing, just as she threw a towel after him.

Maddie enjoyed the walk with Uncle Pierre and Aunt Eleana. The grounds of the château were vast, and Eleana oversaw a large part of the maintenance whilst Pierre focused on the vineyard. But the building gave them much cause for concern. When Léon questioned whether they would consider paying guests, Pierre laughed drily.

"Not as long as my mother is still with us," he said with a resigned shrug. "She insists on keeping the château to ourselves."

"It would make things easier," Eleana added with a wistful smile. "One day…"

Maddie nodded, letting her gaze roam the park. "This could be the perfect getaway."

"It will be." Her uncle winked.

Dinner with the family was a more formal affair, overseen by the dowager. The food, all local produce, was tasty, and Maddie happily tucked into the tenderloin of game with Dauphinoise potatoes and green beans followed by a homemade crème brûlée with a hint of lavender.

Her cousins asked many questions, and she was happy to tell them of her life in York, and of her work, which even raised an approving nod from the dowager.

"And now, are you going to settle in France?" Her cousin Felicia's question took her by surprise.

Meeting Léon's serious eyes across the table, she knew what she wanted. A new challenge. A new life.

Smiling, she said, "Yes, I think so. All I'm missing is a dog!"

Her mother would have been so proud.

Two days later, after Pierre and Eleana had shown them the historic sites in and around Beaune, her paternal heritage, Maddie and Léon were ready to return to Languedoc. There was only one more thing to do, and her relatives had kindly suggested she went without them. She preferred it that way and was grateful for their understanding. So after a lengthy farewell, including a brief embrace and *bises* from the dowager, Léon finally parked the Audi in the car park of the cemetery of Beaune.

"Are you sure you want me to come with you? With Pierre's description, you could easily find the family crypt."

Maddie nodded, blinking back the tears. "Yes, please. I'd like that."

"OK." He squeezed her hand. "Let's meet your father."

Chapter Twenty-Eight

Mid-October, AD 793
Carcassonne

Bellon stepped quickly out of the pouring rain into the hall at Carcassonne. The wind almost blew the door from his grip, and he closed it firmly. Raking his hands through his soaked hair, he spotted Guillaume at the high table, from where they would face the accused, Clovis. A monk sat to the duke's left, rolling out parchments. Guillaume had brought him from Narbonne.

"'Tis a miserable day for a trial." Guillaume's drew his mouth to a fine line.

"It is that," Bellon acknowledged. Straightening his tunic, he considered himself presentable again and walked up to his seat, looking across the empty room. In front of their table stood a single stool for Clovis. "I wish I could face him in a fight." He slumped into his chair.

"You know you can't. The rule of law is important to the king, and if you break it, he might take action."

Bellon snorted. "Do you think I care? This cur murdered my wife and my servants, and he receives the opportunity to defend himself, in words?"

Guillaume sent him a sharp glance. "You have sat in judgement of other men before. It is part of your role as count. Distance yourself from the victims, even your wife – as difficult as it may be."

"It's impossible," he whispered.

The duke put a hand on his shoulder and squeezed. "I can imagine. I can't in all honesty say that I particularly agreed with the lady Nanthild's views, but I respected her."

"Thank you." He knew Guillaume had not been impressed with Hilda's opinions, or her tendency to voice them. His mouth twitched as he remembered her forthright manner.

They looked up as the door opened and Roderic appeared. "Are we ready to let the people in?"

Bellon nodded. "Yes, and ask Dagobert to fetch the prisoner."

Moments later, the hall was bustling, with men and women ushering in to pick the best spaces on the few benches. Many, bereft of a seat, stood behind them, herded into place by several armed guards. The mood was dark. The captain clearly expected some might be angry enough to attack Clovis.

Roderic hovered in the open door, letting the wind sweep in, which whipped the fire in the hearth into a frenzy. "Here he is." He stepped back to let Dagobert pass, dragging Clovis by a chain linked to the man's hands and feet.

Dagobert stopped beside the stool. "Stand here." He positioned himself at Clovis' side.

A sennight in the dungeon had not done the knight any good. He looked tired, dishevelled, his usually clean tunic smudged and torn. Yet the glare in his gaze when Bellon met it was undiminished.

Why did the man hate him so?

"Silence!" He stood, emphasising his order. "Everyone be silent."

A hush fell over the room, and the only sound left was the crackling of firewood in the central hearth.

"Roderic, are all the witnesses present?"

The *majordomus* nodded. "Yes, lord."

"Then please bolt the door. We do not want any disruption of this trial."

Clovis snorted. "Trial? When you've already announced me guilty without a shred of evidence?"

"You will respond when spoken to, Clovis. Until then, hold your tongue!" He returned the glare, then sat. "Be seated."

Those on the benches shuffled until only subdued murmurs remained.

Guillaume stood. "Clovis of Marteuil, lord in the service of Charles, king of the Franks. You are accused of three counts of murder: of the lady Nanthild, countess of Carcassonne; the dame Amalberga, her elderly companion; and Lot, their young guard. How do you plead?"

"It is a trap, lord duke. This man," he pointed at Bellon, "wants me out of the way."

Bellon bit back a retort. Under the table, he balled his hands into fists until the nails dug into his flesh, then slowly released the pressure. It helped. He steadied his breathing.

"Now, why would Bellon, a trusted count in the king's service, want *you* 'out of the way', as you put it?"

"Because he hates me."

"The feeling is entirely mutual," Bellon quipped, earning himself a sharp glance from Guillaume.

"That is not reason enough, as you will find. There are witnesses who have confirmed that you were watching the village at which the lady attended a young woman's difficult confinement."

"Nonsense," Clovis grumbled. "I was travelling along the coast to Narbonne."

"So you are not guilty?"

The soldier raised his chin. "I do, lord duke."

"Very well." Guillaume sat and turned to Bellon. "Would you ask the first witness to come forward?"

"I would. Guisclafred, bring forward the lady Alda." He swallowed back lingering doubts he had about using his daughter as a witness, but she had insisted.

She is so like her mother.

Alda stood to the right of Clovis, facing Guillaume and Bellon. Beads of sweat covered her forehead, and she blinked furiously. Then she took a deep breath.

"You are the lady Alda, daughter of Count Bellon and Countess Nanthild?"

"Yes, lord duke. I am." Her voice showed the dignity of her rank.

"And together with your maid, Rotlinde, you cared for Dame Amalberga, a lifelong companion of your mother, until she passed away."

Alda swallowed hard. "I did."

"That is commendable for one so young."

"'Tis what Mother would have done."

She would have done Hilda proud. Bellon smiled, his heart bursting with pride.

Guillaume coughed. "Indeed, it would. Now, was Dame Amalberga conscious during your ministrations?"

"Yes, she was…near the end."

"And did she say anything to you?"

"What's this? Are you suggesting something to the lass that did not happen?" Clovis rose, but Dagobert pushed him roughly back onto the stool.

Guillaume sighed. "Hold your tongue until spoken to, Clovis. And listen!" He turned to Alda. "Did she?"

She nodded. "Yes. I sat by Amalberga's bedside and wiped her brow and temple when she woke. She was in so much pain."

"I can imagine. Her injuries were horrific, I've heard. Please continue."

"Amalberga grabbed my hand and spoke to me. Her voice was hoarse, but I still hear her words as clear as if she were here now. They were but a few."

"What did she say?"

The shuffling in the room stopped. Alda commanded everyone's attention. Bellon held his breath, then, consciously, he breathed out slowly.

"She said that…that…" Alda's eyes welled up, but then she squared her shoulders, looking straight at the duke. "Amalberga said that man, Clovis, had waylaid them." She spat his name. "Before she knew what happened, he had… had…taken Mother away."

A whimper went up in the crowd, quickly stilled until only a series of sobs remained. Bellon recognised the woman as Theodosia, Roderic's wife, who had often helped Hilda with the household accounts. Her reaction gave him a sense of comfort. Others mourned Hilda's absence almost as strongly as he did.

"The lady Nanthild was taken? How? Where to?"

"By this man on his horse. It was a white stallion with a black spot on his right hind flank, Amalberga said. After he had gone with...Mother, one of his accomplices knifed Amalberga repeatedly, rolled her into the undergrowth and left her to die."

Gasps echoed around the room, followed by cries of "murderer".

"Silence!" Guillaume thundered. After a while, a hush fell over the hall again. "For the record," he nodded to the monk sitting beside him, whose quill scratched furiously across the parchment, "the lady Alda describes the horse of the accused, as I have personally verified."

"She would've seen it during my last visit," Clovis argued, pointing at Alda.

"I could, perhaps, but I did not." Alda glared at him, and Bellon bit back a smirk.

"So we have the knight and his stallion at the scene of the attack."

"The feverish ramblings of an old woman!"

"She was of sound mind. You must believe me, lord duke."

"I do, child. As does your father." Guillaume smiled at her. "I thank you for being such a brave girl, Alda. Your mother would be proud of you. I have no further questions."

"You may retire to your chamber, if you wish," Bellon said to her.

She shook her head. "I'd rather stay, Father."

"So be it. Then rejoin your brothers over there."

"Lord duke. Father." She inclined her head and went past the packed benches to where Guisclafred and Oliba stood with Roderic, Theodosia and other members of their household.

"So this is your proof? The word of a dead woman?" Clovis chuckled. "Wait till the king hears of this mockery of a trial."

Guillaume leaned back. "Oh, he shall. And I'm certain that he will agree with our judgement."

"We have another witness." Bellon raised his voice. "Carloman, step forward."

A stocky man of two score years came to a halt where moments earlier Alda had stood. He inclined his head. "Lord. Lord duke."

"Greetings, Carloman. You live in the hamlet the lady Nanthild was visiting?" Guillaume asked, propping his elbows on the table.

"Yes, lord. My wife and I, we are neighbours of Gunda, the woman who had sought the help of the lady Nanthild." He stared at his feet. "Had she known what were to befall the lady, she'd never have called for her. She has been praying for her day and night."

"But she delivered Gunda's child safely, and both are well?" Bellon asked quietly.

Carloman met his gaze. "Yes, lord. They are."

"Then her visit was not in vain." His words pained him, but it was how Hilda would have seen it.

"No, lord."

"During the lady's visit to Gunda, did you notice anything unusual?"

"Yes, lord duke. This man," he pointed at Clovis, "and two others who looked like mercenaries were lurking on the hillside nearby. They had arrived not long after the lady Nanthild and her companions, but kept themselves hidden in the forest; or tried to."

"That's a lie!" Clovis gnarled.

Carloman shuddered. "I do not lie. You were filling up your flasks with water from our well. I saw you with my own eyes, as did my wife."

Clovis rattled at his chains. "You're a dead man."

Carloman blanched.

"Threatening witnesses won't help your cause, Clovis. On the contrary, I shall regard your comment as an admission of your guilt." Guillaume turned to the witness. "Thank you, Carloman. You can now return to your seat."

"And please tell Gunda that we thank her for her prayers," Bellon added.

The man gave him a wan smile and went back to his seat. His wife took his hand and squeezed it.

Guillaume faced Clovis. "What do you have to say to your accusers?"

"That they're all liars! I am a lord of the realm of the Franks, a trusted soldier for King Charles. You will do well to remember that."

"Are you threatening me, Clovis? Have you forgotten your station?"

"No, but that dog beside you has messed with your head."

Bellon laughed out loud. "Clovis, ever since you first set eyes on the lady Nanthild, your intentions towards her have been very clear. I remember each occasion."

"It should have been me, not a Pagan half-blood like you."

"Bellon is a Christian, Clovis, not a Pagan. Your accusations are ridiculous. Is there anything you wish to say about the day the lady Nanthild disappeared, before we pronounce judgement?"

"You have it all stitched up neatly, haven't you?" Venom dripped from Clovis' voice, and he leaned forward. "This cur gets the title, lands, everything. I've risked my life for the king many times—"

"For which he rewarded you richly, with property and silver," Guillaume finished.

Clovis huffed.

"It kept your wife in comfort, I hear, until she passed away."

"Your wife died?" Bellon raised an eyebrow. That might explain much. Had Clovis abducted Hilda to keep her?

"Yes."

"So you thought you could help yourself to another man's woman?" Rage grew inside him when he saw Clovis' eyes sparkle. The man taunted him. "Where is Hilda?"

"Bellon…" Guillaume tried to calm him.

He stood and leaned over the table. "Where is my wife, Clovis? Is she still alive?"

Clovis chuckled. "You'd want to know, don't you? You, with your fancy fortress," his hands swept a wide circle, rattling the chains, "and your perfect family." He turned to glare at Bellon's children. "But the one thing you're desperate to find out will always elude you."

Bellon skirted the table and reached the accused in three strides. He lifted him off the stool by his tunic, tearing it. "I'm asking you once more. Where…is…she?"

"You'll meet her in Hell one day, your Pagan bitch!" Clovis spat on the floor.

Bellon tightened his grip, his heart pounding in his ears. If only he could wrest Hilda's whereabouts from this dog.

"Bellon! Release Clovis." Guillaume's voice drifted through the fog in his head. Then Dagobert's hand clasped his shoulder.

"He will die, Bellon," Dagobert whispered.

"But not before he'll reveal what he did to Hilda!" He shook Clovis to bring home his point, but the man let out a mad laugh.

"Never! I'll haunt you day and night, Bellon."

"You'll—"

"She cursed me, you know." Clovis' face contorted. "The witch cursed me. She had to pay…"

Rage surged through him. His fists pummelled the accused's chest, and it took Dagobert and Guillaume's combined strength to pull him away from Clovis.

"Where is she?" He fought against their hold of him, but failed.

"Let it be, Bellon."

Clovis laughed. "She cursed me, but you'll be the one who'll suffer for the rest of your days…"

Bellon straightened. "I demand to wield the sword that cuts off his head, lord duke."

Guillaume gave him a long glance, then nodded.

"So be it. Clovis, you have brought shame to the army of King Charles, and to any Christian soldier of the kingdom." He stepped back behind the table and pointed to the scribe. "Let it be known that Clovis of Marteuil, lord in service to the illustrious Charles, king of the Franks, be put to death for the murder of the lady Nanthild, countess of Carcassonne, the dame Amalberga, and Lot, their guard, whom he waylaid on their return home. Count Bellon of Carcassonne will carry out punishment by beheading immediately following the conclusion of this trial. The murderer's remains shall not be buried in hallowed soil, but instead be cut up and scattered across the kingdom, to be placed on pikes by the roadside as a warning to others."

Clovis blanched and crossed himself. "You can't do that."

"I can, and my decision is final. God's sacred earth is no place for the likes of you."

Bellon took a deep breath. Hilda's curse would haunt the man forever.

And him…

Chapter Twenty-Nine

21st June, 2019
The manor of Château de Minervens

"Here, let me get this."

"Léon, I'm pregnant, not ill! I can carry a box of six bottles of wine perfectly well, thank you."

He laughed and picked up another. "I can try."

"Ha! Just a shame I won't be able to enjoy any of this stuff."

"True, but you'll have plenty of chances to catch up once Bump is born and weaned."

"That still means a long time."

"Must be tough being a woman, and all that…"

Maddie tried to aim a kick at him, but he deftly avoided it. "Bastard!"

"No, my dear, that's your heritage." He winked. "Speaking of which, when will Pierre, Eleana and the others arrive?"

"Around 5 pm, Aunt Eleana messaged. Just as well that your mother has organised their rooms and the dinner for tonight. No stress about heading out in several cars." She put the box on a large table set up against a wall inside the *cave*. "Oh, thank you," she said as Paul brought in three boxes. "Please leave it all right here, so we can easily take the bottles we need for tomorrow's fête out."

"No problem." Paul grinned, setting the boxes on the table. Gina had left the winery when Maddie moved in last October, but Paul was a great support in the day-to-day running of the wine-tasting sessions. Now marketing fell to Maddie, and she enjoyed learning new skills alongside her research. She'd discovered that she enjoyed dealing with people face-to-face.

She stopped in the door to the *cave* and scanned the landscape that opened before her eyes – the large yard with the shop annexe set against the wall of the old manor house and the sweeping views over the Cabardès hills and down into the plain.

"Happy?"

She nodded and gently rubbed her growing middle. "Very. Not at all how I envisaged my life to be, but much better than anything I could've imagined." Linking her hand in his, they walked over to where the low wall allowed her to admire the scenery fully. She breathed in the fresh air, enjoying the warm breeze.

Their latest addition to the family, a young black cat called Shadow, jumped up, and she stroked his silky fur, revelling in the droning sound of his purrs. "Hmm, my sweet! You'll be in hiding tomorrow during the fête!"

Shadow looked up at her and meowed.

"I take that as a complaint, then." She laughed, then turned to Léon. "All OK at the gîte?"

After the renovations were completed and Maddie had moved in with Léon, they decided to rent her mother's house to holiday visitors. Mindful of Bernadette, they chose their clients carefully, although they allowed pets, much to her old neighbour's delight.

"Yes, the German couple have settled in fine. They'll come up for a tasting next Tuesday morning, and they bring their Labrador."

Maddie laughed. "I bet he'll be all over the place. Shadow won't know what's hit him."

Another meow confirmed the cat's objection.

"You'll be OK, my boy. Just get Old Susie to chase him."

Léon snorted. "The old girl will likely doze in the shade rather than have a young Lab ruffle her."

"True." Maddie took a deep breath. "She deserves her peace, at eleven." Still stroking the cat, she was smiling at the thought of their rescued Pyrenean mountain dog putting a bouncy young Labrador in his place.

"Lucky girl! No peace for us, though, in the next few weeks. Tomorrow's engagement party, sightseeing with your family, and your new book release – it's all coming together." He wrapped his arm around her. "Just one last thing left to do."

"Bury the cranium?"

"Umm, I rather thought about deciding on a name for this one," he put his free hand on her bump. "Or do you want her to be born nameless?"

She laughed out loud. "We can't have that, can we? Fine. Let's choose one, but later. Aunt Eleana wants to see the cranium before I close the casket. Tomorrow, Bertrand will give her a private tour at the museum where she can see the rest of the bones. But tonight, we'll have our burial ceremony, so the lady can finally rest in peace."

"In the spot you marked in the rose garden?"

"Yes. It's perfect. Calm, surrounded by wonderful scents. Hopefully, she'll be at peace there. I'm so grateful to your parents for their permission."

"You didn't need it, but we all agree it is the best place. OK. If you keep an eye on the preparations here, I'll get a shovel and dig a hole. Where is the casket?"

"Yes, on the desk in the library. It's ready."

"Great. Then I'll see you later." He gave her a kiss and Shadow a final scratch behind the ears and walked off.

Meow.

"Yes, Shadow, you can join us too if you wish." Maddie smiled. The presence of a black cat would make it special.

Late that evening, the waning gibbous moon lit up the path as they left the manor house through the back door in double file towards the rose garden. Apart from Maddie, each family member carried a white candle with a drip protector, to avoid burning themselves or the dry shrubs.

She carried in front of her an open box lined with velvet. Inside, the partial cranium of the ancient lady lay on a small cushion. Tonight, she would be blessed, laid to rest, and hopefully at peace.

As they approached the hole Léon had dug between two large rose bushes, Maddie placed the box on the ground and asked, "Please can we form a circle around her?"

When all stood gathered, she joined in between Léon and her aunt. She then intoned her blessing.

"Here and Now
I invoke the God and the Goddess

I seek your blessing
To shine your light upon your daughter
Who we herewith return to the earth
Her circle of life complete
Banishing the darkness that surrounded her
We bring forth your light
To guide her on her journey ahead
So mote it be."

When silence fell, Maddie stepped forward and, closing her eyes, held her hand over the cranium. It sent a tingling through her fingers and up her arm. After a deep breath, she blinked and reached out to Léon who passed her a sprig of dried lavender. She placed it inside the box and closed the lid, content that she had made the connection.

The circle opened, and she put the casket into the hole, with a final sign of a blessing. Shadow lay beside the opening, peeking in, mesmerised. He felt it too.

Léon joined her and, together, they laid down a single white rose on top of the box. "May you now rest in peace, my dear."

'Nanthild…'

A whiff of lavender hung in the air, but it could have come from the branch Maddie held seconds earlier. She looked up as Léon drew in a sharp breath.

"Your name is Nanthild?"

'Peace…' The scent of lavender grew stronger.

"Blessed be. May your spirit find your family, dear Nanthild. Farewell." Tears stung in her eyes, and a sense of loss rushed through her. "I feel like I lost a friend." She held out her hand and Léon helped her up and wrapped his arm around her shoulder.

"You set her free, Maddie. She is grateful. Paul will fill up the hole, then she can rest."

"We can get a plaque with her name now, can't we?"

"Absolutely. A lovely touch."

"So that was her name – Nanthild?" Beside her, Eleana looked at the box. "Wouldn't it be a fitting memory if you named your daughter after her?"

"You heard her speak, too?"

Léon's mother joined them, nodding. "Yes, we all did. I like Eleana's idea."

Maddie swallowed hard. "Umm…" She glanced at Léon.

"It is a lovely name, and ancient French, I guess," he said. "I like it too."

Maddie smiled as a sense of happiness engulfed her. "Yes, what a wonderful idea!" She lay her hand on her belly.

Nanthild…

***

They turned to walk back to the manor, and Shadow ran up to her, weaving his small body around her ankles. Maddie picked him up and cuddled him, his purrs a warm comfort. She leaned into Léon whose arm encircled her waist.

It was time to return to the realm of the living and look towards the future.

Paul gently shovelled loose earth over the casket, then crouched to pat it firmly into place. Goosebumps rose on his skin when he felt a surge of energy, and he quickly pulled his hands away. All done, he shrugged off the strange sensation, wiped his hands on a handkerchief and returned to the house at a brisk pace. He did not turn to look back.

In the rose garden, the scent of lavender grew.

'Peace…'

Epilogue

Mid-October, AD 793
Carcassonne

Bellon stood on the ramparts, looking out over the plain below, his arm wrapped around Alda. The sun had set much earlier, but a faint red glow remained firmly rooted in the western sky.

"Will Mother be at peace?" Oliba asked.

Bellon looked at him and put his other hand on his shoulder. "I hope so. Wherever she is…"

"We will never know now," Guisclafred, standing beside Alda, whispered hoarsely. He clenched and unclenched his fists.

Bellon ached for his children. Their pain hurt his heart more than anything. Yet, he could not take it away from them. They all suffered too much.

"No, son, we won't. But your mother's curse ensured that her murderer's spirit will roam this earth forever. No heaven for him, no eternal life."

"I'd rather have Mother back." Alda's voice quivered, and she wrapped her arms around his waist.

"So would I, Sweeting." He kissed her temple.

"Look!" Oliba pointed at the dark eastern horizon. "A star!"

"Is it Mother?" Alda asked as they watched it glide across the sky.

Bellon smiled. "I would like to think so, yes…"

And he drew his daughter a little closer to him just as the star vanished.

"My beloved…"

Glossary

À toute à l'heure:	See you later
Au revoir:	goodbye
Bah ouais:	well, yes
Bonjour:	hello; good day (lit.)
Ça va:	how are you?; also a response: I'm fine
Cave Cooperative:	cooperative of wine growers, found in many villages, to share costs.
Certainement:	certainly
C'est tellement bizarre:	it's so weird
Courage:	good luck
D'accord:	OK
Domaine:	vineyard
Enchanté(e):	nice to meet you
Épicerie:	grocery shop
J'écoute:	I'm listening; often used when answering a phone call
Je suis désolé(e):	I'm sorry
La pauvre fille:	the poor girl
Madame:	Mrs
Madeleines:	sponge cake, often shell-shaped
Maire:	mayor
Mairie:	town hall
Maître:	master (lit.); a title used for notaries and similar professionals
Mesdames:	ladies
Messieurs:	gentlemen
Mon dieu:	my god
Monsieur:	Mr
Notaire:	notary
Oui:	yes
Ouais:	yeah
Puis-je vous aider?	Can I help you?
Putain:	whore (lit.); an often used swearword
Quoi?	what?
S'il vous plaît:	please
Suivez-moi:	follow me

Place Names

Aquitania:	Aquitaine, a vast region in south-west France
Carisiacum:	Quercy; seat of one of Charlemagne's palaces and important Frankish town
Iberia:	south-western European peninsular; modern Spain and Portugal
Neustria:	Frankish territory in north-west France, excluding Brittany
Pyrenaei:	Pyrenees
Tolosa:	Toulouse
Vasconia:	Gascony; the region extended from south-west France across the Pyrenees

List of Real Characters featured in Love Lost in Time:

Bellon:

Bellon (or Bello) was born around 755 (or 770 or 780) to unknown parentage. Records show him as first count of Carcassonne and the Razès (some state in 790, others quote the 770s). He is the founder of the Bellonid dynasty and had at least two sons who in turn succeeded him, Guisclafred and Oliba. Other sons are also attributed to him, but there is no evidence of a link.

During Bellon's time, Carcassonne was already an important fortress, with many of its towers dating back to Roman times, and its strategic position north of the Pyrenees helped with the defence against the Saracen expansion from Iberia to the north. It changed hands several times over the centuries.

King Charles:

Born to Pepin the Short, king of the Franks, and Bertrada of Laon around 748, Charles, these days better known as Charlemagne (Charles the Great), went on to reign over a vast area in central and western Europe. He became king of the Franks in 768, jointly with his brother Carloman. On his brother's untimely death in 771, Charles gained the whole kingdom and continued to expand its reach in the footsteps of his father, Pepin, and grandfather, Charles Martel.

The Franks focused on three sides: to the west, and from there on south-west into Aquitania and Vasconia, south into Lombardia (where he became king of the Lombards in 774) and east into Saxony, which was still ruled by Pagan tribes. He married four times and had at least four sons.

On Christmas Day in 800, Pope Leo III crowned Charles *Imperator Romanorum* (Emperor of the Romans), a purely political move to bolster his own fragile position, and which triggered centuries of conflict between Byzantium and Rome.

Charles died in 814 and is buried in Aachen (Aix-la-Chapelle), Germany.

Guillaume (William) of Autun / Gellone:

Born around 755, Guillaume was the son of Thierry IV, count of Autun, of Frankish heritage. He was a cousin of Charlemagne on his mother's side, and spent much time at court. The king put him in charge of battling the Saracens in what is now the south of France and northern Spain.

In 804, Guillaume founded the monastery at Gellone (a river in the Hérault *département*),
to which he retired in 804. Following his death, it was renamed Sant-Guilhem-le-Désert. His will consists of a few curiosities, not least that he left something to his two 'wives' (both named as 'wife' in his testament, although one may have been a concubine), and several children, but not to two named daughters!

Guillaume's life would become legend after his death in either 812 or 814. He was canonised by Pope Alexander II in 1066 and various *chansons de geste*, the epic tales of heroic deeds of the 12th and 13th centuries, sang his praises, most notably of his defeat of the Saracens at Orange, which gave him the nickname 'Guillaume of Orange' (the first of that title).

I also included several minor historical characters who did not play an active part.

Author's Note

Part of the plot of *Love Lost in Time* is based on a true story. In 2016, my husband and I moved to a village in the Languedoc-Roussillon area of France. Not far from our house, there used to be an ancient graveyard dating back to Visigoth times. Many such graveyards dot the whole region, and they are often to be found in remote areas.

But then our neighbours told us of their discovery during renovations of their kitchen: when they dug up their floor, they discovered several bones and a parts of a skull dating back hundreds of years. But the curious thing was that their house was not near the old graveyard! And so the plot was born…

As there are so many traces of Visigoths and early Franks in the area, and Charlemagne has always fascinated me, I began to research the time of the expansion of the Franks south. That's when I came across Bellon, reported to have been the first count of Carcassonne. Little is known of his life, and reports even vary on his year of birth and accession to the county. His wife's name is not noted (except on some dubious genealogy sites), so I took the liberty to make my fictional Frankish lady, Nanthild, his spouse. Bellon had at least two sons, and various records agree on their names: Guisclafred and Oliba, who both succeeded him as count of Carcassonne. Others have been mentioned, but not confirmed. A tenuous link later veers off to Barcelona, but we can't be sure whether those counts were his successors or other men with the same names, which is quite possible.

As for Charlemagne, his army fought the Saracens on several occasions, both along the western Mediterranean coast as well as across the Pyrenees. I have included two pivotal moments from his campaigns: the ambush of Charlemagne's returning army at Roncevaux (Span.: Roncesvalles) in August 778 and the battle near the Orbiel river in September

793, which led to Guillaume/William of Autun (later 'of Gellone') to withdraw. A third occasion – Charlemagne's execution of over 4,000 Saxon 'heretics' – I mentioned in dialogue. To this day, historians regard that particular event as unusual for a king who purported to uphold his own laws. By mentioning these events, I intended to bring a sense of authenticity to the story, to show how uncertain life was in Septimania and across Europe in the late 8th century.

Nanthild's (fictional) story is a sad one, and I found it hard to kill her off. But I needed someone for the bones, so it was her who ended up under Maddie's kitchen floor! Although Christianity had begun to spread, thanks to a large extent to the Frankish expansion across Gaul, Aquitania and Septimania, there were still many tribes, particularly in Germania and in the north, who remained pagan. Unlike the Saracens of the early and mid-8th century who settled in Narbonne and Béziers, and who allowed the conquered Visigoth and Roman inhabitants to maintain their religion, the Franks were not as generous. So making Nanthild pagan at heart added to the dangers to her life.

Cathie Dunn
Carcassonne, November 2019

Acknowledgments

I want to thank my husband, Laurence, for his patience. I'm very grateful for his continuing support of my research and writing, often leaving him on his own for much of the time when I retire to my 'writing cave' aka our office with its partial view of the cité of Carcassonne.

A special 'thank you' goes again to my fellow authors at Ocelot Press. The 'Ocelots' are a very supportive clowder of writing friends, with a wonderful range of stories. Don't forget to check them out!

Un grand merci also goes to my former neighbours, Marie and Omer, in the small village in the beautiful Minervois where we first moved to here in France. When they showed us their treasure of ancient bones, the idea of *Love Lost in Time* was born.

Thank you for reading this Ocelot Press book.

If you enjoyed it, we would greatly
appreciate it if you could take a moment
to write a short review.

You might also like to try books by fellow
Ocelot Press authors. We cover a small range of
genres, with a focus on historical fiction (including
mystery and paranormal), romance and fantasy.

Find Ocelot Press at:
Website: **www.ocelotpress.wordpress.com**
Facebook: **www.facebook.com/OcelotPress**
Twitter: **www.twitter.com/OcelotPress**

Printed in Great Britain
by Amazon

44610781R00163